"Last chance, Merlene."

Tucking his arm into hers, Cody drew her out of the elevator with him.

"Hey..." She pulled away, but the doors had already closed behind them.

"What's going on? I know you have something to tell me."

"And how do you know that?" Furious, she turned to confront him, but was stopped by his probing gaze, a look that brought all of her senses to full alert. Warmth spread outward from the spot on her arm where he had touched her.

"Because I'm a detective," he said.

"Yeah? Well, so am I." And she had never been as aware of a man as she was of Cody Warren at this moment—of his height a full foot over her, of the confident way he stood, of a muscular body full of power and authority. Sexy as hell, and infuriating.

Dear Reader,

I love stories about police officers. Something about that hint of danger swirling around the hero or heroine makes their developing passion so much more intense. During my working life as a court reporter, I encountered many situations that sparked my imagination, the "what ifs" that I enjoy turning into books. Now I attend any citizen police academy I can to help me understand the life of a cop. I encourage anyone who wants to know more about law enforcement to check if their local police department allows a citizen ride-along.

I've learned law enforcement is a perilous job, a career tough on romance, but that love can always prevail. Take Cody and Merlene, the hero and heroine of *To Trust a Cop*. When their worlds collide on a difficult case, at first mutual distrust makes the idea of love flaring between them seem impossible. I hope you enjoy reading their story as much as I enjoyed telling it.

I've met many police officers like Cody, honorable people who always try to do what's right, no matter the cost. I admire and respect these men and women who stay true to themselves while performing an important but difficult job.

Nothing is better than hearing from my readers! Please visit my website at sharonshartley.com.

Be present and stay happy,

Sharon Hartley

To Trust
a Cop

—

Sharon Hartley

HARLEQUIN® SUPER ROMANCE®

Recycling programs
for this product may
not exist in your area.

ISBN-13: 978-0-373-71876-4

TO TRUST A COP

Copyright © 2013 by Sharon Hartley

All rights reserved. Except for use in any review, the reproduction or utilization of this work in whole or in part in any form by any electronic, mechanical or other means, now known or hereafter invented, including xerography, photocopying and recording, or in any information storage or retrieval system, is forbidden without the written permission of the publisher, Harlequin Enterprises Limited, 225 Duncan Mill Road, Don Mills, Ontario, Canada M3B 3K9.

This is a work of fiction. Names, characters, places and incidents are either the product of the author's imagination or are used fictitiously, and any resemblance to actual persons, living or dead, business establishments, events or locales is entirely coincidental.

This edition published by arrangement with Harlequin Books S.A.

For questions and comments about the quality of this book, please contact us at CustomerService@Harlequin.com.

® and TM are trademarks of Harlequin Enterprises Limited or its corporate affiliates. Trademarks indicated with ® are registered in the United States Patent and Trademark Office, the Canadian Trade Marks Office and in other countries.

Printed in U.S.A.

™ www.Harlequin.com

ABOUT THE AUTHOR

Sharon Hartley writes romance stories that revolve around cops and the fascinating, often dangerous people that inhabit their world. A previous career as a court reporter, as well as multiple citizen police academies, provides ideas for her fiction. To calm herself from thinking about cops and robbers, Sharon teaches yoga, urging her students to accept themselves just the way they are. She lives on an island in Miami, Florida, with her husband, a Jack Russell terrorist and hundreds of orchids. Sharon loves to hear from her readers! Please contact her at sharonshartley01@bellsouth.net.

This book is dedicated to my sister, Sandy Clark,
who inspires me every day.
Her strength and determination have taught me
that anything is possible.

CHAPTER ONE

"Yeah, you sing about those cheating hearts, Hank honey."

Merlene Saunders edged up the volume on her car radio. A little down-home music always put her in the mood to catch another cheating husband, and tonight she definitely needed Hank's help.

Merlene picked up her camcorder, aimed it at the front of Patricia and Rick Johnson's graceful Spanish-style home and shot thirty seconds of video. From her vantage point behind a row of live oaks she had a clear view of any vehicles coming or going from the Johnsons' house.

Nothing exciting to record. Just the expensive, lushly landscaped Coral Gables home of a wealthy orthopedic surgeon. A doctor with a nasty little secret.

"Nothing yet," she murmured, and lowered the video camera.

Convinced his recent late hours had more to do with an attractive new nurse than an excessive patient load, Patricia Johnson had hired Merlene to conduct surveillance on her husband of fifteen years. Merlene glanced at the photo of a flashy blonde clipped to her visor. If the woman showed up at the house while Patricia spent the next month in North Carolina…well, that was more than enough proof for the high-strung and very jealous Mrs. Johnson.

But Merlene knew she would need much more to prove infidelity to the satisfaction of a judge, so she'd signed a contract to follow Dr. Johnson around Miami for a month, if necessary, to get the goods on him.

Merlene knew how to trail a subject—and not get caught—and now had a license that made it legal.

Just ask my ex-husband, she thought. Now, there was a doctor who'd thought he could get away with anything. Merlene shook her head to rid herself of thoughts of her ex. She didn't want to believe all men were pond scum, but she'd yet to take a case and discover that the husband had been faithful.

She poured a cup of steaming coffee from her battered Thermos and settled in the seat, her gaze fixed on the Johnson residence. Pat had also promised to recommend her to a friend who did the hiring at a major insurance company if she caught Doc Johnson with his mistress. As she sipped, the strong, hot liquid warmed Merlene. Wouldn't she just love a regular gig tracking down workers' comp cheats? That would be more rewarding that chasing cheating husbands. She'd also liked the idea of saving the feds a million or so in Medicare fraud.

A bead of sweat trickled between her breasts, and Merlene pulled her cotton blouse away from damp skin. Miami in August and hot coffee didn't mix, but she needed the caffeine to stay alert.

She had other props to help, her favorite being Häagen-Dazs Chocolate Chocolate-Chip ice cream slowly melting in a blue cooler. Nothing like a jolt of cool, creamy sugar to keep her focused when she got sleepy. She'd packed plenty of crisp tortilla chips and spicy salsa to munch on. Unfortunately, she didn't have enough light to read.

With a sigh, Merlene took another gulp of coffee. The night promised to be a long one. She glanced in the rearview mirror and froze midswallow.

A large figure moved swiftly toward her car.

She dropped her cup in the console and rolled up the window. All four doors were locked. Her keys hung from the ignition for a quick getaway.

"Damn," she muttered, as the shadowy figure became clearer. As surely as the Grand Ole Opry was in Nashville, a cop of some sort was on his way to speak to her. She'd been able to spot a cop since the age of ten.

No uniform, no marked car visible. Detective, maybe? Could Doc Johnson have spotted her and called 911?

Merlene fished her investigator's license from her purse and waited for the tall, muscular man to get closer. Early thirties, she guessed, and annoyed about something by the way he punched out determined steps. Good-looking dude from what she could tell, but why the blazes would any man wear a tie in August?

He stopped two feet from the back of her car. "Merlene Saunders?" he shouted. "Miami-Dade County Police."

So he'd run her license plate. Of course he had.

She rolled down the window and dangled her investigator's license outside. "I'm unarmed."

The cop approached and grabbed the license. "You're a P.I.?"

Craning her head out the window to see his face, she nodded. "Any chance I could see your ID?"

He flashed a detective's badge, and she barely had time to register the name Cody Warren.

"What's the problem, Detective Warren?"

He handed back the license, placed his hands on her door and leaned forward to look inside. "What are you doing here, ma'am?"

"I'm on a case." She patted the camcorder. "Conducting surveillance."

"Does your surveillance have anything to do with Dr. Richard Johnson?"

"Yes," she admitted.

"Then we have a problem."

"We do?" Merlene stared at Cody Warren, and he glared back with a crystal-blue glare she could easily interpret in the dying light. He didn't want her here.

Well, so what? She didn't want him here, either. Cops made her nervous. Plus, his presence could attract attention from the Johnson house.

"Why don't you hop in and tell me about this problem," she suggested.

He peered into her tiny car, a smile tugging at the corners of his mouth. "I wouldn't want to sit on your nachos."

A rush of heat warmed her face. From the chaos surrounding her, it appeared as if a hurricane had blown through her car.

Well, no one ever said conducting a stakeout was easy.

"No problem," she mumbled, tossing books and snacks into the backseat. She carefully placed the video camera and her new digital camera on the floorboard behind her, then threw her notebook onto the dash next to her binoculars and a deck of cards.

Her compact car became much too small when the cop folded himself into the passenger seat. Damn if his knees didn't almost reach his chest.

"Does this thing slide back?" Warren asked, reaching for a lever beneath the seat. Before she could answer, he sent the seat zooming back, crackling cellophane and pulverizing her half-eaten bag of corn chips.

He glanced at her. "What the hell was that?"

"My dinner."

He retrieved the crushed bag from behind the seat and raised an eyebrow. "Very nutritious."

Merlene lifted her chin. "So I take it you're with the diet

police, Detective Warren. Some sort of special task force to ferret out fat?"

His expression morphed into a scowl. She shifted her weight, knowing she should have curbed her tongue. But that all-knowing male smirk had been too much.

"So what's your interest in Richard Johnson?" Detective Warren demanded, now all business.

"I've been hired to keep track of his activities."

"By who?"

"That's confidential."

He scrubbed his fingers against his chin, and Merlene heard an unmistakable scratch that meant he hadn't shaved in a while. Long day?

Wishing cops didn't always make her uneasy, she studied the detective in the fading light. He had an angular yet handsome face, a strong, confident jaw. His nose featured a slight bump, and she wondered if it'd been broken in a fight on the job. From the way he dominated space in the Toyota, he had to be at least six-two. The cotton shirt across his torso confirmed an iron-flat stomach, not an ounce of fat anywhere on him, probably because he never ate junk food.

Good for him.

"Is something wrong, Mrs. Saunders?"

Merlene jerked her gaze to Warren's face. He watched her with a frown. Lord, what was the matter with her, checking out his body? She swallowed. "I'm wondering why the police are interested in Dr. Johnson."

Cody shook his head. "Mrs. Saunders, the Miami-Dade Police would greatly appreciate your discontinuing surveillance of the doctor."

"Why's that?"

"Let's just say your presence here could jeopardize a lot of work. Interference with a police investigation is something we take seriously."

"By sitting here I'm interfering?"

"Possibly."

"Are you going to give me any details?"

"No, ma'am."

Merlene sighed, knowing she had to do as he asked. Her boss's number-one rule was to stay out of the way of the police. She snapped the cover over the camera lens. "Sure, Detective, whatever you say."

He nodded. "Good."

Merlene stared through the windshield at the doctor's house. "What did you do, you bad boy?" she asked softly, then picked up her notebook and entered the time.

The detective planted one foot on the grass, preparing to exit, then paused. "Did you get anybody on tape tonight?"

Merlene shook her head. "Nobody went in or out after I followed him home."

"All right. The sooner you leave, the better."

She smiled at his profile and tapped the pen against her cheek. "I'll bet you're worried that if he sees me following him, he'll know you guys are onto him. Am I right?"

Without answering, the detective pulled himself from the car and walked around to the driver's window. He held out a business card. "If you get anything you think might be helpful, I'd appreciate a call. My cell's on the back. It's always on."

Merlene accepted the card. "If you won't tell me what's going on, how will I know what's helpful?"

His steely gaze bored into her. "I think you'll know. Thanks for your cooperation, ma'am."

"Oh, sure. No problem." She flipped the card against her thigh as he moved away. Why were the police always telling her what to do? As a child, they'd hassled her family with threats of family services and foster homes but never offered a bit of help.

Merlene tossed the card onto her front seat and started the car. She knew better than to get in the way of the police. Besides, she had other methods to keep track of Doc Johnson.

SOMETHING WAS WRONG. Dead wrong.

Cody couldn't shake a gnawing feeling in his gut that he'd missed something important. Where was Dr. Richard Johnson?

Months of work to make this case, to put away a dirty doctor who didn't care who he prescribed narcotics to or what bogus diagnosis he made—not as long as he got a big check from an insurance company—and now the whole damn thing threatened to fall apart.

Waiting for a traffic light to change, he wondered what hole Dr. Johnson had vanished into. Could his disappearance have anything to do with the Saunders woman's surveillance? An image of the intriguing female private eye he'd encountered the night before flashed through his head. How could a woman who dug for dirt to pay the bills manage to look all wide-eyed and innocent?

The check he'd run on her came back clean. No outstanding wants or warrants, and he wished *his* credit report looked as solid. She worked for D. J. Cooke Investigations, the man and the firm both reputable, and no one had ever lodged a complaint against her license. The licensing board promised to double check with Cooke and get back to him.

Yeah, maybe her activities had nothing to do with Johnson's vanishing act, but he didn't believe in coincidences. A P.I. is on Johnson's trail one day, and he disappears the next? Had to be a connection. He'd warned his lieutenant they needed twenty-four-hour surveillance to always keep track of the doc's whereabouts. Damn budget cuts were undermining a lot of investigations these days.

"What the…" He swore under his breath as he turned

the corner, spotting the P.I.'s vehicle secreted behind a tree across from Nurse Cole's apartment building. Merlene Saunders had inserted herself square in the middle of his case again. This time he'd question her more thoroughly.

"Detective Warren," Merlene said when he leaned in the passenger window. "We have to quit meeting like this."

He jerked open the door. "You and I need to talk."

"Have a seat," she murmured.

Feeling as if he were squeezing into a bulletproof vest, Cody eased into the small car.

"You know," she said, "it's hard for me to blend into the surroundings when you're always hanging around my stakeout."

He slammed the door. "Who are you working for?"

She shook her head. "That's confidential information."

"Must be the wife. She's worried about the doc and Nurse Linda Cole, whose apartment you're watching."

He studied Merlene's face but wasn't sure if he'd nailed her game.

"So what can you tell me about Nurse Cole?" Merlene asked.

He shrugged. "I'd rather hear what you can tell me about Dr. Johnson."

"Truth is…nothing. Yet." She lifted a video camera from the backseat and aimed it at the apartment. A large emerald-cut diamond glittered on her right ring finger. "Haven't got anything but test footage to prove I've been watching their sorry butts. Never have caught them together."

"How long have you been on them?" he asked.

"How long do you think?" Merlene lowered the camera. A faint red mark encircled her eye where the camera had pressed into her pale skin, and Cody resisted an urge to touch the spot, wondering why he wanted to smooth away the distrust shimmering in her eyes.

"Five days," he guessed. "I'll bet Mrs. Johnson hired you before she flew to Blowing Rock. She thinks the doc is fooling around and wants you to prove it, right?"

Merlene smiled, and the curve of her lips brought a curious sparkle into smoky-gray eyes. Damn but she had a beautiful smile. Shining, almost-black hair fell to her shoulders.

"Am I interfering with a police investigation again?"

Yes, and he needed to get his mind back on business. "If you're spotted, you could blow months of work. Cooperation would be greatly appreciated."

She glanced at him sideways, looking doubtful.

"I already showed you my badge," he said.

"Cooperate how?"

"We'll trade information."

"Trade? Yeah, right. Cops just love to trade." She raised the video camera again and pressed the record button.

"What are you recording?"

"I make a video record of all my activities to substantiate my bill."

"Good plan," he said. Hell, she talked like a pro. Time to throw her off balance—find out if she actually was one.

"So what does your husband think of your line of work?"

"I don't have a husband."

"Divorced?"

"You know," she said, placing the camera in her lap, "you are absolutely the rudest man. First it's my diet and now my marital status?"

He caught her gaze and held it. Beneath delicate brows, her eyes had darkened to an opaque, deeper gray.

She looked away, glancing toward the apartment. Cody admired her flushed cheeks as he chose his next words. Too bad if she didn't like his probing. It was his job to stir things up and see what kind of reaction he got.

"Guess what," she whispered in a husky voice. "Linda is on the move."

He shifted his gaze. Nurse Cole hid behind large, white sunglasses and a floppy straw hat, but there was no mistaking the woman climbing into a white BMW.

Merlene started the car and shoved it into gear.

CHAPTER TWO

"HEY!" CODY SHOUTED as the car lurched forward.

"I've been hired to watch her, remember?" Merlene shot a sideways glance at the detective as she accelerated and found him staring at her, mouth open. Yeah, maybe she shouldn't have taken off with him in the car, but if she'd waited to get rid of him, she'd have lost her subject. No way was she losing her subject. Linda Cole could be on her way to meet Dr. Johnson.

"You are unbelievable," he said, fumbling the seat belt across his lap.

"Just cooperating with your investigation."

"Then don't follow so closely," he said.

"Thank you, Detective, for your professional advice, but I've never been made on a tail." She kept her gaze fixed on the road, but the heat of his scrutiny made her squirm. At least the car's movement created a rush of cooling air.

"And how many tails have you been on?"

"Probably less than you," she admitted as she stepped harder on the gas. "So Nurse Cole is involved with whatever the doc's into?"

"You know I can't answer that." Cody peered at the speedometer.

"What happened to trading information?"

"Don't speed," he said.

"I'm not speeding." Okay. So she was—but only a little. Merlene stayed well behind the BMW as she followed the nurse toward Miller Drive, holding out her right hand to test the blessedly cold air blasting from AC vents.

"She's probably just going to the grocery store," Merlene muttered. "Won't even have time to cool the car down."

Warren loosened his tie. "Glamorous work."

Suppressing a laugh, she thought of the khaki shorts and sleeveless cotton blouse she wore, her usual surveillance uniform. Some glamour. In case she needed to follow a subject to a more formal atmosphere, she always kept a skirt and jacket hanging in the backseat. A good investigator was always prepared.

"I hope she is going to meet Johnson," Warren said.

With both vehicles caught by a red light, Merlene scribbled the time and mileage in her notebook. "Why?"

"Because he didn't show up at his office today."

She raised her head. "Are you saying you don't know where he is?"

He rubbed a hand over his chin. "Not at the moment."

"Why don't you have him under surveillance?"

"Good question," Warren said.

"Well, well. I guess you should have let me stay last night," she said, not even trying to keep satisfied amusement out of her voice. She couldn't help but enjoy this turn of events. "I'd know his location if you hadn't run me off."

Warren answered with a strangled noise.

The BMW turned south on Galloway Road, and Merlene stayed with it.

"How long have you been a private investigator?" he asked.

"Two years. I work with D. J. Cooke Investigations."

Warren nodded as if he knew where she worked, which she didn't like one bit. But of course he'd probably verified her license was current and she'd paid all her fees. Fortunately her boss was a stickler for those kinds of details.

"I didn't know D.J. was still around," the detective said. "Tell him I said hello."

Was that a note of respect in Warren's usually overbearing tone? "You know D.J.?"

"He's a good man."

"He is, isn't he?" She adored her boss, a distant relative from Missouri. He'd taught her how to follow a subject and not get nailed. D.J. was semiretired now, bothered by too many medical problems, but she'd heard tall tales of his exciting career, first as a cop and then a P.I. "Did you ever work together?" She'd love to hear another war story about D.J.'s time on the job.

"My dad knew him," Warren said in a flat voice.

She threw him a look, but he stared out the windshield, his eyes fixed on the vehicle in front of them.

"Linda is turning into Norman Brothers," he said.

"Shoot." Merlene drove slowly past the gourmet grocery, confirmed that her subject had parked in its lot, then turned around at the next intersection.

"I don't see Johnson's car," Merlene said as she drove through the jammed parking lot.

She maneuvered the Corolla into an empty space, then reached into a zippered sports bag in the backseat and selected a red wig.

"You're going to follow her in?" Warren asked.

"Unless you want to." Gathering her long hair into a bun, she tugged the wig securely over her head. The detective leaned against the passenger door to watch.

Hating that his scrutiny made her self-conscious, she checked herself in the rearview mirror, rearranged the wig with quick fingers, then grimaced at her pale face surrounded by a mop of hideous red hair.

Oh, definitely a glamorous job, she thought, angry with herself for caring what she looked like.

"Cole might meet the doc here," she said. "Haven't you heard the grocery store's a hot spot to pick up dates?"

"Speaking from experience?" he asked, quirking an eyebrow.

"There you go with rude questions again."

He grinned. "That's one hell of a wig."

"It works." She placed tortoiseshell frames with clear lenses on her nose. "I don't want Dr. Johnson to recognize me."

"The doc won't meet her here."

"Probably not," Merlene agreed, "but it's my job to confirm that. Stay put and keep the air-conditioning running."

Without waiting for an answer, she stepped out of the car and breathed a sigh of relief. Detective Warren's presence made the compact car feel like a toy.

CODY LAUGHED AS he watched Merlene half run across the lot and enter the grocery. Stay put? Where did she get her nerve? He should have arrested her for kidnapping him.

But he enjoyed the feminine sway of her hips, thinking good things definitely came in small packages. He smiled, guessing this was one lady who never resorted to the grocery to meet members of the opposite sex.

And a meet at a produce market wasn't Richard Johnson's style, especially since the good doctor wasn't having an affair with "Nurse" Cole. Linda Cole had been hired only as a player in Johnson's elaborate game of fraud and deceit. No wonder the wife got suspicious, considering how much time her husband spent with the bogus Florence Nightingale.

She'd be more likely to hook up with Sean Feldman, the attorney mastermind of the scheme, but a survey of the parking lot didn't reveal either of his vehicles. Too bad. Merlene could have recorded Nurse Cole and Feldman together. That would be one nice piece of evidence against Feldman, the lawyer who filed lawsuits based on the phony injuries diagnosed by Dr. Johnson, allowing them to fleece insurance companies out of millions. Usually by quick settlement so the insurers didn't have to even bear the expense of a trial. What an easy con.

So where was Doc Johnson? Had he gotten wind of the coming bust and rabbited? If so, he hadn't cleaned out any accounts. Didn't seem likely since he'd made a fortune off his various schemes, including a lucrative pill mill in Hallandale where any addict with an itch could get a prescription for a fee. Cody shook his head, thinking about the greedy physician who'd supplied narcotics to his sister's husband.

Cody still searched for answers when Linda exited the store and loaded brown paper bags into the trunk of her white BMW. She lit a cigarette, dropped the lighter back in her oversize purse and climbed behind the wheel.

Moments later Merlene slid into the driver's seat and yanked off the wig. "Oh, that itches." She scratched her head, her own dark hair cascading to her shoulders in waves.

"You look better with your own hair."

She stopped scratching and looked up, gray eyes suspicious. "Thank you."

"You're welcome."

She shoved the car into gear. Neither spoke for a moment as she followed the BMW into traffic.

"Looks like she's headed home," he said.

"She didn't speak to anybody in there except the clerks." Merlene sighed. "Just a routine trip to get groceries."

Silence filled the car again. He studied Merlene's face, trying to figure out why she intrigued him. He liked her, despite her interference. No question she was a looker. She had a fragile, porcelain look, although her attitude was anything but docile. She appeared to be a competent detective, but she was wasting her time attempting to catch Linda Cole and Dr. Johnson together in a romantic tryst. He ought to tell her and save her some effort. She had to be frustrated. He sure as hell knew how that felt.

Plus, he couldn't help but believe her constant presence around the players in his case had somehow changed the game, had caused Johnson to vanish. The sooner she moved on to other surveillance, the better. This wasn't just another case to him. This case involved a doctor more interested in cold, hard cash than healing patients, some of them patients like his brother-in-law.

"Have you recorded anyone going into the doctor's house?" he asked.

She shook her head. "Nope. He's pretty damn boring, if you ask me. His wife is probably well rid of him."

"Because he's boring?"

"He's a crook, too, right?"

Cody nodded. "Listen… Mrs. Saunders…"

"Don't tell me. I'm interfering and you don't want me to mention anything about a police investigation to my client."

"Actually, I've decided to help you," he said. "I'll save you the headache of following Cole around."

"Oh, yeah?"

"Yes, ma'am."

"Then call me Merlene." She tossed him a look. "I don't answer to Mrs. Saunders. That's my ex's mother, thank you very much. Not me."

Amused by her prickly tone, Cody relaxed against the seat. He'd known her marital status, but now he knew how she felt about her ex.

"So how are you going to help me?" she asked.

"You're wasting your time chasing Linda Cole. Dr. Johnson isn't romantically involved with her."

"My client thinks otherwise."

Cody nodded. "He's spending a lot of time with her, but

only to make money, not love. They won't meet outside the office." He watched while she turned the information over in her mind.

"You're sure?" she asked.

"We've got them on audio, and it's all been pure business."

"Interesting." Merlene remained quiet for a moment. "But not good enough for my client. She wants concrete proof, and I can't exactly tell her my info came from the cops, now, can I?"

"I'd appreciate it if you didn't," he said. Merlene's sarcasm bothered him, but he wasn't sure why. She seemed to take particular delight in antagonizing him. Hey, he was trying to help her.

"I don't know."

Fascinated, he watched her absently twirl a strand of thick hair around a long, graceful finger, the diamond ring flashing with her movements.

"I'll run it by D.J." She dropped her hand to the steering wheel and narrowed her eyes. "But don't feed me any nonsense about you pulling my license if I don't back off. I know you can't do that. It takes months…probably a year to suspend a P.I.'s license."

"I didn't say one word about suspending your license."

They'd arrived back at Linda's apartment. Without speaking again, Merlene pulled in next to his white, unmarked unit.

"Are you going or staying?" he asked, not caring that he sounded sharp.

"Going. For now. I'll let D.J. tell me what to do. I trust him." She met his gaze as if daring him to object.

"Fine," Cody said. "I don't want to say, 'See you around,' exactly, but…"

She crossed her arms. "I won't promise to stay out of your way."

"Then I guess I will see you around."

"LICENSING BOARD?" Merlene stared at D. J. Cooke behind his cluttered desk. She'd thought her boss looked more tired than usual. Now she knew why. "What do you mean you've heard from the licensing board?"

"Something about your client's husband," D.J. said with a sigh. "Interference with the police. They're sending an investigator out next week to interview me."

"They're starting an investigation?"

"Routine, I'm sure," D.J. said.

"Damn that Cody Warren," Merlene muttered. "I knew he was nothing but trouble."

"Cody Warren?"

She nodded. "That's the cop who rousted me off surveillance on the Johnson case."

"Cody. Doggone it. That's a name I haven't heard in a dog's age."

In spite of her annoyance, Merlene grinned at D.J.'s wrinkled face. Her boss always resorted to Ozark slang on a trip down memory lane.

"He remembered you, too," she said. "He said you were a good man. His exact words." She stared at her lap, organizing her notes from the surveillance. "That's the only nice thing he said all day. I should have known he'd pull something like this."

D.J. made a clucking sound. "Little Cody. I'm glad he stuck it out."

"Well, he's not little anymore," she said, remembering the way his white shirt had stretched across a muscular back.

D.J. didn't seem to hear her. "It sure was rough on him there for a while."

She raised her gaze. "What was?"

D.J. sighed. "Bad business. His dad was a longtime beat cop and got caught shaking down shop owners for protection money. Cody was a rookie when the scandal broke."

"He seems to have survived." So she and Cody had the same rotten luck when it came to their parents.

"I can't rightly recall what happened to Bill Warren, but Cody became a cop who plays it strictly by the book." Tapping his glasses against his cheek, D.J. swiveled in his chair and looked out the office window. "He worked in homicide for a while, then asked for assignment to the fraud division."

Merlene followed his gaze outside to a suburban backyard. Two small brown squirrels chased each other around the gnarled trunk of an avocado tree. Her boss conducted business out of his home now, taking only an occasional case, allowing Merlene to work as many surveillance jobs as she could land.

She watched the squirrels fuss at each other. *Probably squirrel husband and wife,* she thought. But at least one of them still wanted the other.

D.J. coughed. Not liking the sound, she shifted her gaze back to his face and really didn't like what she saw. D.J. looked exhausted. No, more than that. He looked sick, his face as pale and white as his hair.

"Hey, are you okay, boss?" she asked softly.

"Fit as a fiddle," he said with the wave of a thin hand. "Don't worry about me." D.J. swiveled back and placed his forearms on the desk. "I've handled much worse problems in my career."

She nodded, thinking he definitely didn't need the stress of a Division of Licensing inquiry at this stage in his life.

"What should I tell Mrs. Johnson?" she asked.

"You've never seen the doctor and the nurse together away from the office?" D.J. asked.

"Never."

"Call your client. Tell her you've got nothing. Let her make the decision."

Merlene nodded. "Good enough. I'll even offer to refund some of the retainer."

"Is money part of the problem in this marriage? From the home address, I thought they were loaded."

"Could be. I definitely get the feeling the doc keeps her on a tight leash," Merlene said. "And I remember what it's like to be divorced, broke and unemployed. Scary. Maybe she's got nobody to help her. If it weren't for you, I don't know where I'd be right now." D.J. and his wife had been there for her when she hit rock bottom after the divorce.

"You'll always be fine, Merl. You've taken care of yourself since you were knee-high to a grasshopper."

She smiled at yet another of his country clichés and then shrugged. "I'm also thinking her husband might soon be in jail. That's my next question. Should I tell her the cops are investigating Dr. Johnson?"

"No. If she calls her husband and tips him off, it could torpedo an important case. My policy is to always cooperate with the police."

Merlene nodded. "I wonder what he's done."

With a thoughtful smile, D.J. leaned back in his chair. "Probably some kind of fraud. Or selling narcotic prescriptions to bogus patients. Maybe he's become addicted himself. Doctors can be quite creative."

"You don't have to tell me that," she said as she stood. "Remember, my ex was one of the great creative healers of all time."

D.J. chuckled, which turned into a cough as he waved Merlene out. "Good luck on the Harris case tomorrow."

She turned back. "Thanks. You know how much I hate testifying."

"Are you ready?"

She sighed, wishing tomorrow and her court appearance were already over. "I've typed my report and been over it four times."

D.J. nodded. "Good. Make sure you can prove chain of custody on the video. Judge Robinson is a stickler for details."

"You got it. I'll check in with you tomorrow."

Merlene stole a last look at D.J. as she exited his office and paused in the doorway. A tickle of worry nudged at her thoughts as she watched him struggle to take a breath, an effort which prompted a deep cough.

No wanting him to watch her hovering, she stepped out of his view, but waited in the hallway until his hacking ceased and she knew he was okay.

Moving toward her car, she wondered about D.J.'s health. Of course, he hated it when she fussed over him, but, damn, how could she help worrying? Seemed he was deteriorating a little each day. Well, too bad if he didn't like her nagging about his meds. She'd keep reminding him anyway.

WHEN MERLENE'S TIRES crunched gravel in the driveway of her Coconut Grove home, she wished all her problems were as simple as proving the authenticity of her evidence. Her video of a philandering John Harris had never left her possession and certainly hadn't been tampered with. The pickiest judge in the country would have no basis to exclude her absolute proof of infidelity.

But she was more worried about D.J. Anyone could tell his cough had worsened, and she suspected he hid something from her. He didn't act worried about the investigation triggered by Detective Warren, but maybe that was a ruse, too. Were they in serious trouble with the licensing board thanks to Warren?

But they hadn't done anything wrong, so why would they be?

And she dreaded talking to her client. She'd rather keep trustworthy records anytime than talk to a distraught wife about discontinuing surveillance on her jerk of a husband. All of this mess thanks to Cody Warren. The nerve of that man. So he'd really gone after her license.

Her mood lightened as she walked across the shaded front yard, savoring the scent of blooming gardenias. She'd bought this small, eighty-year-old house after her divorce from Peter, the only real home she'd ever had. To her, home meant safety, a refuge, a place to hide. She'd never felt any of those things while living with Peter.

After unlocking the front door, she collapsed onto her green leather couch and tossed her briefcase onto the cushion next to her. No way to hide from calling Mrs. Johnson tonight.

The phone rang before she'd had time to slip off her shoes.

"What have you found out about my husband and that woman?" Pat Johnson demanded. Merlene closed her eyes and took a deep breath. "Nothing yet, Pat. In fact, I've seen no evidence at all after five days."

Mrs. Johnson lowered her voice, as if conveying a sensitive government secret. "I think Rick is in Ocala."

Merlene sat up. "Ocala?"

"We have a horse farm in Marion County, one of his little hobbies. I rarely visit, but I think he and that slut nurse are there together right now."

"No, Pat. The nurse has been in her apartment all day. I was sitting out front. Listen, I'll give you back half the retainer if you want to call this off."

"Absolutely not. I know I'm right. Stay on it, Merlene, please."

Merlene cringed at the insistence in Pat's voice. "Pat, I

hate to see you waste your money. I think there's a chance that—"

"That he's involved in something illegal?"

Merlene rose to her feet, clutching the cord. "Why do you say that?"

"I'm not stupid, and I have an office key," Pat said. "Ever since that Linda Cole took over Rick's office, billings have doubled. I think she's gotten him involved in something, well, frankly, sordid. I have a feeling it's not…legal." Merlene waited as Pat sucked in a breath to regain control of her voice. "That's why you have to…to prove their affair, so I can force him to break it off, get rid of her." After another pause she said, "I have two children, Merlene. They need their father."

"But, Pat…"

"I'll double your fee."

Merlene stopped pacing. So money obviously wasn't a problem for Mrs. Johnson. She sighed. "All right, Pat. I'll do my best. Tell me why you think your husband is in Ocala."

"Because I got a call from a friend. He's been seen in town. Alone, thank goodness. I want you to drive up there and check it out. Maybe his nurse is going to meet him there."

"I guess that's possible," Merlene murmured, although if Cody were right, that definitely wouldn't happen. But who was she to argue with her client?

"I'll leave tomorrow afternoon," Merlene said, now thinking with pleasure of a visit upstate courtesy of Pat Johnson's expense account. The scenery in northern Florida reminded her of the Midwest—more woodsy, a lot less people crowding the roads. More room to breathe. She could leave as soon as she finished her testimony in the Harris divorce. The trip would provide a much-needed break from city life.

"Even when he comes back to Miami I want you to stay

on this," Mrs. Johnson continued. "I need to get absolute proof of his infidelity. Remember what I told you about my friend at Union Farm Insurance. One word from me and the job is yours."

"Of course I'd appreciate that, Pat." If she could nail a high-billing insurance gig, maybe D.J. could finally retire.

"Then do not let my husband out of your sight. Have you got a pen? I'll give you directions."

"Trouble," Merlene muttered when she'd disconnected, staring at the address she'd jotted down, wondering if it would be hard to find. Her client might want her to stay on the case, but Detective Warren would not be happy. No indeed.

She relaxed against her sofa cushions, her thoughts drifting to Cody Warren. She couldn't stop thinking about the man and his piercing blue eyes that noticed everything. What was really strange was how she actually liked how they circled each other, seeing who would give up information first. Enjoying that kind of conversation made absolutely no sense. He'd probably turn out to be another macho cop convinced he knew everything, one who didn't care who he hurt as he shoved his way through life.

No, that wasn't fair. After all, he had clued her in about the doctor and his nurse. He didn't have to do that. He could have let her spin her wheels for weeks chasing the pair trying to catch them together. But then he'd probably told her so she wouldn't keep sticking her nose into his big case.

His case. She sighed, tapping the pen against her chin. D.J. always cautioned her not to interfere with active police investigations. And she supposed his case was important, would in some way protect the citizens of Miami-Dade County. For sure Cody acted as if he thought the case was vital, although he wouldn't tell her anything specific.

So should she clue him in about Johnson being in Ocala?

After all, he'd helped her. How had he put it? Trade information? Actually, telling him might be fun since he didn't know where the doc was. Did the cops even know about the horse farm in Ocala? If so, had they bothered to look there?

She wrapped her arms around her knees and smiled, deciding to find Cody before her drive to North Florida. How would Mr. Don't-Interfere-with-My-Case Warren react when she supplied him information he didn't have? She nibbled at her bottom lip, picturing how he'd respond to her news, how those eyes would drill into her. Maybe she could get more details out of him about what the heck was going on with Dr. Johnson, why the cops were so hot to find him.

She'd follow D.J.'s advice and not reveal to Pat Johnson anything Cody told her. Still, her client already suspected something was up and blamed Nurse Linda Cole. But Cody insisted the nurse and the doctor were not involved romantically.

So what was really going on?

CODY RECOGNIZED HER by the maddening sway of her hips and the bounce of that amazing cascade of hair. He knew he'd run into Merlene Saunders again but hadn't expected it to be so soon, and definitely not in the lobby of the Miami-Dade County Courthouse.

What was she doing here? For sure not following Nurse Cole for Pat Johnson. The nurse had shown up in Dr. Johnson's office this morning like clockwork.

He was anxious for his conference with the prosecutor on the Johnson case, but seeing Merlene made him want to slow down and find out what she was up to.

"Hold it," he shouted, and stuck his hand into the closing elevator. The doors jumped open and he squeezed in the crowded car beside her.

"Morning," he said, letting his gaze wander over her tiny but shapely form. She did indeed look good.

"Detective Warren," she said.

He smiled down at her, noting her briefcase and a professional navy blue suit. Leaning over, he spoke close to her ear. "If I didn't know better, Merlene, I'd say you were a lawyer ready for trial."

She switched her briefcase to the front of her body and grasped it with both hands. "I'm here as a witness."

"Ah. Keeping Miami-Dade County safe from cheating husbands?"

Smoky-gray eyes shifted from the elevator door to meet his gaze. Her discomfort was easy to read. "And to think I'd decided to help you."

Damn. He'd forgotten she had no sense of humor. "Help me?"

She shrugged and raised her chin.

The elevator stopped on six, and he nodded at two smiling clerks from Judge White's office as they exited. "Ladies."

When the doors closed and the car resumed its upward motion, he turned back to Merlene. "How are you going to help me?"

Although all eyes focused politely elsewhere, he knew the remaining occupants of the car listened to their conversation. Merlene knew it, too, and shot him a chilling glance, one meant to shut him up.

He caught her gaze and smiled. She hesitated, then shook her head. Pleasure slid past Cody's defenses as her full lips curved into a tentative smile. She faced the burnished metal doors again.

"Never mind," she said. "Maybe I'll call you later."

"Why not talk now?"

"I'm due in court."

He studied her profile, thinking she was as lovely in the

harsh, artificial light of the elevator as she had been in the softer, muted shadows of early evening. A subtle, warm fragrance of citrus—was it lemon or orange?—hung in the air.

As the car slowed down for the tenth floor—his stop—he said, "Last chance, Merlene."

She threw him an unreadable look. "Good luck, Detective."

Tucking his arm into hers, he drew her out of the elevator with him.

"Hey…" She pulled away, but the doors had already closed behind them.

Cody released her arm and threw her a grin. "Now you know how it feels to be abducted."

"This is not the same and you know it."

"No?"

"No." Merlene jabbed the call button, but at this busy time of the morning in this old building it would take forever for another elevator to arrive. She was already nervous about testifying, and now she'd probably be late. Damn Cody.

"I need to be on the twelfth floor in about two minutes," she said, "and now—thanks to you—I'll be late."

"Maybe you should have left home earlier."

She punched the button again, knowing her impatience wouldn't hurry the machinery in the least, wishing she could jab her finger into Cody's chest instead.

"What's going on, Merlene? I know you have something to tell me."

"And how do you know that?" Furious, she turned to confront him but was stopped by his probing gaze, a look that brought all of her senses to full alert. Warmth spread outward from the spot on her arm where he had touched her.

"Because I'm a detective," he said.

"Yeah? Well, so am I." And she had never been as aware of a man as she was of Cody Warren at this moment, of his height a full foot over her, of the confident way he stood, of a muscular body full of power and authority. Sexy as hell, and infuriating.

Turning back to the elevator, she looked up at the light. At least a car was descending. But of course it stopped on twelve—her floor.

She took a deep breath and let it out slowly to calm herself. "Did you ever find Dr. Johnson?"

"No. We still don't know where the hell he is."

"I might know."

He took a step closer. "Yeah? Where?"

"His wife thinks he's in Ocala. I'm driving up this afternoon to check it out at her request."

"She thinks he's staying at the ranch?"

"Exactly." So Cody knew about the ranch. Of course he did. She took a sideways glance at him and decided he looked confused. Yes, this was fun.

"Why would the doc go to the ranch in the middle of the week? He had a calendar full of patients."

"I don't know why, but a friend spotted him in town and my client wants me to investigate. She thinks he's there with Nurse Cole on some sort of romantic getaway." Merlene shrugged. "We know different, of course, but I couldn't convince her."

Cody ran a hand through his thick, sun-streaked hair. "Going to Ocala right now makes no sense."

"What do you mean? Why doesn't it make sense?" She'd given Cody some good info. Maybe he'd share some in return.

"Did you tell Pat Johnson about the police investigation?"

"I know better than that." She sighed. Cody loved to answer a question with a question. Great strategy to wiggle off the hook. And once again, she learned nothing.

"I was wondering if that's what made Johnson disappear," he said.

"Well, if he knows, I promise that info didn't come from me."

"Thanks," Cody said. "I appreciate it."

"I can tell you this, though," Merlene said. "Pat suspects her husband is into something illegal and that our Nurse Cole led him down that crooked path."

Cody laughed. "Yeah, women are a bad influence."

"Not funny. She's worried about her kids."

"Yeah, I'm aware he has kids." He shook his head and after a pause said, "Ocala doesn't add up."

"Maybe not," Merlene agreed, "but as long as my client pays my bill, I do what she asks."

Cody jammed balled fists into his pants pockets; body language that told her he was really worried about something. What was it? Damn. Why wouldn't he tell her anything?

"Do you carry a gun?" he asked.

"A gun?" She stabbed the lit elevator button again. "For surveillance? I don't think so."

"Surveillance is all you do?"

"That's all I'm interested in doing. Besides, D.J. says don't carry a gun unless you plan on using it."

He nodded. "Good advice. Listen…watch yourself."

That unexpected comment caused her to face him again. "Do you know something I don't? Is there something special I should look out for?"

His blue eyes searched her face. For a moment she thought he was going to give her something, but then he tightened his jaw. "You're in a profession that could be dangerous. Just be careful."

"I'm always careful."

He nodded, looking doubtful. "Call me when you get back."

"What for? Wait. You actually expect me to report in? Tell you what I found in Ocala?"

"Cooperation is a good thing, Merlene. Remember?"

The elevator doors bounced open, and she stepped into the crowded car.

"You have my card," he said. "Call me." He held his hand to his ear, mimicking a phone.

She stared at him as the doors closed between them and wanted to stamp her foot in frustration. She would have, too, if this elevator hadn't been as full at the last one.

So this overbearing man screws around with not only her license, but D.J.'s license, and then expects her to call him with a report? Amazing. The nerve. Especially since he hadn't shared a thing of use with her.

Detective Cody Warren was driving her crazy.

CHAPTER THREE

CODY CHUCKLED AS he pushed open the door to the tenth-floor conference room. No question an encounter with feisty Merlene Saunders always lightened his mood. Too bad they'd met under the strained and tense circumstances of this serious case. Maybe he could look her up later and they could start over.

He'd like that. The question was: would she?

Inside the room, he found Assistant County Attorney Rafael Alvarez at the head of a long wooden conference table cluttered with files, books and paper. The prosecutor had summoned Cody and his partner to the courthouse this morning for a strategy session on the Johnson case. Jake Steadman, his partner, was tied up in a deposition but would join them later if he got finished in time.

Alvarez wasn't looking at his papers, though. He stared out the window wearing an solemn expression.

"Hey, Rafael," Cody said. "What's wrong, man?"

Rafael turned to face him with a grimace. "Cody. Yeah, well, I've got some bad news. I'm not sure I quite believe it myself yet."

Cody sat down beside Rafael. "What?"

The prosecutor used a pen to nudge his cell phone on the table before him. "Just got off the phone with my supervisor."

"I'm listening."

"We're done, man."

"Done?"

"They've pulled the plug on the Johnson case."

Cody felt blood drain from his face as he stared at Rafael. He'd thought this meeting was to discuss an arrest, not an ending to the investigation.

"Pulled the plug? Is that some kind of a sick joke?"

"It's no joke, man," Rafael stated with a shake of his head. "Believe me, I wish it were."

"But you can't end this investigation. My partner and I have put in six months of hard work."

"And you know the hours I've logged," Rafael said. "It's not me, Cody. It's coming from the top guns. As of now, I'm off the case. Reassigned." Rafael stood and jammed his scattered papers into a brown leather briefcase. "I've got to get back to my office. I suspect when you return to your station you'll find that you've been reassigned, as well."

"What's going on?"

"Off the record, I think Dr. Johnson got to someone. I saw him leaving the federal building early this morning."

"You saw Johnson in Miami today?"

"Right. Around eight."

"You're certain?"

Rafael paused in his quick movements. "Why? What do you know?"

Cody also rose. "I got a tip that he was in North Florida."

"No way. Johnson was with Tony Menudo, an FBI agent I know."

"He was with a fed?"

"Yeah, and Tony was treating him like a confidential informant." Rafael reached out and shook Cody's hand. "I'm sorry, man. We were almost there."

"Yeah. Thanks, Rafael," Cody said. "But I'm not giving up on nailing this bastard."

"See you on the next one," Rafael said.

Frustration and fury raged inside Cody as he strode toward the elevator. He rotated his shoulders to release the tension. Didn't help. What he needed to do was jog about twenty miles. Or punch something.

What the hell was going on?

But he knew.

Most likely Doc Johnson had buddies in high places. Slimeballs always did. Johnson had gone to his friends and struck some kind of cushy deal. Oh, maybe he'd get a few months, maybe even a year in a nice country club prison, but he wouldn't do any hard time. Maybe he'd have to pay a stiff fine, but nothing a wealthy physician couldn't easily handle. Before long, Johnson would return to his old life and continue to enjoy his illegally obtained riches. Within months of release, he'd start another lucrative fraud.

Hands on his hips, Cody stared down the hallway and tried to calm his rushing thoughts. What would his lieutenant say? Had Montoya already assigned him a new case? Not that he didn't have plenty of other open cases to work.

What about Jake? Cody placed a quick call to his partner to let him know the latest development. Jake's cell was off for the depo, but Cody left a voice mail that their conference had been cancelled.

He knew Jake would be equally pissed when he learned the reason. They'd worked hard to develop the evidence to convict Dr. Johnson. And now it was over. All that work for nothing.

Cody shook his head. Damn. So Johnson had returned from his trip to Ocala…if he'd ever gone there. Jealous wives often overreacted, read more into a situation than really existed. Maybe the good doc had never even left town.

When the elevator pinged its presence, Cody entered and punched the button for the twelfth floor. He needed to find Merlene and save her a long, pointless trip.

To his knowledge Dr. Johnson had never been violent, but not so the other players in this fraud. He hated the idea of her going after Johnson by herself. Yeah, she seemed competent enough, but the woman had no idea what she was getting into.

There was a hell of a lot more to this case than a wandering husband. Maybe it was time he told her. What did it matter? Wasn't his case anymore.

INSIDE A CAVERNOUS wood-paneled courtroom, Merlene jotted careful notes as her client's soon-to-be ex-husband whined out his side of the story. She didn't want to make any mistakes when called to testify. Lawyers loved to confuse, to trip up witnesses. There was probably a class in law school on how to do that.

She'd thought she might be sequestered, not allowed to hear the other witness's testimony until sworn in, but her client's attorney informed her there was a chance the case could settle thanks to her surveillance. Merlene secretly crossed her fingers. She certainly hoped so. She hated testifying.

But, man, had this Mr. John Harris ever changed his story since his wife had filed for divorce. At first he denied any wrongdoing, but he couldn't do that under oath once he'd viewed her video of his frequent visits to his secretary's town house.

Poor guy. She thought Harris might actually cry. Not that she had any sympathy for him. She remembered Carol Harris's tears when she watched the video that confirmed a wife's worst suspicions. Because of Merlene's surveillance, John Harris would have to cough up a lot more money per month for his wife and kids.

Of course he could afford plenty of alimony and child support. She'd seen his income tax returns for the last three years. She'd never realized one person actually made that much money.

Judge Robinson summoned the lawyers up to the bench for a sidebar conference no one else could hear. Were they about to settle? Glancing at her watch, Merlene hoped she'd be called soon or they reached an agreement. She planned to leave for Ocala by one, but that wouldn't happen at the pace this hearing plodded along. She might have to wait until tomorrow.

As happened all too often, her thoughts drifted to Detective Cody Warren, he of the piercing blue eyes and wide shoulders. No question Cody made her nuts. She couldn't remember ever responding to a man the way she did to him. And it made no sense. How could he infuriate her but make her feel totally alive and glad to be with him at the same time? And Cody was likely married. Men that looked like him always were.

She glanced at John Harris, who still waited in the witness chair. Out of nowhere she hoped Cody wasn't a cheating husband like this man.

An envelope thrust into her lap jarred Merlene from her thoughts. As she glanced up, her breath caught when she found Cody standing to her left. He smiled and winked, then hurried up the aisle. She turned in her seat and watched him exit the double swinging doors.

She took a quick glance around the courtroom. The judge and counsel were still engrossed in their bench conference. She took a deep breath. No one else had even noticed Cody.

Relieved that he hadn't waited around to watch her testify, she slashed open the envelope with her pen.

In large spidery scrawl he'd written: "Meet me before you leave for Ocala. After three I'll be at Tamiami Little League Park. Find me. It's important. Cody."

Her heart racing from his startling appearance, she read

the note over and over. He'd underlined "important" twice and used an exclamation mark.

Cody wanted her to meet him at a Little League park? What could be so important?

And who did he think he was? Her boss?

She bit her lip as she slipped Cody's note into her briefcase. If she postponed her trip until three, it would put her into Ocala after dark. But the hearing hadn't even resumed yet, and from the amount of questions the judge was asking the lawyers, it looked like it might be a while before the testimony resumed. She'd already considered the option of postponing a day.

Should she find Cody later? Of course D.J. would want her to cooperate.

Still, when would cops ever stop telling her what to do? This one in particular enjoyed ordering her around, making her life miserable. Merlene crossed her legs and edged down her skirt, wondering how her spirits could possibly lift because she anticipated an afternoon meeting with Detective Cody Warren.

If she were honest with herself—always hard to do when it came to Cody Warren—she liked the idea that he'd sought her out and wanted to meet with her. She liked it too much. Was it about the case? Of course. What else could he want to see her about? She doubted he found her as attractive as she found him. No way would his steady cop's heart race as hers just had if she showed up unexpectedly in his life. She'd practically had to fan herself with her notebook when she saw him. She could tell herself her reaction stemmed from nerves over her imminent testimony, but that wouldn't be the whole truth.

Yeah, she'd meet Cody later. She wanted to know what was up. Heck, she looked forward to another one of their standoffs where they jockeyed for position and each other's information. Jockeying for position? That thought brought up all kinds of erotic notions and rocketed a shiver down her spine. What was wrong with her?

Judge Robinson banged his gavel and called the hearing back into session. Merlene shook her head and forced her attention away from images of a naked Cody Warren.

THE CRACK OF a ball slamming into a bat echoed through Tamiami Park. Merlene paused next to a game in progress as the image of her little brother punching a mitt flooded her memory. Donny had loved to play first base more than he'd loved to eat, and she'd loved watching him.

She took a deep breath. How long had it been since she'd remembered the fun of watching kids playing baseball? Too long.

She relaxed as she inhaled the sweet fragrance of freshly mowed grass. Four or five boisterous games were in progress on fields surrounding her. A carnival atmosphere enlivened a park full of squealing kids and boastful parents. Oh, look at that young catcher in his bulky uniform. Merlene laughed, remembering how once in a pinch she'd subbed as an umpire for Donny's game. What a disaster that had turned into.

A light breeze ruffled her hair and brought the fragrance of fresh popcorn and cotton candy. Donny's usual after-game snack had been a lime snow cone. She closed her eyes and tasted the sweet-tart flavor of her little brother's favorite treat.

After a nostalgic moment or two absorbing this familiar all-American scene, Merlene remembered why she'd come.

Right. Back to business. So how would she locate Cody? No help but to look for him game by game.

With fingers entwined in a tall chain-link fence behind home plate, she searched the closest field, figuring Cody must be coaching his son's Little League team. Of course, the man was married and had kids. The absence of a ring never meant a thing. She ignored the nagging sense of disappointment that accompanied her thoughts.

She considered leaving without finding him. How embarrassing that she'd allowed her imagination to take off like a runaway train.

But no. What did she care if the man had ten kids? She'd come on business, pure and simple. And, damn, she wanted to find out what was so important.

At the third game she visited, she looked up at a tap on her shoulder.

"Keep your eye on the shortstop. We're convinced he's headed for the majors."

"Yeah?"

Cody towered over her, his eyes hidden by dark sunglasses. "No doubt about it."

Merlene judged the shortstop in question to be around eight or nine, his hair a similar light brown color to Cody's. The boy focused intently on the batter, his face screwed into a tight ball of concentration.

She also tried to concentrate on the game but found Cody's long, muscular legs distracting. He wore tan coaching shorts and a blue shirt that emphasized the width of his shoulders.

"Heads up, Charlie," Cody yelled.

The shortstop grinned when a pint-size batter swung nowhere near the ball.

"That's strike two," Cody said. "When this team is out, Charlie will be first up."

She nodded at the batter. "That kid's not standing close enough to the plate." Her brother had had the same problem his first year.

"You're a baseball fan?"

"I used to be."

The little boy missed again, and she felt a twinge of pity as he fought tears. Poor little guy. Donny'd hated it when he struck out.

"Third out," Cody said.

Ten small players raced toward the dugout. "Is that talented shortstop your son?" she asked.

"Nephew."

Nephew? Interesting. "Is your son here, too?"

"I don't have a son." He faced her and grinned. "Thanks for coming. How'd it go in Judge Robinson's court?"

"Other than not getting called until after lunch, fine." Looking up, she smiled back, liking the friendly expression on his angular face. Damn, but Cody was tall. *Okay. No son, but what about a daughter?*

She sighed. "I'm just glad my testimony is over."

He led her away from the game to a concrete bench in the shade of a large oak. The bench and the ground below were covered with oak leaves. Cody brushed the debris away.

"Testifying is never a picnic," he said as they sat. "Believe me, police hate going to court, too. It's time away from our regular duties, and I'm sure you know how defense lawyers try to destroy our evidence, make us look bad."

At his mention of cops, familiar suspicion bumped into her good mood. So why was Cody acting so nice? He obviously wanted something. No one ever did anything for free, especially not cops.

"Are you going to tell me why I'm here?"

"Relax, Merlene. You don't have to rush off to Ocala. Dr. Johnson is back in Miami."

"What? Are you sure?" She searched his face, wishing she could see his eyes behind the glasses.

He nodded. "I confirmed it myself even though I've been reassigned. He's at his office this afternoon."

"Reassigned?" she asked. "What does that mean?" When

he leaned toward her, the scent of fresh grass and clean masculinity curled around her senses.

"That you're free to watch your favorite doctor as much as you want. He's no longer under active investigation by my department."

"But why? Has he been cleared of whatever you thought he'd done?" Which Cody still hadn't told her about, by the way. Was he about to tell her now?

"No, ma'am. I didn't say that. In fact, I was hoping you'd tape the comings and goings from the good doc's house for me."

"What? Come on, Cody. You have to tell me what's going on."

Cody removed his sunglasses and ran a hand through his hair. "I don't know why yet, but I've been pulled from the case. So has the county attorney my partner and I've been working with." He leaned back and caught her gaze. "Guess what? It's not because of budget cuts."

"Wow." Merlene thought hard and came up with only one explanation. "Dr. Johnson must have powerful friends."

He nodded. "That's what we think. So if you stay on him, at least I'll still receive some information."

"Because his friends can't call me off," Merlene said, nodding. "And I suppose you'll want a full report?"

"I wouldn't mind."

The complete irony of the situation caused a laugh to bubble up from deep in her chest. She tried to stop herself but couldn't. At the confusion on Cody's face, she clamped a hand over her mouth. "Sorry," she murmured.

"My case is a disaster, and you're laughing?"

"Because you chased me away twice and now…now you want me back." She shook her head. "I never thought I'd live long enough for the police to ask me for help."

"At least something I say can make you smile." He startled her by raising his hand, but merely brushed a lock of hair away from her face, then dropped his hand to her shoulder.

She sucked in a quick breath but didn't move.

"Do you know you have a beautiful smile?" he said.

She didn't reply, only felt the weight of his hand resting on her shoulder.

His eyes searched hers, and an unfamiliar yearning shot through her as he leaned closer. His hand inched closer to her neck. She found herself shifting in his direction. Was he going to kiss her? She suddenly wanted him to. Wanted him to more than she'd wanted anything in a long time.

"Hey, Cody," a voice shouted. "Get back over here. Charlie's up next."

She stiffened, and Cody dropped his hand.

He angled his head toward the ball field. "Want to come with me to watch my nephew at bat?"

"No!" She jumped to her feet, furious with herself for letting down her guard. "No, no. I can't. I have to go."

He stood beside her with a frown. "Slow down, Merlene. You don't have to drive to Ocala, remember? Since you haven't got anywhere else to be, why not enjoy the game with me?"

"Thanks, but no. I—" She looked around, searching the bench so she didn't leave something behind. Like her good sense. Or maybe she could find an excuse for why she had to run away from him. And, Lord, she needed to. Her flesh burned where he'd touched her. She resisted the urge to stroke the spot.

"I have to catch up with Dr. Johnson again," she said. There. That was the truth. "My client wants me to maintain constant surveillance on her husband."

"But I wanted to—"

She stuck out her hand to shake his. He took hold and squeezed, so she quickly withdrew her arm. She needed to get away from Cody before she did something really stupid. "Thanks for letting me know about Dr. Johnson, Detective Warren."

"Sure," he said. "Why don't you—"

"Really, I appreciate it. But I've got to get back to work."

Refusing to meet his gaze again, she fled toward the parking lot. When she got to her car she unlocked the door and collapsed inside.

What had happened to her just now? For those few moments it was as if Cody had put her into some kind of a trance. She frowned. No, not exactly. She'd been conscious of every hammer of her pulse, exquisitely aware of him, silently urging him to take her into his arms and kiss her.

She glanced back the way she'd come. At a baseball field. In front of children.

Dear heaven, what was wrong with her?

Long ago she'd promised herself to never, ever lose control of her actions. Losing control was what had happened to her parents when they drank. She'd learned to never let anything but logic and common sense rule her life.

So obviously she had to stay away from this detective if he could make her forget where she was with a mere touch.

MERLENE SIGHED AND stretched her legs, trying without success to get comfortable in the Toyota's bucket seat. What was that old country song about being back in the saddle again? Yep, that was her. And nothing doing at Doc Johnson's house—as usual. This promised to be another long night. She'd have to remain on this stakeout until after midnight.

After a conversation with her client, she'd resumed surveillance on the good doctor, picking him up again at his office where Cody said he'd be. Johnson arrived home after dark and hadn't budged since.

And her mind wouldn't budge from thoughts of her encounter with Cody Warren this afternoon at the ballpark. Now that she'd calmed down, in hindsight she wished she hadn't run away like a big chicken. She'd behaved like a scared little girl who'd never been kissed.

Well, truth was she'd never been kissed by somebody as exciting as Cody. What must he think of her, running away like that?

She lightly stroked a finger across her shoulder, tracing the path of his touch, remembering the flood of sensation he'd aroused. Part of her wished he had kissed her. She rubbed her finger across her lower lip. What would kissing Cody feel like?

And, really, how could a simple touch, a hand resting on her shoulder, make her behave so crazy? Maybe her reaction had more to do with the haunting emotions the baseball field had dredged up, bittersweet memories of her younger brother.

Yeah, right. She laughed at herself. *Blame poor Donny.* Of course, that was it.

She did the math and realized this year Donny would be twenty-two years old. Imagine that. What would he be doing now? Would he be in college? Working? She liked to think he'd have beat the odds and made the major leagues in baseball. He could even have kids of his own.

A loud bang on the car door jerked Merlene from her reverie. Startled, she looked up to find Cody grinning at her through the open window.

Placing her hand over her racing heart, she closed her eyes. How had he snuck up on her like that?

"Unlock the door, Merlene."

She opened her eyes to glare at him, but he was already at the passenger door waiting to climb in. She reached across the front seat and flipped the lock.

"You scared me half to death," she accused as he positioned himself in the small seat. A delicious spicy aroma floated from the brown paper bag he carried.

He shrugged, obviously unconcerned by her fright. "You should be aware of what goes on around you at all times, Madam Detective. Especially at night. Maybe it's a good thing you don't carry a gun."

She bristled at his words even knowing he was right. "Did you come to give me a lecture?"

"No. I brought you dinner." He held the paper bag in front of him and rattled the contents. "Smells good, doesn't it?"

Yes, it did smell good, and she hadn't had a decent meal all day. She'd been too nervous about testifying to eat breakfast or lunch and had only grabbed some cheese crackers to nibble during the surveillance.

"What is it?" she asked, eyeing the bag.

"My sister Annie's homemade vegetable soup. When I told her I was coming by to check on you, she insisted I bring you some. She saw us talking at the game this afternoon."

"That was nice of her." Merlene swallowed. And nice of Cody to bring her food, especially considering how she'd acted this afternoon. What was with him? This was probably a bribe meant to insure her cooperation. For sure cops loved cooperation, but so far it had traveled mainly in one direction.

"You don't need to check on me, you know. I'm a big girl."

He pulled a clear plastic container filled with a thick liquid from the bag. Heat had condensed moisture underneath the lid. "Better eat before it gets cold."

She gave in to her hunger. No sense letting homemade soup go to waste.

"Okay, thanks." When she pried open the lid, steam and an appetizing hint of garlic spread into the car. Cody handed her a spoon, and she took a tentative taste, closing her eyes as she savored the flavorful, warm broth. Best soup she'd had in ages. Of course, she couldn't actually say it was better than her mother's since her mom never made soup that didn't come from a can.

"What about you?" she asked between sips.

"I already ate. My sister's a great cook, isn't she?"

Merlene nodded, enjoying the soup too much to answer, not caring that Cody watched every spoonful she placed in her mouth. She hadn't realized she'd been so hungry.

He smiled, then glanced toward the Johnsons' house. "Anything going on tonight?"

"Uh-uh," she mumbled, shaking her head.

"You need to be more careful around Johnson. He's involved with some dangerous people in high-stakes insurance fraud and pill mills."

"Pill mills?" Merlene asked. She'd read about that scam in the paper lately. "You mean he provides painkillers, narcotics to addicts when they're not truly sick?"

"Bingo. Very lucrative for the physician, but people are dying because of greedy doctors. It's a huge problem in Florida."

She nodded, wondering about the hard set to Cody's jaw. "I'll record any cars coming or going, report the tags to you."

He glanced at her again. "I like how you set up in a different location this time. Smart."

"D.J. taught me well."

Cody rubbed his hand across his chin. "D.J. was a good cop."

"Oh, you think so?" she asked, unable to keep the sarcasm from her voice.

Cody cocked a brow at her tone. "Yeah, I do."

"Well, I doubt if he'll appreciate your praise since the Division of Licensing is investigating him…thanks to you."

Cody narrowed his eyes. "What are you talking about?"

"You didn't know they're sending out an investigator because of your complaints?"

"Complaints? All I did was confirm you had a valid license."

"Well, guess what? A call from the cops worries the regulators in Tallahassee."

Cody sighed. "I'll see if I can call them off."

"Good." Her outrage cranked down to a simmer, Merlene took another bite of soup, spilling a drop on her blouse. She reached for a crumpled napkin and said, "D.J. hasn't been feeling well lately."

"Sorry to hear that. How did you hook up with him?"

"He's a distant relative. My mother's second cousin, I think. They were close as kids. He moved away from Joplin and made good, though."

"Joplin?"

"Joplin, Missouri. Once the proud home of the Bob Cummings Motel, its only claim to fame until the tornado last year."

"Your home, too?"

"No, not my home," she murmured. "But I was born there." Merlene gulped the last bite of soup and placed the container in her console next to a half-eaten bag of cheese crackers.

"You moved to Miami and looked up D.J. so you could make good, too?"

She shifted in the seat and looked out the window. Seated like this, Cody was too close. "Not exactly. I moved here when I got married. I looked up D.J. afterward."

"Ah, the husband. I'm curious about what he thought of your career choice."

"Not much, since I chose it so I could catch him in bed with his lover." There. She'd said it. She raised her chin and gave Cody a direct look, daring him to say the wrong thing.

"I see."

She sighed. "It was a long time ago."

"Well, did you?"

"What?"

"Catch him in bed with his lover?"

She nodded. "Like I said, D.J. taught me well."

"Was your husband a police officer?"

"No." She issued a short laugh. "Another no-good doctor."

"So since you were so good at surveilling people, you decided to make a living at it?"

"Made sense, don't you think?"

"Hell of a way to choose a career."

"It wasn't my first choice." After a pause she said, "Did you always want to be a cop?"

"From the time I was about ten. My dad was a cop."

"Yeah, D.J. told me. That's nice that you ended up doing what you always wanted," she said. "Most people don't get that in life."

"So what was your first choice for a career?"

Damn, she'd left herself wide open for that question. "An impossible dream."

"Why impossible?"

"Never mind." She leaned her head against the seat back.

"You can't do that, Merlene. You have to tell me."

"You don't want to know."

"Yeah, I do."

She sighed and wrapped a strand of hair around a finger.

"Come on."

Wondering why she was dredging up ancient history, Merlene gazed toward the Johnson house. "I wanted to be a singer, specifically a country singer. I ran away to Branson, auditioned for every music hall in town, but all I ever did was wait tables. What a mistake." She examined the ring on her right hand and wondered why she still wore it. To remind her how miserable her marriage was?

"That's how I met Dr. Peter Saunders."

"Ah. You're a singer?"

"That's just it. I'm not." She shook her head. "I can't even carry a tune. When I was seventeen I thought I could, but believe me, what happens when I sing isn't music."

"I like country tunes," he said. "Sing something for me."

"No way, Detective." She held up both hands. "I knew better than to tell you."

He grinned at her. "Coward."

You got that right. I'm a big fat chicken who might start clucking any minute.

"Forget it." As she reached for her notebook on the dash, her arm brushed against his shoulder, the same arm he'd touched this afternoon. Warmth again spread out from their contact. Did he feel that spark, too? She felt her belly muscles contract and thought about their almost kiss this afternoon. Being in a confined space with this man was definitely a bad idea.

Taking a deep breath, she checked the time and entered her status into the log. She needed to refocus.

"Did you find out why you've been yanked off Johnson's case?" she asked.

"There's rumor," Cody said, "but nothing concrete."

Or maybe you're refusing to tell me, she thought, tossing the pad back to its place.

"You should have stayed and watched the game," he continued. "In the fifth inning my nephew hit a triple."

"Hey, that's great," she said, and meant it. "I'll bet he was thrilled."

"He was. And I think you enjoyed yourself at the park today, too."

"Yeah, I got a kick out of watching the kids. It'd been a long time."

He nodded. "I thought so."

She caught his gaze and held it, again wondering why he'd really come tonight. "You're observant. D.J. says that's the mark of a good detective."

"Is that a compliment, Merlene?"

She rested her head against the seat, watching him. "Maybe."

"Well, thank you, ma'am."

"Don't let it go to your head."

"Too late," he whispered. "It already has." He cupped his hand around her neck and pulled her toward him, lowering his mouth to hers.

CHAPTER FOUR

MERLENE SURRENDERED TO the tide of pleasure sweeping through her, oblivious to anything but the power of Cody's kiss. Magic, that's what it was. Sweet, soul-stealing magic she was powerless to resist, had no wish to resist.

He made a husky noise, a rumbling deep in his throat. Arms corded with muscle gathered her close. He was warm, strong, solid as an ancient oak. She arched toward him, needing to get closer, wanting to feel the safety of his strength crushed against her.

Until an insistent, shrill beep echoed through the Toyota.

She stiffened and pulled away. Cody eased her back against her seat but didn't release her.

"Ignore it," he growled.

She swallowed. "It's D.J. He'll be worried." She cringed at the catch in her voice but grabbed her cell phone.

"Oh, well…if it's D.J.," Cody muttered as he slumped against the passenger seat.

A green light glowed in the dark car when Merlene flipped open her phone. What had just happened? Her heart galloped as she focused on the keypad. Fighting to control her trembling fingers, she punched in D.J.'s speed number. He answered immediately.

"What's going on, Merl?" D.J. barked. "Why didn't you answer?"

"Nothing is going on, D.J. I couldn't get to my phone in time." No need to tell him why.

"You scared me a bit," her boss said. "I got plumb worried."

"Sorry. But everything is fine. The doctor arrived home around nine and is probably tucked into bed for the night. I'll go on home around midnight as usual, get some sleep and be back here before he leaves for work tomorrow."

"Sounds good," D.J. said. "Talk to you tomorrow."

"You feeling okay?"

"Fine." D.J. hung up, and the tone of the off button sounded in the quiet car.

"He likes to check on me," Merlene said. Watching the light of the numbers dim, cold reality settled over her. What would have happened if D.J. hadn't called her? She needed to get Cody out of her car.

"You'd better go," she said.

Cody turned to her with a frown. "What's wrong?"

What's wrong? What was right? Good Lord, how could she make out in a car like a hormone-impaired teenager? During an assignment, no less.

"I'm working, and you shouldn't be here," she said. "Now who's the one interfering?"

His brows arched. "What?"

"You heard me. You're interfering with my investigation, distracting me from the job."

"Come on, Merlene. I'm keeping you company on a boring stakeout."

"What would your precious police department think about me crashing one of their stakeouts and seducing an officer on duty?"

He opened his mouth to speak, then tightened his jaw without speaking. She looked away, recalling how easily she'd given in when he'd urged her lips apart. Furious with herself for succumbing to his potent attraction, she searched for the quickest way to make him leave. So what would piss him off? She could ask for money. That should work.

"How much is the Miami-Dade P.D. willing to pay for help with your little problem?"

"Pay?"

She shrugged. "I don't work for free." Yeah, maybe this was a lame idea, but the best she could come up with on short notice. Next time she'd know better than to unlock the car door.

"You know damn well I've been pulled from the case. I can't pay you. I hoped you'd cooperate."

"Typical of the police." She folded her arms across her chest and stared out the windshield. "All take and no give." Her cheek tingled from the scratch of his beard. She longed to run her fingers where he'd touched her. She didn't dare look at him.

"What the hell are you talking about?" Finally he sounded angry. Took him long enough.

She shrugged. "Money talks. I have bills to pay."

He lifted her hand and wiggled the finger with the diamond ring. "Doesn't your ex-husband pay your bills?"

She snatched her hand back. "That's none of your business."

She held her breath waiting for his reaction.

"No," he said, dragging out the word. "I guess it's not." He opened the car door, then paused and glanced at her over his shoulder. "I'll be sure to tell my sister you liked the soup."

Merlene watched him walk away, surprised by the tears stinging her eyes. With him gone, her car felt empty. Lonely. Lifeless.

Her heart felt empty, too. Like a big pit she'd seen once in the Ozark Mountains.

She hated the look on his face when she'd asked for payment. Now he obviously thought she was a greedy witch. She only asked for money to get him out of the car.

But she would make the video he requested and send him a copy. He might call her to say thanks, but she suspected there was a good chance she'd never see him again after this little episode. Who could blame him?

The thought that she'd never see him again made her sorry she'd answered D.J.'s call.

She'd been hungry most of her life. Sometimes for food, always for love. When very young, often escape from freezing weather was what she hungered for most. But when Cody kissed her she'd felt…full, as if she finally had enough of whatever she needed. Well, at least she couldn't imagine needing anything else during that kiss.

Problem was, this new sense of fullness was addictive. How could anyone resist a feeling that made you feel so good, even if lasted only briefly?

Yeah, and wasn't that the way drugs worked? She thought of the pill mills Cody had told her about tonight, and how her client's husband helped make addicts out of good people. What would be so wrong with letting herself go with Cody? Just enjoy his company and see what happened? She'd been resisting him solely because he worked in law enforcement, following her years-old logic that told her all police officers had to be jerks.

She knew that couldn't be true. Not all of them, anyway.

Cody definitely wasn't a jerk. Jerks didn't bring you vegetable soup. Jerks didn't tell you how evil pill mills were connected to your case. And how could a jerk kiss like that?

Anyway, he *had* shared information with her. Probably about as much as she'd shared with him.

With him she felt so…what was it? Alive. New. With Cody it felt like the past didn't matter, that she didn't have to be that hungry little girl from Missouri. She could be somebody different, somebody new.

STOMPING BACK TO his car, Cody decided Merlene Saunders had a chip on her shoulder that stretched all the way to Branson, Missouri. Why did everything in life always come down to greed? Cody jerked open the driver door and slammed it behind him.

Oh, but he knew why. People always want what they don't have. His old man had wanted way, way too much, more than he could ever get on a cop's salary. He understood exactly what desperate yearning had done to his hardworking father, and it was never going to happen to him.

Cody cranked the engine, his angry thoughts now focused on his dad. What had happened to him to make him turn? He knew his father hadn't been dirty his whole career. For a treat, his family used to eat in a neighborhood café near their home on Friday nights. What was the name? Smitty's, named for the owner. Money was always tight, but Smitty had some kind of deal for early diners. His mom raved about the meat loaf. He and Annie loved the outings because the early-bird meal came with dessert, one of the choices being their favorite: hot apple pie.

Smitty usually came out to say hello and every time offered to pick up the entire check because his dad was a police officer. But his dad always paid the bill, refusing to take anything from Smitty. Not even a free cup of coffee.

"But it's just a way to say thanks," Smitty would say. "Really nothing. Cops put their life on the line every day."

"That's my job," his dad had always responded seriously. "And it's my privilege to uphold the law."

Cody remembered practically bursting with pride because of his dad's honesty. He'd decided right then he wanted to grow up and be exactly like his dad. Be honest. Be a cop. Uphold the law.

And he'd wondered a million times since what had happened to make Dad change. He'd even considered the idea the refusals had all been for show in front of the family. If the wife and kids hadn't been there, would Dad have let Smitty pay the tab?

Cody maneuvered his vehicle onto the roadway. He'd never know. He'd never know what it was his father had wanted so much that he had to turn crooked, forced him to end his own life.

Merlene Saunders sure as hell wanted something. Probably another rich doctor who could buy her more flashy gems to adorn her skin, skin that in his opinion needed absolutely no help from bling.

Now that his initial anger had ebbed, a heavy sense of disappointment weighed him down over what had happened with Merlene. He liked Merlene. He liked her sassy attitude, even if it drove him nuts, and she was definitely easy on the eyes. He'd been looking forward to getting to know her better.

For sure kissing her had been a pleasure. He shifted in the seat, remembering how she'd felt in his arms. Yeah, he'd like to get to know her a lot better, but not if money was what spun her world.

Why hadn't he noticed such a materialistic streak in her? Had he been so blinded by her beauty? Missing a trait like that sure as hell wasn't like him. She'd even called him observant, which had led to that fabulous kiss.

Well, the department wouldn't pay her, and he wasn't about to. He never had money left over from a paycheck anyway, didn't have a dime saved anywhere, didn't want to be a slave to possessions, didn't want to end up like his dad.

Money talks. Yeah, right, it always does.

How could a woman come apart like warm honey in his arms and then freeze into a sheet of ice in seconds? Why had Merlene pushed him away? She was interested in him. He *would* have to be blind not to have picked up on the signals, the way she secretly checked him out. Even his sister had noticed their mutual attraction this afternoon.

Annie! Damn. He'd forgotten that his sister and Charlie were bunking with him tomorrow night while their home was tented for termites. She'd asked for the couch, but of course he'd give them the only bed in his one-bedroom apartment.

Annie had reminded him about the plan this afternoon, and he didn't have any food in the house. He glanced at the digital clock on the dash. After ten. Too late to pick up groceries now. He'd have to make time tomorrow. Nah. Better yet, he'd order pizza. Charlie would love that idea.

He probably should straighten up the place, though, maybe run the vacuum. If not, he'd have to listen to Annie grumble about how he should get married, have kids, settle down. Cody sighed. Fat chance that would happen anytime soon. The only women he met were on the job.

Like Merlene. Would he ever see her again? Did he want to see her again? Hell, yes. What was it about her? Merlene might be greedy, but he'd never been this intrigued by a woman.

CODY OPENED HIS door to his sister and nephew the following evening, hoping a little family time would improve his mood. He needed a distraction so he could stop thinking about one certain female private investigator.

He and Charlie talked baseball stats and who would make the playoffs over a pepperoni pizza, boring Annie to eye rolling, until she announced since tomorrow was a school day, Charlie had to go to sleep.

"Look at this place," Annie said, as she collapsed onto the sofa beside him after her son had reluctantly crawled into Cody's bed. "When are you going to buy some furniture?"

"This place is good enough for you and Charlie to crash in," Cody said, glancing around the small, sparsely furnished room. His secondhand belongings suited him fine.

Annie sighed. "Don't get huffy. You know we appreciate not having to pay for a motel. Besides, Charlie insisted. He wanted to talk to you about sports, sports and more sports."

Cody nodded. "And we know sports are way over your head, Annie Oakley."

She punched his shoulder. "Annie Oakley! Nobody can call me that but you, Cody Wyoming."

He grinned at his sister over the strange names their mother had cursed them with. Thank God Annie was better now, finally able to smile again, enjoy life. She'd had a difficult couple of years after her husband had overdosed on pain meds following complications from back surgery. Pills he'd obtained from another unscrupulous doctor. Yeah, just hand over the cash and the doc was only too glad to provide relief. Mark had been a damn good man, but one with a low threshold for pain. Addiction sent him on a downward path that had spiraled out of control.

Annie plumped a cushion behind her and turned to study him. "So now you can tell me more about that gorgeous new girlfriend who came to the game yesterday. Where did you meet her?"

"She's not my girlfriend."

"Yeah? The two of you seemed awfully engrossed in each other." Pinching him lightly in the ribs, she continued, "You almost missed Charlie's turn at bat."

"Strictly business, Annie." He knew eagle-eyed Annie had noticed his interest in Merlene.

"Why is everything always business with you, Cody? You need to lighten up."

"I take my work seriously."

Annie waved her hand. "Everyone knows that. You've spent years trying to make up for Dad's mistakes. It's time to stop and get a life."

Cody glared at Annie. First she ragged him about Merlene and now their father. If he didn't love his sister, he'd arrest her for disturbing his peace. "I've got a life, thank you very much."

"What life? You work constantly and don't own a thing so that, God forbid, you won't become attached to anything. You even drive a county car. I'm wondering what you do spend your paycheck on. You must have a mint stashed away."

"Not everyone worships money. I don't need material things, Annie. They're not important."

"Please." She held up her hand. "You talk like some wigged-out new age guru when I know what you really like is to watch grown men bash each other's heads in on Sunday afternoons. But that's only if you're not at work trying to arrest felons and bash heads yourself."

"I'm sorry you think so little of police work," Cody said in his most wounded tone.

"It's not that." She sighed. "Cody, you don't have anything to prove. No one thinks you're going to end up like Dad. And buying a few nice things wouldn't mean you're greedy."

"I'm happy with what I've got."

"Hey, it's me, your sister. I know how badly you want kids. If you don't settle down and get married, you'll never have them."

"I'm twenty-nine. I've got plenty of time." He closed his eyes. He'd had this conversation with his sister too many times. Hell, yes, he wanted kids, but she didn't get how hard his job was on a relationship. Or how important his job was to him.

"Did you at least give her my soup?"

"Yes, I gave her your soup. She enjoyed every drop." An image of Merlene placing her delightful lips around a spoon loaded with veggies flashed into his mind. He'd enjoyed every drop right along with her.

Annie nodded. "Good. Now call her up and ask her out." She tugged on her thin, straight blond locks. "I'd give anything for hair like that."

He stood, now pushing away a mental image of Merlene wrapping dark hair around a long, graceful finger. Annie wasn't providing a distraction. She was making him think about Merlene even more.

Call her up and ask her out? If he did, would she accept?

He stood. "It's been a rough day, Annie. I'm sorry, but I've got to get some shut-eye."

Annie rose beside him. "I hate that we've thrown you out of your bed. Are you sure?"

"I'm sure. Go to sleep."

She grinned at him. "You don't fool me, Cody. You just don't want to listen to me nag anymore."

"You got that right. See you in the morning, Annie."

"I hope you don't have one of your horrible nightmares tonight."

"Good night, Annie."

"You should buy a condo," she said, moving to the bedroom. "You can't rent forever."

Merlene reached for her video camera when a dark-colored sedan pulled into Doc Johnson's driveway. She glanced at her watch. Almost midnight.

Definitely not Linda's BMW, but she'd record the license

plate for Cody. She zoomed in on the rear of the car until she got a good image of the numbers as the car doors opened.

Two men dressed in dark slacks and casual jackets exited the vehicle and moved toward the front door. Merlene lost them when they moved behind a hibiscus hedge.

She lowered the camera. Strange. Who would visit Doc Johnson in the middle of the night? She'd planned to leave in another few minutes.

She jotted the plate number and a description of the vehicle in her notebook. Tomorrow she'd call Cody with the information.

He'd still be furious with her for throwing him out of the car last night, but that was tough. The man knocked her rational brain patterns out of whack. She needed to stay away from him.

Why did she find Cody so bone-meltingly sexy? She doodled his name on the side of her notebook, then scratched it out. She'd be fine as long as she didn't see him. Or think of him.

Her head jerked up when a loud crack sounded from the Johnson house. Then another, and another.

She froze, recognizing the noise. Gunshots.

Her heart pounded inside her chest. When she remembered to breathe, her inhalation sounded shaky in the quiet of the car. What the hell was going on inside that house?

She picked up the video camera and refocused on the car in the Johnsons' driveway. The same two men rushed toward the vehicle as Merlene hit the record button.

One carried a gun.

Her mind racing, she continued to record as the sedan careened out of the driveway and raced north on Granada Avenue. The car skidded while making a sharp left turn, bounced off a street marker, then disappeared.

Merlene lowered the camera, took a deep, painful breath, then exhaled with a whoosh. She glanced back at the house.

She had to call the police. This was one time when she had no choice. Still…she hesitated. Every time the cops got involved in her life, disaster followed.

If she called the police, it would blow her surveillance of Dr. Johnson clear to Missouri…but she had to do something. She couldn't just sit here and ignore what she heard and saw.

One of the men had waved a pistol. What if he'd shot somebody? Like Dr. Johnson.

She dug in her console for Cody's card.

He answered on the third ring with a groggy "Hello."

"Cody, wake up. Something's happened."

"Merlene?"

"Yes," she whispered. "I—"

"What's wrong? Where the hell are you?"

"I'm in front of Doc Johnson's house and—"

Merlene paused as she heard a female voice questioning him in the background. Cody told the woman to go back to sleep.

Damn, a woman was with him. She shut her eyes. What the hell was she thinking to call Cody? She knew better.

"What's going on?" Now Cody sounded wide-awake.

"Never mind," she said. "I shouldn't have—"

"Talk to me, Merlene."

"I think someone just shot Dr. Johnson."

CODY RACED FROM his apartment in West Miami to Coral Gables, barely slowing down as he sped through intersections. Merlene had sounded terrified, the first time he'd ever heard anything but bravado in her voice.

All he could think about was getting to her.

Johnson's neighborhood remained quiet as he pulled up

beside her Toyota. He'd monitored the Gables police frequency, and no one else had called in a disturbance.

He eased himself into the tiny seat beside her.

"Thanks for coming," she said, eyes wide, cellular phone in her right hand.

"Let me hear it again," Cody said.

She related the story exactly the same way the second time.

"What if he's in there bleeding to death?" She closed her eyes. "I should have called 911."

Cody placed his hand on her shoulder and squeezed. "Hey, take it easy."

Her chest rose as she inhaled deeply. "You didn't hear that loud crack. You didn't see those men run away."

He released her and opened the car door. "I'll check it out. Wait here."

Exiting the car, he wondered why the hell he was bending the rules for Merlene. He'd known her...what? Less than a week and he was about to peer in the front window of Dr. Richard Johnson's house, a man that two days ago was the subject of an investigation he'd been abruptly ordered to terminate. He'd played it strictly by the book for years and now—

A car door closed behind him. Cody whirled around.

"I told you to wait in the car," he growled as Merlene moved close. A flicker of distrust flashed through her eyes, an expression he'd analyze later.

"I'll make a better witness if I see what's going on. Besides, you might need me." She clutched her cell phone as if it were a lifeline.

He stared into her stubborn face and couldn't think of how to dissuade her.

"This is my client's house. I have her permission," Merlene insisted. She dug in her pocket and held up a key. "I've never used it, but Pat gave me this just in case."

"You have a key to this house?"

"So it's not trespassing, is it?"

He shook his head. "I don't even want to think about that."

He turned and moved through the front yard. Merlene stayed with him.

"Do you think we'll be able to see anything through the front window?" she whispered near his ear. "There's a light on in the foyer."

He held up his hand to slow her down, then edged forward. "We won't need your key. The door is wide-open."

CHAPTER FIVE

MERLENE ENTERED THE DOOR behind Cody but slammed into his chest when he turned to block her view.

Too late. She'd already seen a pool of dark blood spreading from a body sprawled in the white marble foyer—a grisly image reflected endlessly in the mirrored walls on either side of the chilly room.

Dr. Johnson's body. She shivered. This couldn't be happening.

Cody swore. "Go outside," he ordered. "You don't need to see this." Then he knelt to feel for a pulse.

But she didn't move, couldn't move. She felt frozen, as if the cold had seeped into every cell of her body.

She knew the doctor was dead even before Cody performed his grim ritual. The amount of blood left no question.

"Oh, God," Merlene breathed.

Cody gently pried the phone from her hand and led her to a porch step. "Wait here while I call this in. We can't disturb the scene any more than we already have."

TWO HOURS LATER, still sitting on a narrow step of the Johnsons' front porch, Merlene found herself in the center of an active crime scene. At least twenty cop cars—most of them marked and with their blue lights flashing—surrounded her. Some of the vehicles were from the Coral Gables Police, some from Miami-Dade County. Even a Florida Highway Patrol cruiser had come for some strange reason.

An hour ago the medical examiner's van had arrived. Two men had entered the house pushing a gurney draped with a white sheet. They hadn't come out yet, but she knew they'd eventually remove Dr. Johnson's body. She guessed they were still processing evidence, likely taking photos, making drawings.

Yellow crime-scene tape flapped in a light breeze around the Johnson premises. She knew they'd placed the barrier to keep out nonpolice personnel. Scores of curious neighbors huddled on the other side, speaking to each other, staring at the house, at her, no doubt speculating about what had happened. Trucks from all the local television stations had already shown up, too. Vultures come to pick on the bones of the dead.

Merlene closed her eyes, wishing she could block out the chaotic scene. How had this happened?

"Here you go, Mrs. Saunders."

She opened her eyes. Officer Garcia had brought her the coffee he'd promised. Finally. She lifted a plastic lid to find black, thick liquid swirling in a white take-out cup. Steam wafted into the night air. No cream, but that was the least of her worries.

"Thanks, Officer Garcia."

"You're welcome, ma'am," the heavyset officer said.

He'd been with her since the police vehicles began arriving. Maybe he was her handler, assigned to keep an eye on her. She'd been over the chain of events three times with various detectives. She knew they were looking for inconsistencies, hoping to trip her up.

Merlene took a sip of the bitter brew and felt warmth slide into her empty stomach, but knew nothing could fill the cold, empty space created by the horrible image of Dr. Johnson's lifeless body.

"We won't keep you much longer, Mrs. Saunders," Garcia said.

She glanced at Cody. Jaw locked into a grim scowl, he stood on the other side of the yard surrounded by five or six uniformed men. No doubt he'd told his story several times, as well. But while Coral Gables' finest treated her like a suspect, they afforded Cody endless respect.

Of course the video would prove the arrival and hasty departure of the murderers, but she hadn't yet mentioned its existence. No way would she turn over the recording before she'd reviewed it first. Evidence could get lost, and she needed to make a copy for her client. And to protect herself. Merlene took a hesitant sip of dreadful coffee, her mind racing. She needed to figure out the best way to handle a tricky situation.

Cody had been pulled from this case for a reason. What if one of the cops here was involved? She couldn't take the chance.

Garcia flipped back a few pages of his small spiral-bound notebook. "Detective Warren vouched for you, Mrs. Saunders, but we still have to confirm your story with Mrs. Johnson. We've been unable to reach her."

Merlene hated the idea that anyone would call Pat at three-thirty in the morning. Poor Pat. What a way to find out your husband had been murdered.

"You're not planning on leaving town, are you, Mrs. Saunders?"

"Hey, lay off, Tito." Cody stepped to her side. "Mrs. Saunders has done nothing wrong. She called me immediately. The body was still warm."

Still warm. She covered her face with her hands. *Still warm.* "I can't believe this."

"If you're through here, I'm going to drive Mrs. Saunders home," Cody said, reaching to help her up. "Come on, Merlene."

She started to object as she pushed herself up but bit back her comment. Cody was right. She shouldn't drive right now. She was too shaky.

"What about my car?" she asked.

"It'll be safe until tomorrow." Cody took her arm and guided her toward his vehicle.

Her thoughts churned as they crossed the dark yard in silence. They ducked under the yellow ribbon, and continued toward his car, blue lights flashing in disorienting circles around them. Since there were police cars everywhere and likely would be for a while, her car should be fine. Still, she couldn't leave without her camera or at least a dupe of the video.

She needed to think. Why couldn't she come up with a plan? Because she was so very tired. Her feet felt like fifty-pound weights as she trudged toward Cody's car.

Cody opened the passenger door of his unmarked vehicle, and she collapsed into the seat, undeniably glad to be with him on this awful night no matter what. She'd worry about why later.

He slid behind the wheel, slammed his door, then turned to her. Their gazes locked, and she couldn't look away.

"Are you all right?" he asked in a quiet, steady voice.

She forced a smile. "Am I acting that scared?"

"It's only natural you'd be shook up."

"You probably see scenes like that all the time," she said, glancing back to the house, wondering if Cody could be in trouble for being at the murder scene of a man he'd once investigated.

"More often than I like." He shrugged and also looked toward the Johnson residence.

She hadn't considered how phoning him could drag him

into problems, create a difficult situation for him at work. But she saw it now.

"Right now I hardly know my name," she said. That at least was the truth.

He squeezed her shoulder as if to encourage her. "I'll drive you back tomorrow to get your vehicle," he said.

She nodded. "I'm too drained to argue. I can't remember ever being this tired."

Cody almost said something, then shrugged and started his car. She closed her eyes and settled into her seat. Before the car moved, she sat up straight.

"Wait," she said. "Please."

"What?"

"I need to get my purse out of my car."

Before he could stop her, she ran toward her Toyota. She knew she had to work fast or arouse Cody's suspicions. The video camera lay on the passenger seat floorboard. She opened her purse and jammed the camera inside. Thank goodness the compact equipment fit. She covered her binoculars with her jacket, grabbed the textbook for her education class and moved toward Cody's car with the items cradled in her arms.

"In case I can't sleep tonight," she told him when she'd climbed back inside, indicating the book.

Relief flooded her when Cody nodded and accelerated onto Granada Avenue. Thank goodness, he didn't notice anything amiss.

After a moment she asked, "The murder has something to do with your investigation, doesn't it?"

When he didn't answer, Merlene swiveled to look at him. A muscle worked in the side of his jaw. He focused on the road, gripping the steering wheel with both hands.

So Cody wasn't going to tell her what was going on.

That figured. She'd watched a murder practically happen

under her nose, but from now on she'd be kept in the dark. Always that one-way street.

"You're not going to tell me anything, are you?" she demanded.

"I'm sorry. I can't. Not yet."

"Damn you," she muttered. But she shifted in the seat and tamped down her frustration. She wasn't telling him everything, either. And Cody *had* been a big help on this terrible night, getting to her quicker than she could have imagined. Had she even thanked him?

Cody ran a hand through his hair. "Hey, I don't know what's going on yet."

They remained silent for a few miles. Merlene broke the silence with, "Who'll call Pat?"

"We have a protocol to follow in cases like this. Officers will break it to her as gently as possible."

Yeah, right, she thought, remembering the cops who had broken it to her that her parents had been killed in a head-on collision. Streetlights flowed by Cody's car in a blurred streak as she recalled the uniformed officers on her front step, sunglasses blocking their eyes so she couldn't tell if they held any sympathy.

Both her mom and dad had been dead drunk, though, so probably hadn't felt a thing. But she'd been fifteen years old, trying to take care of a twelve-year-old brother. She'd felt plenty. She took a deep breath and exhaled slowly. None of that was Cody's fault.

"Turn here," she instructed. "I'm the third house on the left. What time tomorrow?"

"How about noon? That way you can sleep late."

"Thanks," she said. "And thanks for coming tonight. I don't know what I would have done if…" she trailed off. What would she have done?

"You're welcome." Cody placed his hand on the small of

her back and walked her to the porch. He turned her to face him after she'd unlocked the door, his hands settling on her upper arms, his thumbs gently stroking.

"Are you sure you're all right? You've been quiet."

She nodded, raised her gaze to meet his and wished she hadn't. His eyes searched hers, full of worry, full of kindness she didn't know how to deal with. Not when her video camera hung heavy on her shoulder.

Warmth spread from his hands to her center. Damn if she wasn't falling under his spell again.

"You should take a hot bath before going to bed," he said.

"What?" Cody short-circuited her thought processes when he stood this close. Words never registered the way they should.

"A hot soak will help you relax. You need to get some sleep."

She parted her lips, and his warm, soft mouth briefly touched hers before she could speak. He gathered her close, lightly smoothing her hair.

She allowed her purse to fall to the porch and clung to him, reaching for a source of strength in a crazy, brutal world. She'd remember the trouble he'd caused D.J. tomorrow, the trouble she'd caused him, but right now it felt good to be enfolded in his warmth, to feel safe and protected, to be comforted.

He lifted his head. "Do you want me to stay?" he asked. He tucked a lock of hair behind her ear, meeting her gaze. "I could sleep on the couch."

"What about the woman in your apartment?" The words popped out of her mouth before she could stop them. Where had they come from? She hadn't thought about that soft female voice since the phone call to Cody hours ago. From offhand comments during her interrogation at the Johnsons' home, she knew Cody wasn't married. But that didn't change the fact that a woman waited for him at home while he'd offered to spend the night with her.

He frowned. "My *sister* is used to me working crazy hours."

Merlene stepped out of his embrace, startled by her pleasure at learning the woman was his sister. Damn, but she was a wreck to even think about that.

"Thanks, Cody, but I'll be fine."

"You're sure?"

"Of course. And thanks again for the ride home."

"Okay. I'm beat, too. See you tomorrow."

She nodded and grabbed her belongings from the ground. "Right. See you tomorrow."

"Sweet dreams," he murmured, pushing open the door for her, holding her gaze for another second.

She leaned against the door after she'd locked it and closed her eyes, wishing she'd asked him to stay. She didn't want to be alone tonight.

The weight of the camera in her purse pulled at her conscience. How had everything gone so wrong so fast?

Her client's husband was dead. Murdered while she had him under surveillance. What kind of an investigator was she? And until she produced the video to prove her innocence, no doubt she was the focus of the investigation, the police's prime suspect. She'd have probably been arrested if Cody hadn't vouched for her.

And she'd caused a bad situation for him, too, no doubt requiring him to make a lot of explanations to his department. By now he'd probably concluded she was nothing but trouble, and maybe he was right. Even so, he'd been kind to her tonight. Sweet, even gentle.

She needed to stay away from him. For his sake as well as her own.

THE NEXT MORNING, after her third cup of coffee, Merlene called D.J. to fill him in on the previous evening's disastrous activities. She'd watched the video twice last night before going to bed and several times this morning. Then she'd made a copy and stashed it in a box under her bed.

"The recording is good," she told her boss. "I'm sure the police can make an identification. I'll give the camera with the original to Detective Warren later today."

"Make sure you do that," D.J. said. "Have you spoken to Mrs. Johnson yet?"

"That's my next call. I'm not looking forward to that conversation."

"Do you need a lift to get your car?"

"No. Cody said he'd—" Merlene hesitated. "Yes, I do. Thanks, D.J."

The less she saw of Cody the better. Besides, if he walked her to her car, he might notice the camera wasn't in the seat. He might wonder about that later when she produced her video, claiming she had forgotten. Cody was sharp, observant. He'd remember.

D.J. said, "I'll be there in an hour. Call your client."

Merlene replaced the receiver and immediately tried Cody's cell number. She got voice mail and left the message that she didn't need a ride back to the Johnsons' home. She left a similar message with a clerk at his precinct.

She stared at the phone, knowing she should call Pat Johnson, but kept seeing her husband's dead body sprawled across a white marble floor. Who would want to kill him? She believed Cody when he said he didn't know any details. And he'd been wonderful last night. His kiss had been different from the first one. He'd been tender, soothing, as if he understood her uneasiness and wanted to reassure her, to give her some of his strength.

And she was withholding information from him.

She shook her head to clear tumbling thoughts. Wrong. She was useful to him, that's all, and vulnerable because of the murder. Maybe Cody only pretended to be helpful when it suited him. Had he called off the regulators beating down D.J.'s door? Police had all the power, and they could do whatever they wanted with it.

Her mind flashed to the image of her brother's battered body on a cold steel table in the morgue. As next of kin, it'd been her duty to identify Donny. She hadn't wanted to, had been afraid to even go in the room. But there'd been no one else. She'd hoped and hoped and prayed the corpse wouldn't be Donny, that a mistake had been made. But it was him.

Now her last memory of her little brother was him laid out on a death table with that terrified expression on his pale, young face.

She dared not forget Detective Cody Warren was a police officer. Problem was, the mere sound of his voice on a recording stirred a dangerous longing. She needed to crush that longing into oblivion. There was no chance anything could develop between them. They were too damn different.

Merlene grabbed the phone again and punched in Pat's number in North Carolina.

"How's your client?" D.J. asked on the way to retrieve Merlene's car.

"There was no answer at her number in North Carolina. I tried her cell, but that went to voice mail. She's probably staying with friends who are protecting her."

Merlene considered how Pat must be feeling…or maybe she'd been sedated into never-never land. Her client had been totally focused on catching her husband with a mistress, but she'd be grieving over a cold-blooded murder.

With a pang, Merlene remembered two young children who'd now grow up without a father.

"Bad business, this," D.J. said. "I don't like it. Maybe it's time you started taking those teaching classes full time at Miami Dade College. At the rate you're going, you won't finish for another ten years. Your surveillance career was only supposed to be temporary."

"I can't afford full-time tuition."

"The hell you can't." D.J. smothered a cough. "What about the settlement from your husband? Are you going to let it sit in the bank until your funeral?"

"There's not much left after I bought my house. Just some emergency cash."

And that cash was going to remain in the bank where it belonged, because she was never going to be dirt-poor again. Never. She wouldn't, couldn't allow herself to ever again have no food, no one to turn to, no money to pay the power bill. At least she didn't have to worry about keeping the heat on in Florida too often, one of the reasons she'd been eager to move.

Some bitterly cold nights she and Donny had huddled together fully dressed under so many blankets they could barely move beneath all that weight. Even so, they could still feel the chill. Frigid weather never stopped Mom and Dad's boozy parties, though. Hey, the party must go on... until inevitably her parents got into a loud fight, sometimes a violent one, which caused the police to show up at the front door making all sorts of threats.

D.J. didn't realize how bad it had been. He'd been in Florida during the really bad years. Why tell him now? He had problems of his own.

D.J. snorted in disgust. "I swear, Merl, you're the tightest person I ever knew. Your mother, bless her soul, used to say you'd hear her robbing your piggy bank all the way from school. You'd hit the door running when you got home to count how much was missing."

Merlene didn't smile at the familiar story. "After a while, I learned to hide my piggy bank. If I hadn't, Donny and I wouldn't have had lunch money."

"The booze ruined your mom, Merl," he said softly. "She was a good girl."

Merlene shrugged. Good girl? Maybe once, in distant fading memories, those two words might have fit her mother. Had that really been her mom who had held her in church, smoothed her hair and whispered softly not to be afraid of the loud singing? That memory didn't jibe with ones of a bleary-eyed, frightened thief who spent every dime on cheap whiskey. If her father hadn't started slipping her cash from his paycheck, no one would have eaten by the end of the week.

"Have you heard from Tallahassee and the licensing board?" she asked, needing a change of subjects.

"Merl, please don't worry about that nonsense. I can handle matters just fine."

"I know, I know. Are you feeling okay, D.J.?"

"Fit as a fiddle," he said in his most chipper tone.

"You're using the inhalers the doctor gave you?"

"Of course."

"Good." But she didn't like the grayish tint of his skin. Or how frequently he coughed. She suspected his chronic bronchitis caused by years of smoking had flared up again, but he hated it when she inquired about his health.

When D.J. turned on Granada Avenue, Merlene saw police units still in the Johnsons' driveway. Yellow tape still hung at the perimeter of the yard marking the crime scene. She looked around for Cody's unmarked car but didn't spot it.

D.J. pulled in next to Merlene's Toyota.

"Keep me informed, Merl."

"Will do, D.J. Thanks for the ride."

Seated behind the wheel, Merlene shoved aside her jacket and glared at her surveillance notes and binoculars. Guilt ate at her stomach like acid. When had she become such a big, fat liar?

She picked up the notebook and flipped to the last page where she'd jotted the time of her last recording—11:54 p.m., just as the sedan arrived. She'd recorded the license number, which would be corroborating evidence to her video. She stared at the front of the Johnson house, remembering the two men walking to the front door, reliving the terrible sound of gunshots.

As soon as she got home she'd call Cody and tell him about the video. She'd have to act all sorry and embarrassed, which shouldn't be too hard to manage since she *was* embarrassed by what she'd done. She felt rotten about her little white lie, especially since he'd been such a gentleman last night. And maybe the fib wasn't exactly so little. Would he be able to tell she was hiding something? Probably. Those piercing blue eyes didn't miss a thing.

But if she had turned the recording over to the police last night without making a copy, she'd never have seen it again. She wouldn't be able to play it for her client, and really the evidence was her client's property, wasn't it? Pat had paid her to conduct the surveillance.

No, she could never explain to Cody that she didn't trust the police, that she feared they might lose her evidence and proof of what had happened last night. Would he think she was being greedy and maybe wanted a payoff for the video? She didn't want anything. The authorities should have the evidence. She planned to hand it over freely, if a little late.

She sighed, wishing her life, this case, hadn't become so complicated. Who knew what was right or wrong anymore? All she knew was she felt like dirt for keeping the truth from Cody. She wanted to be honest with him. She now believed he was different than other cops. Or anyway, he sure didn't behave like the other cops she'd run into. Even if he got D.J. into trouble, she knew he was basically an honest man who always did what he thought was right.

She didn't have to always agree with those actions.

"YOU'RE TELLING ME that you just—what—forgot?" Cody stared at Merlene. She perched on the edge of her couch, plucking at the hem of her shorts. "A video of a murder somehow slipped your mind?"

"Don't take that tone of voice with me, Detective. I'd never seen a man with huge holes blown in his chest before."

Expressive gray eyes dominated her fragile face, and he wondered if she'd gotten any sleep last night. He sure as hell hadn't. He'd been disappointed by the message that she didn't need a ride to retrieve her car, then mystified when she'd called back and said she had something important to show him.

He hadn't needed an excuse to hurry over to see her.

Damn. A digital recording. He should have asked her about one last night. Suspicion edged into his thoughts. How could she have forgotten? He scrutinized her face, searching for deception. Could she be hiding something? She was excited. That much was certain. The pink color in her usually pale cheeks told him that.

He sat on the couch beside her. "Have you reviewed it?"

She nodded and picked up a remote control device. "I downloaded the file to a DVD. It's set up for you to view."

"Any good?"

She shrugged. "See for yourself." She aimed the remote at her TV, turning it on with a quick click. "I always expose a few minutes of tape every hour on the hour to prove I'm doing my job. This begins with the sequence I shot around midnight. I was about to go home."

Cody placed his elbows on his knees and leaned forward when a surprisingly clear image of the Johnsons' house appeared on the small television, the house numbers and front door clearly visible. Merlene had good equipment. The date and time flashed in the bottom right-hand corner of the screen.

Her voice repeated the date and time and that nothing had occurred in the past hour.

After a quick blip, a dark-colored late-model Buick Regal pulled into the Johnsons' driveway. Merlene zoomed in on the license plate, speaking on the tape about rude late-night visitors. With backs to the camera, two men exited the vehicle and moved to the front of the house. No way to ID either one of them.

The next image that flashed on the screen jerked crazily, and labored breathing had been recorded by the camcorder. The same two men reappeared in the frame, rushing back to the Buick.

Cody gripped the arm of the couch and swore softly under his breath, recognizing the tall, heavyset driver: Neville Feldman, Sean Feldman's brother. Just as he climbed into the vehicle, Neville glanced toward the street and directly into the camera. Merlene had captured him perfectly.

Brother Neville's role in the con was to solicit people involved in car accidents and steer them to Dr. Johnson. Johnson diagnosed major injuries, promptly billing insurance for unnecessary treatment. And then came the lawsuits filed by brother Sean Feldman for pain and suffering. Insurance companies usually settled out of court because, in the long run, that was cheaper than paying legal fees.

Merlene had a tough time keeping the camera steady as the escaping car swerved out of the driveway and raced north on Granada. But she'd done good. Damn good.

"Back it up," he ordered.

Merlene fumbled with the remote and rewound to the image of Neville Feldman exiting the house.

"Freeze that frame," Cody said.

Neville's round face stared directly into the camera, shadowy but easily identifiable. His right hand clutched a Glock semiautomatic.

"Gotcha," Cody said.

"Do you recognize him?" Merlene asked.

"Damn right, I do." Cody stood and grinned at Merlene. "Sweetheart, you're amazing."

As dimples deepened in her cheeks, he let this bit of good luck sink in. He wondered what kind of deal Sean Feldman would try to cut to worm his brother out of this surefire conviction. Who cared if he couldn't get these scumbags for fraud? First-degree murder would do just fine.

When her moist lips spread into a pleased grin, Cody's heart lurched at his double good fortune. Merlene might not smile often, but when she did, she set his world on a major tilt.

Pulling her from the couch, he wrapped his arms around her slim waist and squeezed. He lifted and twirled her around the center of the room, breathing in her feminine, lemony fragrance while he lightly kissed, then nuzzled the delicious warmth behind her left ear. Man, she felt good.

"Put me down." She didn't sound convincing, but he replaced her feet on the tile floor. She swayed against him, and he didn't release her.

"Dizzy?" he murmured into her hair.

"Yes…I guess."

She clutched his shoulders tightly, pressing her fingers into his back, and he lowered his mouth to hers. Her lips were soft and parted easily. She tasted of strong, sweet Cuban coffee. A welcoming, husky noise escaped her throat, sending a wave of heat through him. He moved his body into her softness.

She ducked her head and stepped away as if she'd been burned.

He held on to her. "Hey, Merl…"

"Cody, please." She shook her head and took a deep breath. "Whether we like it or not, we're now working together on this case. Let's not complicate things."

He tipped her chin and confronted eyes as gray as a battleship. "This isn't very complicated."

"It is for me."

"Then how about if I explain what's going on?" he said.

"That's all right." She stepped away. "I think I understand."

He sucked air deep into his lungs. At least *she* understood. He wasn't even sure what they were talking about anymore. Reluctantly, he let her go.

"So," he said.

"What?" She turned back to him.

"So I'm not your type?"

She gave him a disbelieving sideways glance that told him all he needed to know. He was definitely her type. He reached for her again but stopped himself.

The problem was he didn't have a big enough bank account.

Merlene would never let herself get involved with a poor working slob, especially not a cop. She'd made that perfectly clear, believing his profession to be full of—what was the term he'd heard her use?—*pond scum*. She liked huge diamonds and hefty divorce settlements. He'd looked up her divorce record in the county clerk's office. Interesting file. Her neat home contained modern furnishings but nothing ostentatious or flashy. She might like money but was careful what she spent it on.

He suppressed a stab of disappointment knowing he'd see plenty more of Merlene Saunders. As the pretty lady said, they were working together on the case.

"Okay, then. So…thank you," he said.

She eyed him questioningly. "For what?"

"For the recording, of course. Thanks to you, a very bad man is looking at a first-degree murder rap and no way to beat it."

Her eyes widened. "You think so?"

"Not with this video." He ejected the DVD. "But you know the D.A. will need you to authenticate the evidence at trial."

"Yeah, I understand. But that should be months away."

"Not necessarily."

Brows knit together, Merlene stepped farther away from him. She rubbed her left hand up and down her right arm, worry etched all over her now-pale face. He let her retreat. Too bad. Having her in his arms had been the nicest thing to happen to him in a long time. But this evidence changed the whole case. Hell, it changed everything. He'd need to put out an APB, notify the Coral Gables department, get an arrest warrant started on Neville Feldman. They needed to identify the second suspect traveling with Neville.

He'd check in with Merlene later. They had plenty of unfinished business to… He hesitated, catching the nervous way she nibbled her lower lip.

Truth was she had reason to be worried. Neville Feldman had been convicted of second-degree murder at the age twenty-three and served ten years in Raiford Penitentiary. If this scumbag caught wind of the video, he'd try to find its maker. He'd want to get rid of the evidence, and that meant getting rid of the videographer. Neville might not be crazy enough to think he could get away with two murders, but at this point what did he have to lose?

Merlene needed to be careful.

Cody dropped the disk in an evidence envelope. "Remember, Merlene, without your testimony, this recording is useless."

"WHAT DOES THAT MEAN?" Her thoughts rushing in a thousand directions, Merlene stared at Cody. Too much was happening. She felt as if she were floating around the room again, a wild ride in Cody's strong arms. She needed to get her bearings.

"It means I want you to be careful."

"Why?"

Cody moved closer. "The guy in the video, the driver?"

She nodded, wondering if she could stop Cody from kissing her a second time. She'd been right. Kissing him was addictive.

She took a deep breath to focus. "Neville Feldman, you called him?"

Cody nodded. "He's a convicted murderer—not someone to take lightly."

"Why isn't he in jail?"

"He served his time. Listen, I'm not trying to scare you. Your name won't be released to the public, so Neville won't be able to find you."

"Good," she said, wondering how Cody had switched from kissing her to police business so quickly. Pushing him away had been harder than she cared to admit. She'd been seconds away from dragging him into her bedroom. Not that he gave any signs of resistance.

"I just don't want you to take any foolish chances," he continued.

"I won't. What will happen next?" she asked, at a loss for anything else to say.

"I'll log your recording in at the evidence vault," he said.

She slid her hands up and down her arms to keep them busy, closing her eyes against the memory of his erection pushing into her belly. She'd never experienced anything half as erotic in her life.

What was it about Cody that caused her hormones to go into double overdrive? And how could she respond so strongly to him? She should still be furious with him for calling the authorities down on D.J.

Well, if he could be all business, so could she.

"I want to go with you to log in the disk," she said.

"Why?" he asked, turning away.

She gulped for air. A rush of oxygen ought to clear her head. Damn Cody. Why *did* she need to go with him?

"Chain of custody," she explained. "Lawyers love to attack technical stuff like that. If I'm with you when you check in the DVD, no one can say the recording was tampered with."

Cody swiveled to stare at her, blue eyes cold. "Why don't you come right out and say you don't trust me?"

She blinked at the harsh edge to his voice. "What?"

"Is it just me, Merlene, or law enforcement in general?"

She watched a muscle contract in his jaw and realized she'd offended him. Offering what she hoped looked like an apologetic smile, she said, "I trust you, Cody, even if you did release the wrath of Tallahassee on my agency. I don't know why, but I do. I have a cautious nature. D.J. says it's the Missouri Mule in me."

When he didn't reply, she deepened her smile. "Besides, I like D.J., and he used to be a cop."

He focused on her face for a long time, not answering. Finally, he shook his head. "You drive me nuts."

She straightened her shoulders. "Not intentional, I assure you."

He winced. "That only makes it worse."

CHAPTER SIX

AT FIVE O'CLOCK that evening Merlene settled herself on the sofa to watch the evening news, anxious to learn what the media reported about the Johnson murder. Cody had broadcast the license number of the murderer's sedan in a police bulletin, so the police were searching everywhere.

She was dying to know what was going on. Had the car been located? If so, Cody hadn't called, and she wondered if he'd bother to keep her informed on the latest developments. Probably not. When she'd last seen him, some internal switch had been turned on and he'd become all cop.

She'd followed him to the station in her own car. Inside, he'd been aloof. Polite, but his mind obviously elsewhere. They'd registered the video with a snarky clerk, and Cody had pocketed the receipt.

"Satisfied?" he'd asked, eyebrows raised, in a hurry to move on to other business.

"Can I have a copy of the receipt?" she'd asked.

"Why do you need one?" the clerk asked.

"For my records."

"I haven't got time," the clerk said, turning away.

"No biggie," Cody said with a glare at the clerk. "I'll make you a copy," He'd taken her to a huge photocopier, keyed in a code and handed her a copy. Then he'd showed her the way out and disappeared behind a locked door with a quick wave. Some goodbye.

Merlene raised the remote to turn on the television. No

question Cody could be nice when he tried. He'd definitely been pleased by her recording. Fortunately, he hadn't focused on her delay, but she had seen a shadow of doubt cross his face.

The phone rang as the early version of the evening news began. Merlene paused the broadcast so she could resume watching later, and checked caller ID, hoping to see Cody's number.

Pat Johnson. Finally. She'd been trying to reach her client all day.

"I'm so sorry for your loss," Merlene told Pat.

"Thank you," Pat said in a choked voice.

"Is there anything I can do?"

"Yes, Merlene, there is." Pat sounded exhausted and drained. "I've taken the liberty of couriering you a key to our ranch in Ocala. I want you to drive up and make sure it's safe for the kids."

"Safe? What do you mean?"

"We need to move in up there for a while until the police give me back the Gables house. They say it's still a crime scene, so we can't get in."

"I'm sorry." Of course that was true. She'd confirmed that herself this afternoon.

"As soon as the police release my home, I'll need to have it thoroughly cleaned. I'm sure you understand I don't want my children to see any signs of their father's blood," Pat said.

"Certainly," Merlene murmured.

"But since Rick was seen in Ocala earlier in the week, I don't know what that house looks like. I'm wondering if he…" Pat trailed off, swallowing a sob. "I want you to check it out, make sure everything is okay, that there's nothing the kids shouldn't see."

"Of course, Pat. I'll leave as soon as I get a key."

"You've been a tremendous help at this terrible time, Merlene," Pat said in a flat voice. "When it's all over, I promise to make the trouble worth your while."

After disconnecting, Merlene ached for her client. What a tragedy. And she admired Pat's clear thinking, doubting she'd be able to make logical decisions the day after her husband had been murdered. When you have kids to think of, you do what you have to do, she supposed.

As expected, Dr. Johnson's murder was the lead news story on every channel. Merlene thumbed a remote from her couch, hoping one of the local stations would provide new information. Cody hadn't told her squat.

She'd already analyzed what little she knew and concluded the murder had not been an aborted robbery. No way. Doc Johnson had opened his door to his visitors. She remembered hearing voices, people having a conversation. No one had even sounded angry.

On the screen, a uniformed spokesperson gave the official police response. Graphics on the bottom read, "Media Relations Specialist."

"What can you tell us about this brutal murder?" a female reporter asked.

"At present, the investigation is still ongoing," the uniformed man said.

"Do you have a motive?"

"The investigation still ongoing," he repeated. "We are asking the public to please call in with any tips."

And that was it from the official media relations guy. Nothing but the usual vague nonsense. None of the stations had anything more than video shots of the Johnson home with official vehicles parked in the front yard. One channel speculated about a disgruntled patient, since the murdered man had been a physician.

The media didn't even know about the insurance fraud yet. But they would, and soon.

Merlene sifted what she knew through her investigator's brain one more time. Since Cody alleged the doctor had been involved with Nurse Linda Cole in some sort of fraud, maybe his partners had gotten wind of the heat. The cops had been closing in on them.

So what if someone had spotted her surveillance activity and got nervous? Could Pat's jealous suspicions have inadvertently caused her husband's murder? Oh, God, what a horrible thought. Merlene closed her eyes. That meant she had helped bring about a man's death.

She opened her eyes and stared at the muted screen. She was indulging in blatant speculation like the vultures on TV. The only thing she was certain of was that Johnson's murder must be connected to Cody's investigation. It'd help if she knew more details about his case.

She relaxed into the plush green cushions of her sofa and punched off the remote, wishing she'd stop obsessing about Detective Cody Warren. Fortunately, she wouldn't see him for a few days. As soon as FedEx delivered a key, she'd leave for Ocala to check out the ranch for her client.

Yawning, she stretched out her legs and nestled her head against the arm of the couch. She'd barely slept in the past twenty-four hours. Her eyes drifted shut and her thoughts again drifted to the murder scene and how kind Cody had been under horrible circumstances.

SHE JOLTED AWAKE to her phone's piercing ring. Gooseflesh dotted her arms as she reluctantly abandoned her dream and the erotic sensation of Cody's tongue flicking across her naked breast. A shiver of longing swept through her.

Propping herself on one elbow, she tried to focus. Light streamed in through her front window. Morning. What was she doing on the couch? She reached for the phone but dropped the receiver with a thud on the table. She grabbed it and said, "Hello."

No response.

"Hello?" she repeated. "Who is this?"

No answer...then a dial tone. She checked the caller ID display and squinted at "Unavailable."

"Great," she muttered, and slid the receiver back onto its base. Maybe dropping the phone had somehow severed the connection and whoever called would try again. Maybe her client had forgotten something. Or changed her mind, no doubt a grieving widow's prerogative.

She sat up and rubbed her temples. Waking to that shrill noise had caused a headache and ruined such a pleasant dream. More than pleasant. She nestled back into the cushions and closed her eyes. Maybe she could fall back asleep and pick up where they'd left off.

The phone rang again. Sitting up, Merlene stared at the white contraption. "Unavailable" again appeared in the caller ID screen. Definitely not Pat. With her hand hovering above the receiver, she decided at the last second to allow her machine to pick up.

No one responded to her recorded greeting.

Probably kids playing games, she decided. Not that she'd ever done anything so foolish, but then she'd never gotten the chance to behave like a kid.

The phone rang for the third time while Merlene showered. Again an unavailable number. Again no one left a message.

She briefly wondered if the hang-ups were kids after all. Could the phone calls be more sinister? Should she be worried about the repercussions of the video she'd made? Ridiculous. No one even knew who she was. Only the police knew about the video. Shaking her head, she decided Johnson's murder had turbocharged her overactive imagination.

Still waiting for delivery of the key to Pat Johnson's Ocala ranch, Merlene used the rest of the morning to study. She had enough trouble understanding Introduction to Language Development without phone games, so she turned off the ringer and allowed her ancient but perfectly serviceable machine to take messages.

CODY GLARED ACROSS a battered wooden table at the flushed face of Sean Feldman. At least forty pounds overweight, Feldman had loosened his tie and rolled up his sleeves to compensate for the lack of air-conditioning in the tiny interrogation room.

"One more chance, Feldman," Cody said. "Where is your brother?"

"And I'm going to repeat, Detective, that I don't know where Neville is. I haven't seen him or spoken to him in two days."

Feldman had willingly come in for questioning and denied any involvement in Doc Johnson's murder. Cody believed him.

"Tell me again about your last conversation with Neville."

"All I know is my brother had an appointment with Johnson the night the good doctor was killed."

"What was the meeting about?"

"I don't know. Ask Neville when you find him." Feldman mopped a white cotton handkerchief across his damp face. "Hey, can't we get some air in here? I'm dying."

Cody sat back. He could push the attorney only so far, but could Neville have really acted on his own? Not likely. Of the two brothers, Sean was definitely the mastermind.

Jake, his partner, stuck his head in the room and motioned Cody outside.

Feldman waved at the door. "Go on. Your partner has

some news for you. And while you're out there, turn on the air. If I have a heart attack..."

Cody closed the door to block out Feldman's voice and joined Jake in the hall.

"City of Hialeah found the shooter's car abandoned in the parking lot of Westland Mall," his partner said, stroking his mustache. "It's clean. No prints, not a single link to the Feldmans."

Cody nodded. "What we expected."

"Something else." Jake handed Cody a pink business card. "Vanessa Cooper from Channel Eight somehow got wind of the video. She's digging hard to find out anything she can, including the identity of the videographer."

Cody swore. "Any idea where the leak is?"

Jake shrugged. "It'll take time to find out. But you'd better prepare Mrs. Saunders. They may not have her name yet, but the existence of her video will be on the noon news."

Lieutenant Montoya joined them carrying a white plastic cup of *cafecito*. The tiny container looked especially small in the big man's fingers. "What's happening with Feldman?"

"He's giving me nothing," Cody admitted.

His boss nodded. "Of course not. So why did the Saunders woman withhold her video for twelve hours? We lost valuable time because of that delay."

"She said she forgot about it," Cody said.

"Not f-ing likely," Jake said.

Cody shot his partner a look but had to agree.

"Damn suspicious," Montoya said. "I think the woman knows more than she's saying. Didn't she have a key to the Johnson house?"

"Yes," Cody said.

"God, I hate private cops," Montoya said. "Nothing but a giant pain in the ass."

Cody silently agreed Merlene could be that.

"You and Steadman are on special assignment back to Homicide because of your familiarity with this case. Keep me informed of your progress," Montoya said. He moved toward his office but turned back.

"And keep an eye on Mrs. Saunders. I don't trust her."

Cody couldn't reach Merlene. He tried all morning but talked to nothing but a recording device.

Around two in the afternoon he got a call from D. J. Cooke.

"Cody. Good to talk to you," D.J. said.

"Been a long time, D.J.," Cody said.

"How's tricks?"

How's tricks? The old-fashioned words stirred unsettling memories. His father had used that expression. "I'm good," Cody said. "How about yourself?"

"Well, I been better, Cody. I'm damned concerned about our mutual friend."

"Merlene?"

"I can't get ahold of purty Miss Merl and wondered if you knew anything."

Pretty Miss Merl. Cody liked that. "Yeah, I left a message myself. I don't think she's home, and she's not answering her cell."

"But that's just it. She's supposed to be. She's waiting for a package. I don't like it."

Cody sat up. "I'll check it out."

MERLENE ANSWERED HER door wearing faded blue cutoffs and a sleeveless T-shirt that made her eyes more blue than gray. She wasn't wearing a bra.

"Why aren't you answering your phone?" he demanded.

Merlene opened the door wide, stretching cotton fabric across her nipples. "It's good to see you, too, Detective Warren."

Relief that she was okay and sassy as ever fought with irritation over her careless attitude. As he followed her into the living room, the relief won. Faded denim had never looked so good.

"Kids were playing games with the phone," she said, "so I turned off the bell." She raised a large book from the dining room table. "I was trying to study."

"D.J. tried to call and got worried."

Lifting one rounded hip against the table edge, she said, "D.J. called you?"

Cody nodded. "I couldn't get through, either."

She hugged the textbook close to her chest. "Were you worried?"

Hell, yes, he was worried, but he wasn't falling into that trap. Let a woman know you care and they turn it into a lethal weapon every time.

"Can we sit down, Merlene? I need to talk to you."

Motioning him to the couch, she sat, her eyes wide. "Have you arrested the guy in the video?"

He sat beside her. "Not yet."

"Cody, you've got to tell me what's going on. I'm going crazy trying to figure it out."

He grinned as he relaxed against the leather cushion. "I suppose I ought to get some satisfaction out of that."

Her mouth popped open. "You're pleased that I'm going nuts. Thanks a lot."

Watching her expression, Cody decided it was time for Merlene to know the whole story. Yeah, maybe Montoya didn't trust her, but his boss never trusted private investigators. Usually Cody found her easy to read, and he could make up his own mind from her reaction.

"If you'll be quiet, I'll tell you what you want to know."

She ran her thumb and index finger across her lips to mimic a zipper, then raised both eyebrows.

Cody smothered another grin. "All right. Pay attention."

She rolled her eyes.

"We knew that Dr. Johnson had hooked up with a sleazy ambulance chaser named Sean Feldman we've been after for years. Sean's brother, Neville, the ex-con I told you about, hustles patients from minor fender benders, slips and falls—all kinds of accidents, some bogus, some not—and sends them to Johnson. The good doctor diagnoses life-threatening, very expensive medical problems and/or permanent disability. Sean Feldman files suit on behalf of unhurt patients, then insurance companies dangle major bucks to make it all go away."

"Wow," Merlene said, looking as if she'd burst with excitement. "The patients don't get all the money, do they?"

"Very little of it," Cody said.

"So what part did Linda Cole play?"

"Her job was to process the fraudulent insurance forms."

"Then Johnson wasn't cheating on his wife."

Cody shrugged. "Probably not with Linda. We were close to making arrests when the doc disappeared."

"When he went to Ocala."

Cody nodded. "But the trip was a smoke screen. Dr. Johnson got wind of the coming bust and made a deal with federal prosecutors. He agreed to testify against the Feldman brothers for a promise of a reduced sentence. I didn't know that until this morning."

Merlene drew her legs under her. "That's why you were called off the case."

"Right. The feds needed time to put their case together."

"So you think the brothers decided to get rid of Doc Johnson before he could talk."

"Bull's-eye. The driver in your video is Neville Feldman, the attorney's brother. But now he's off the radar. We found the car, but so far it's told us nothing."

"Have you talked to his brother, the lawyer?"

"For several hours." Cody ran a hand through his hair, recalling Sean Feldman's arrogance during a long, miserable interview.

"Sean has an airtight alibi the night of the shooting. He claims ignorance about Johnson's murder and hasn't talked to Brother Neville in several days. He also claims that Neville had an appointment with Johnson the night of his murder."

"That could be," she said. "I remember thinking that someone let them in, but landscaping hid the entrance."

"Too bad."

"So who was the guy with Neville in the video?"

"We don't know, and Sean isn't saying. I brought some pictures of Neville's known associates for you to look at."

Her lips curved into a half smile. "Like mug shots?"

Cody nodded. "Yeah, a mug shot lineup."

"I'll try, but I'm not sure I could identify anybody." Her smile deepened. "Well, I'm just your regular star witness, aren't I?"

"Yeah," Cody said, "You're my star witness. But there's more."

"What?" She raised her brows, wrinkling her forehead.

"Channel Eight broke the story of your video on the noon news, and they're digging to find out who you are."

Her eyes widened, her surprise as genuine as it had been when he relayed the insurance scam. Cody believed her.

"But how could that happen?" she asked.

He nodded at her phone. "You didn't tell anyone, did you?"

"Of course not." She narrowed her eyes. "The answer is your department has a leak. It's just a matter of time before they get my name."

"Possible."

Merlene moved toward the phone. "Maybe Channel Eight already left a message."

Cody listened to two messages from D.J., one from himself and a half dozen hang-ups.

"Well, they haven't found me so far," she said, clearing her ancient machine with some difficulty.

"Why don't you have voice mail?"

She shrugged. "Why spend money I don't have to?"

"You've never had hang-ups like that before?"

"No," she said, twirling a ribbon of hair around her thumb. "Do you think the calls have something to do with the case?"

Who knew anymore? Cody glared at the phone. This case had more twists than a woman's mind, and he'd never been able to successfully navigate a maze.

No one should know Merlene's name this early in the game—barely twenty-four hours since her video came to light. He'd been careful not to tell Sean Feldman.

"Do you think the hang-ups are related to the Johnson murder?" she asked, interrupting his thoughts.

"I don't see how," he answered. One thing for sure. He wanted Neville Feldman behind bars before Merlene's identity got broadcast for John Q. Public to feast upon and tear apart.

"Let me see your photographs," she said.

Cody pulled the photos from his briefcase and spread them across the dining room table, grimacing at the group—variations on unshaven, flinty-eyed, tattooed lowlifes. As Merlene sat down to examine them, the doorbell rang.

"Finally," she muttered.

"Hold it." Cody moved quickly toward the front window, peeked through the blinds, then nodded for her to answer the door.

Surprised but impressed by his caution, Merlene signed for a small package from a FedEx deliveryman.

"You'll be relieved to know I'll be off your radar for a few days," she said, returning to the table.

"Where are you going?"

"Ocala." She ripped open the envelope and produced two keys. "Mrs. Johnson wants me to check out the ranch, make sure it's safe for her and the kids. She's not real anxious to move back to their house on Granada until it's cleaned up, but wants to be closer to Miami."

"When are you leaving?"

Merlene glanced up at the obvious disapproval in Cody's voice. Why would he care if she went to Ocala?

"Tomorrow morning. Do you have a problem with that?"

She tried to look away when their gazes locked, but something in his cool blue gaze held her. No, not cool. Warm. Worried. Could he be worried about her?

Cody reached back and rubbed his neck. "No problem," he said. "Just be careful."

"Count on it, Detective." She sat down at the table and studied the pictures Cody had placed in two neat rows. Nobody looked the least bit familiar. Wait… She picked up a photo of a fortyish, dark-haired man.

"This was the driver," she said. "I'm sure of it."

Cody moved closer. "Good work. That's Neville Feldman. Keep going."

She tried to concentrate on the images, but became hyperaware of Cody and the spicy scent of his aftershave. He leaned over her, one hand on the back of her chair, one hand resting on the table. Warmth slid into her tense muscles, along with the languorous sensation of being wrapped in his protective embrace. His breath fluttered a wisp of her hair, tickling her cheek. Her breasts rose and fell dangerously close to his muscled forearm. Her gaze strayed to his fingers and neatly trimmed nails. How would those hands feel cupped against her—

"Does anyone else look familiar?"

She dragged her attention back to the photographs. After a moment, she picked up a picture of a young man with stringy blond hair sporting a sly smile.

"I can't be sure, but maybe this one," she said.

Cody's fingers brushed hers when he took the photograph. "Ray Price." Cody nodded. "He and Feldman served time together."

She stared at the photo. "Yeah, that's him. I'm sure."

"Time to pay Mr. Price a visit and determine if he has an alibi the night of Johnson's murder," Cody said. "If not, you'll have to do a live lineup when we find him."

"Will you be there?"

"Of course. Don't worry. He won't be able to see you."

"Just like in the movies," she said, trying to make light of the idea of identifying a murder accomplice. Nothing about the process seemed funny, though.

He shoved the photographs back in his file. She liked the confident way he moved, felt reassured by the strength of his well-toned body. How had her life gotten entangled with Cody Warren's so quickly? She'd known him less than a week and yet he felt strangely like…what? The quick brush of his fingers had caused her pulse to take off like a baby dove attempting first flight. Still, she felt safe with him.

Loud ringing broke into her thoughts and they both turned to look at the phone by the couch. She checked the caller ID.

"Unavailable," she said. "Like before."

"Let your machine answer."

She did as he instructed, but the connection went to dial tone without a message.

"See. I got sick of it," she said, watching Cody for his reaction.

A muscle in his right jaw twitched. "You're probably right," he said. "Most likely kids."

AN UNEASY FEELING settled in Cody's gut on the way to his unmarked police cruiser. Again something was wrong. What was with all those calls? He surveyed Merlene's quiet neighborhood, comparing what he'd observed on arrival with the scene now.

Nothing looked out of place. Nothing different.

He didn't think the calls were kids playing a prank. Too many calls, and no cop believed in coincidences.

He glanced back once more to Merlene's home and frowned. The front and sides were lined with lush, attractive foliage—an easy location for anyone to hide.

Too bad she didn't have a dog. Or an alarm. Shouldn't a P.I. have a damn alarm? Neville Feldman would have no difficulty surprising Merlene in her sleep. Could those mysterious hang-ups be him calling to figure out her schedule?

Cody hesitated, his hand on the car door, and admitted to himself that he was worried about her. He'd warned her, but would she take the situation seriously? Feldman could have other methods to unearth who'd made that video. She definitely wouldn't appreciate his security suggestions.

The idea of her being in danger lit up every protective instinct he possessed, made him want to camp out on her front step. What was it about her that made him feel that way? She surely didn't ask for his protection. Hell, she much preferred to push him away.

He jerked open the door and slid into the seat. She might not like it, but until she left town he'd keep an eye on her. Lieutenant Montoya wanted him to, anyway—just for another reason.

AFTER A LONG, hot shower, Merlene shrugged on an extra-large cotton T-shirt and stretched her bare legs out on the comfy couch. At least she'd be dressed for bed tonight if she conked out in front of the TV again. Nestled against the cushioned arm of the sofa, she brought a cup of steaming chamomile tea to her lips and ventured a tentative sip of the warm, honeyed brew.

Tomorrow she'd say goodbye to the big city. She'd packed a small suitcase with a change of clothing and planned to leave first thing in the morning. Her plan was to be gone only one night, but leaving the turmoil of the past few days behind would be heavenly. Maybe some distance would allow her to gain control over her attraction to Cody. The man managed to drift into her thoughts constantly. But how could she stop thinking about him with the constant developments in this crazy case?

Like her discussion with Pat Johnson a few hours ago when Merlene had phoned to confirm receipt of the ranch keys.

"Oh, good," Pat had said. "By the way, you'll be pleased to know I gave you a fabulous recommendation today."

"What do you mean?" Merlene asked, thinking her client's words sounded slurred, like she might be under the influence of a sleeping pill or tranquilizer.

"I've been telling people up here about the excellent work you've done for me, and someone wanted your name and number. I gave them a glowing report about you."

"Someone?" Merlene repeated. "You gave out my name to a person you don't know?" Huge alarm bells clanged inside her skull.

"To a friend of a friend. Well, the agency's name. After all, you are going to need a new job after the trip to Ocala."

Immediately after that disturbing conversation, Merlene had double checked every possible entrance to her house. No one could get in without making a lot of noise, but still she felt uneasy, exposed. If she was honest, she had to admit that the new widow hadn't sounded particularly bereft.

Merlene sighed and took another sip of the warm tea. But everyone grieved differently, and her client was likely sedated. To lose a husband, even a cheating one, in such a brutal manner…

The door chime startled Merlene back to reality. Who the heck? She placed her eye over the tiny hole in the front door and got a distorted view of Cody Warren, his arms propped on either side of the doorway.

Annoyed at the quick gallop of her heart, she pulled her T-shirt lower on her legs and opened the door.

He strode into the living room full of deadly purpose. When he reached the couch, he pivoted to face her. "In an hour, Channel Eight is going on the air to report that you videoed two men arriving at the Johnson house seconds before his murder."

"How did—"

"They spotted your car in their live report from the murder scene and ran the plates. It didn't take long to find your P.I. license. Vanessa Cooper is on the way to set up a remote." He took a deep breath. "We need to leave ASAP in case Neville Feldman watches the news."

Merlene hugged her arms and gaped at him. "You think he'll come *here?*"

Cody shrugged. "The hang-ups could have been Neville."

A chill ran the length of her spine. "Pat gave some man my name and number. He told her he was impressed with my work on the case and had another job for me. I considered he could have been a reporter, but…" Merlene trailed off. "She's promised help with future jobs. She thought she was giving me a good recommendation."

Cody's face tightened. "Yeah, a recommendation for a

death sentence. It could easily have been Neville. He'd have all Johnson's numbers." He glanced around the room. "Is that your bag for the trip tomorrow?"

Merlene nodded. Good Lord. Her life was spinning out of control.

"Good," he said, his gaze raking her naked legs. "Put on some clothes and let's get out of here."

She opened her mouth to object but stopped herself. If a gun-toting murderer was looking for her, she definitely didn't want to be where he expected to find her. And who better to be with than a man with a gun of his own?

"Give me one minute."

CHAPTER SEVEN

"Where are we going?" Merlene asked when they'd pulled out of her driveway.

Cody accelerated onto Bird Road. "I want you to spend the night at my apartment." She'd turned to reach for her seatbelt, but swiveled to face him. "Your apartment?"

"The building has good security. No one can easily get inside."

She didn't speak for a few moments, then said, "I don't know."

Merlene's nervous tone pulled Cody's attention back to her. She still wore the oversize pink T-shirt but had pulled on black denim jeans to hide legs that... Cody swallowed, imagining the long expanse of smooth thighs now hidden from his view. No matter what she wore, the woman created an urge to touch her.

He'd expected an argument about where she'd spend the night.

"What don't you know?" he asked, his gaze on headlights in the rearview mirror.

"Is this some kind of witness protection program?"

"Do you want to change your identity?" he asked, returning his attention to traffic.

"Very funny."

"I'd just feel better if you got out of town clean tomorrow." He glanced in the mirror again.

Merlene adjusted the mirror out her passenger window and peered behind them. "Are we being followed?"

"Maybe. Don't turn around, but that Jeep has been back there since we left your street. If he stays with us on the next turn, I'm going to lose him."

"Lose him?" Cody felt Merlene's gaze boring into him. "As in a high-speed chase with screeching tires, flying hubcaps and...and bullets zipping past my ear?" She reached overhead and tightened her seat belt.

"I sure hope not," he said. "I wouldn't want to lose my star witness."

He shot her a glance. She sat ramrod straight with her hands clasped tightly in front of her. So much for his lame attempt at humor.

Giving in to the need to touch her, he smoothed her silken hair and let his hand fall to her shoulder. He hadn't meant to frighten her.

Or had he? If she'd handed over the video the night of the murder things would be different. "You've been watching too much TV," he said.

"Maybe."

She closed her eyes, and he squeezed her shoulder to reassure her. She sighed, her muscles relaxing beneath his fingers.

He returned his hand to the steering wheel, unsure which surprised him more—the fact she actually seemed to trust him or that her confidence could make him feel so good. Hell, just being around Merlene made him feel good.

He glanced in the rearview mirror again.

He executed three quick, confusing turns and knew they'd lost their tail...if there'd been one. As they drove toward his apartment in uneasy silence, he wondered if Merlene had affected his judgment. Was he looking for trouble in shadows?

He'd discovered he couldn't stomach the thought of her

being exposed to danger. When Channel Eight called for confirmation of the identity of the videographer, he'd known he had to protect Merlene from Neville Feldman. Lieutenant Montoya believed the leak came from a clerk in the evidence vault, a man they'd been suspicious of in the past. Cody remembered the clerk, not a sworn officer, had given Merlene a hard time when they'd logged in her recording.

He'd deal with the man later if the department didn't.

She wouldn't like it, but he'd decided to go with her tomorrow. Now he had to figure out how to convince her without terrifying her. Maybe Feldman wouldn't pick up her scent, but, damn, what if he did? She'd be an easy target for a killer like Feldman.

Besides, he knew the Ocala area. When his brother-in-law was alive, they'd regularly fished in the Ocala National Forest at his lakeside cabin, which was still available since Annie couldn't make up her mind whether to sell.

A cabin hidden in the woods was the perfect place for them to spend the night.

Cody viewed his own home in a new light when he opened the door for her. Hell, maybe his sister was right. The place did appear a bit, well, sparse. Except for a fairly new high-def TV resting on a black metal stand, the only other furniture in the living room was a well-worn cloth sofa. He took the few meals eaten at home at the Formica counter between the living room and the kitchen perched on a bar stool.

He dropped her bag and locked the door behind them.

After she'd surveyed the apartment with bright and curious eyes, she turned to face him, her usually pale face flushed.

"Are you all right?" he asked, startled by the color in her cheeks.

She nodded. "I'm fine." Her words sounded husky, deeper

than her usual voice. She met his gaze. "Where do you want me to sleep?"

"In my bed." Cody motioned to a door off the hall.

She raised her brows but didn't avert her gaze.

"I'll be on the couch."

"Ah," she said. She glanced at the sofa, the only place in the room to sit except the floor.

"Make yourself comfortable." Cody grabbed her bag and carried it into his bedroom.

When he returned, she remained in the center of the room, her huge leather purse still slung over her shoulder. "Maybe I should call D.J. and stay with him," she suggested.

Loosening his tie, Cody sank onto the sofa. "That's the second place Channel Eight will look for you." He leaned back and locked his hands behind his head. "No one will connect you with me."

Her gray eyes sought his. He knew she was searching, considering, trying to figure out if he had a hidden motive. Something must have happened in her life to make her so distrustful. He wanted to know what it was.

"You're safer here," he continued.

Her mouth curved into a hesitant smile. "Yeah, okay."

"Okay," he repeated. He knew he ought to look away but couldn't.

She glanced toward the bedroom door, then back at him. "Are... Will you be going to sleep right away?"

He laughed. Obviously she had no clue how hard it would be to sleep thinking of her in the next room tucked into his bed. "No," he said. "I need to catch the eleven-o'clock news."

Nodding, she dropped her purse from her shoulder and let it fall to the carpet. "I'm so wired over this whole mess I won't sleep at all tonight."

"You need to rest."

"Fat chance. Do you really think Neville Feldman will come after me because of that damn video?"

"It's a possibility. With you out of the way, the video would be worthless as evidence. The state needs you to authenticate it."

"I scribbled the license tag in my notebook. That's evidence, right?"

"But that would need your verification, too."

"You could find other proof he's the killer."

"Maybe. And the prosecutor could arrange a deposition to preserve your testimony, but that'll take time. The video is a sure thing." He shifted to his right and patted the sofa beside him. "Come sit down."

Nibbling on her lower lip, she stared at the space next to him on the couch but didn't approach.

He wished he could interpret the little flickers of wariness crossing her face. "Are you afraid of me?"

She clasped her hands behind her and walked around the room. "I wasn't in Cody Warren's witness protection program before I met you."

He caught his breath at the teasing note in her voice. She seldom allowed herself to be so playful with him. Instead of joining him on the couch, she moved into the kitchen.

"Are you hungry?" he called. Damn, did he even have anything to feed her? Why did he never have food in the house? That needed to change.

"No," she yelled back. "I couldn't eat."

"Thirsty? I think I've got a beer."

She reappeared in the doorway. "I don't drink."

"Not even water?"

"Okay, yeah." With a sheepish grin, Merlene took a step toward him. "I do drink water."

Fascinated, he watched her slim hips fluidly sway from side to side.

He followed her into the hall, wondering what she was so damn curious about. She poked her nose into the bedroom, then stepped into the bathroom.

Standing just outside the opening, he gripped both sides of the frame. "Why don't you tell me what you're looking for?"

Her gaze swept the tiny room. "Clues," she said.

"Clues?" he repeated.

She nodded, then looked up into his eyes and smiled.

"Into my personality?" he asked.

Amused gray eyes searched his. "Something like that."

He took her hand and led her back to the couch. "Okay. So you might be afraid of me, you don't drink and you're looking for clues. I've learned a lot about you tonight, Merl." He hesitated. "It is okay if I call you Merl, isn't it?"

"SURE." MERLENE SQUEEZED her fingers in her lap wishing there were somewhere else in the room to sit. It was dangerous to be this close to Cody. She should go to bed and get away from him, but she didn't want to be alone. His solid presence comforted her, made her feel safe. Wasn't that why she'd agreed to stay here tonight?

Besides, she also wanted to watch the late news.

As long as he didn't touch her, she'd be fine. When their flesh connected, a current arced between them, shocking her with its intensity. Did he feel it, too? She glanced at him, taking in his muscled shoulders, powerful arms and legs. God, but the man was gorgeous, impossible to resist. Addictive.

Part of her wanted to curl up on his lap and kiss him until she was breathless, and part of her wanted to smack him.

She scooted to the edge of the couch and again surveyed the barely furnished apartment.

"Did you just move in?" she asked.

"I've been here three years."

"Three years?" Merlene shook her head. "You must have been a monk in another life."

"I live simply."

At the harsh edge to his voice, she threw him a quick look. Man, was he touchy about money.

"Listen, thanks for taking me in tonight," she said. "I know you didn't have to."

"You're welcome." He flicked on the television. "Time for your fifteen minutes of fame."

Johnson's murder remained the lead story. Slender, blond-haired Vanessa Cooper stood before the Johnsons' stately home, microphone in hand. In a serious voice she announced Channel Eight had learned exclusively that Merlene Saunders, a local private investigator, had recorded Dr. Johnson's murderers coming and going from the residence, but that the police had so far made no arrests. A note of disapproval hung in her words. Her bright red lips curved into a knowing smile as she promised her listeners that Channel Eight was making every effort to obtain a copy of the video.

When the broadcast moved on to other news, Cody clicked the set off and turned to her with a stubborn set to his jaw. "I'm going with you tomorrow."

Merlene stared into glacier-blue eyes. Going with her? Her heart hammered against her ribs at the idea of traveling anywhere with Cody. Staying with him tonight was risky enough. "To the Johnson ranch?"

He nodded, looking in no mood for an argument, which scared her. Why so determined?

"Why?" she asked.

He ran a hand through his hair, then shrugged. "My lieutenant wants to know what's at the ranch. It's a whole new ball game with Johnson's murder. We've got a lot of loose ends."

"I see." But she didn't see. Without a warrant, he couldn't

use anything he found at the ranch. It was ridiculous for Cody to go with her unless... Her mouth went dry. Most likely he wasn't telling her everything. Was he using her? Maybe he didn't trust her.

"Should I be frightened?" she asked.

He didn't answer right away. Her shoulders tensed. Was he deciding on a lie? Perhaps he wanted her scared and vulnerable.

No, that wasn't fair. She was jumping to conclusions again. Old habits.

"You should be...careful," he said, emphasizing the last word.

"So you do think I'm in danger?"

He sighed. "Probably not, but I don't want to take any chances. You're my star witness, remember?"

She swallowed hard. "Could I have that glass of water now?"

Cody looked questioningly at her but rose. She heard the refrigerator door open, and he yelled, "I have orange juice, too."

"No. Water is fine. No. Make it juice."

Needing to think, she closed her eyes and slumped against the couch. Did she want Cody to go with her to Ocala? For protection from the Feldman brothers, you bet. But did she really need it?

The truth was she felt almost as much of a threat from him. She already teetered on the brink of losing control around Cody, and they'd have to stay in a motel at least one night. Should she trust him? She certainly couldn't trust herself. She'd lost control of her life ever since Cody Warren had shown up on her stakeout of Richard Johnson.

She was hiding from reporters and possibly murderers. With everything going on she should be terrified, but had never felt more alive.

She stood and accepted a plastic mug full of OJ when he returned. "So what time are we leaving in the morning, Detective?"

Cody acknowledged his victory with a smile. A dangerous, cocky smile. "As soon as you wake up. We'll grab some breakfast on the road."

"Sounds good." How had this happened? She'd known this man less than a week and was about to go on a road trip with him.

AT ONE IN THE MORNING Cody gave up all hope of falling asleep. He'd listened from the couch while Merlene brushed her hair, washed her face, completed all the fascinating rituals women go through to prepare for bed. He'd rather have watched. He'd wanted to run his hands through her thick, silken hair while brushing it gently away from her face.

Now he burned to climb into his cool, clean sheets and pull her against him until they were hot and sticky.

Hoping she'd fallen asleep, he punched on the TV, keeping the volume low. Thank God for cable on sleepless nights.

After a few moments Merlene poked her head into the room. Cody sat up, covering his briefs with a blanket.

"Can't sleep?" he asked.

"Uh-uh." She moved toward him, her gaze flickering over his bare chest. "Can I join you?" Her voice sounded unsure, as if she were doing something she shouldn't.

"Sure."

She tugged her T-shirt low over her thighs and sat beside him. "TV always puts me to sleep. I'll be out in ten minutes."

He nodded. "Good. You need rest." He pulled on his T-shirt, wanting to put her at ease. Then he shared his blanket with her, reaping the reward of her increasingly regular smiles as he spread the covering over her bare legs.

"Thanks," she murmured.

At first she laughed self-consciously at the late-night talk-show host, only meeting Cody's gaze on occasion. Once, when surprised by a joke, she touched him unexpectedly. Gradually she relaxed, her body sinking deeper and deeper into the cushions, closer and closer to his. Soon she yawned and her head dropped against his shoulder.

When her breathing became regular, Cody switched off the TV and closed his eyes, inhaling deeply of her sweet warmth. He nuzzled his cheek against her dark, shining hair. God, it was soft. He could lose himself in her and never come up for air.

But her safety was his responsibility. He'd gotten Merlene into this mess by asking her to record vehicles coming and going from Dr. Johnson's. He knew she fought her attraction to him, tolerated him only for protection, pushed him away with bristling accusations that he'd tried to yank her P.I. license. He'd never get past her barriers.

Besides, she wasn't looking for romance, and surely not with a cop. He needed to remember that before his emotions got tangled up with unrealistic fantasies. Again, he wondered about her past, what had created her distrust. Had to be something. Maybe he'd learn some details tomorrow on the long drive north.

And he needed to remember his boss suspected Merlene knew more than she admitted about the murder. Of course, Lieutenant Montoya never trusted private detectives, but the man kept harping on the troubling point that she'd withheld the video for over twelve hours. Why had she done that? Could she really have forgotten?

As Jake had said, *Not f-ing likely.*

Cody positioned her comfortably on the couch, gently lifting her head to lay a pillow underneath. She smiled and murmured something when he covered her with one of his mother's hand-sewn quilts.

He went to his room and crawled between his sheets, her soft lingering fragrance filling his senses.

THE NEXT MORNING they were on the road by nine. Cody pulled into a fast-food drive-through for breakfast and coffee at nine-fifteen.

Last night she'd been too nervous to pay attention, but now Merlene decided the interior of a police cruiser had some interesting bells and whistles. Like a laptop perched on a pedestal convenient to the driver's seat. The cover remained closed, however, and the police radio silent.

So was Cody on the job or a pleasure trip?

He didn't say much for the first hour or so. They argued a bit about whether to take the Florida's Turnpike, an expensive toll road, when she preferred to drive the interstate and save money. He'd also insisted on taking his vehicle, claiming hers could be recognized.

She didn't mind. This boat was tons more comfortable than her little bucket.

She made a few stabs at conversation, but he seemed lost in thought. Probably about the case. Or maybe he wasn't a morning person. Bored, she eventually opened a Florida map to plan their route.

"What are you studying?" he asked.

Merlene looked up, dizzy from trying to read while traveling sixty-five miles per hour—the speed limit, of course—on I-95.

"I'm looking at the map," she said, holding it up.

"No. I mean the book at your house. You said you were studying yesterday and that's why the phone was off."

"I'm taking education courses at Miami Dade College."

"You want to be a teacher?" Surprise dripped from his words.

"I know it probably sounds dull to a cop who craves danger, but I like kids." With a shrug she added, "And I'm beginning to think I'm not cut out for this surveillance gig."

Cody frowned and made a clucking noise. "I hate to see you give up on a promising singing career."

She laughed. She couldn't help it. The man sounded sincere when she knew he was teasing. Hard to imagine she'd reached a point in her life where she could tolerate a cop kidding her about music.

She said, "Keep that up and I'll sing for you as punishment."

He grinned at her. "Promise?"

"No!" She shook her head. "Forget I said that."

"What do you want to teach?"

She studied Cody as he drove, a bit unfair since he had to keep his eyes on the road. Why did he ask so many questions? Before long this man would know more about her than any other person on earth. Maybe he already did.

Maybe the real question was her compulsion to answer, tell him about her past. Why did she want him to know who she really was? What did it matter?

"I'm planning a class on how to thoroughly annoy the local police," she said.

He exhaled loudly, the sound closer to a snort. "You're already well qualified to teach that course."

Merlene watched the flat Florida landscape zoom past the car. Cody didn't know the half of it.

They remained quiet a few miles and then he broke the silence again. "Why don't you tell me about these past experiences of yours that have made you so cautious?"

"Are you always so nosy?" she asked, hoping to sidetrack him onto another subject.

"Hey, you look for clues your way, and I'll do it mine."

He had her there. Last night she'd been blatant with her investigation of his apartment but hadn't been able to stop herself. Not one photograph or personal item that didn't scream *utilitarian* had been visible. No signs of female influence.

She couldn't figure out Cody Warren. He generated an aura of cold police professionalism, but she sensed an undercurrent of kindness and—what? Loneliness. She wanted to ask about his father but waited for the right time. If there ever could be a right time.

"Come on," he urged. "We've got a long drive ahead of us."

She sighed. "You don't want to hear my hard-luck story."

"I wouldn't have asked if I didn't."

Still she hesitated, unsure exactly how much to reveal.

"Look, my childhood was…completely different from yours."

"How do you know that?"

She looked at the road ahead. "Because your dad was a cop while my family had constant run-ins with the law. My parents drank," she said, "a lot. And cops were always coming around threatening to take me and my little brother away. My mom and dad needed me to take care of them, so I had to play games, lie to the police so they'd leave us alone."

She glanced at him to gauge his reaction. His expression hadn't changed.

Hating that she was on the verge of tears, she sucked in a deep breath. How long would it take before she could speak of her family without crying? She didn't want Cody to feel sorry for her, but if she told him the whole story…

"Is that why you don't drink?" His voice was kind, but sympathy only made her feel worse.

She nodded, relieved he didn't press for details, surprised that she'd been able to talk to Cody about her parents. How odd that she felt better for telling him. "I watched what booze did to my mom and swore it would never happen to me."

"You're lucky. Most of the time kids of alcoholics end up drunks, too."

"I don't feel lucky. I guess you had a picture-perfect childhood," she said. "It's probably hard to relate."

"I don't know anyone who had a perfect childhood," Cody said.

"I guess not." She relaxed into the seat, feeling strangely lighter than she had a few minutes ago. Cody didn't judge. She liked that about him.

"My dad was a strict disciplinarian. There were times I hated him."

"Yeah? I can't even imagine having a cop for a father. I'll bet that was tough."

"Tough," he agreed. "But having a mother with a Western fetish was worse."

"Western fetish?"

Cody nodded in such a solemn manner, Merlene couldn't figure out if he was serious or joking.

"I'm going to reveal a horrible family secret," he announced.

"What secret?" she asked, mystified by his tone.

"Guess what my sister's middle name is."

"Your sister's middle name?" What gibberish was he spouting now?

"Oakley," he said.

"Annie Oakley," Merlene repeated. "Cute. So why aren't you John Wayne or Roy Rogers?"

"Mother wanted Wyatt Earp, but my father forbade it."

Merlene turned to face him, propping her elbow on the seat behind her.

"So what is your middle name?"

"Wyoming," he said.

"Cody Wyoming Warren." She grinned. "Child abuse. No doubt about it."

He nodded. "I knew you'd understand."

"Your mom liked movies about the Old West?"

"Loved them, and so do I. How about you?"

"I never got to watch any." She shrugged. "I should rent one. Maybe you can make a recommendation."

"No TV when you were growing up?" he asked.

"Usually either broken or in the pawnshop." She continued to study him. "Is your mom in Miami?"

Cody switched to the left lane to pass a slow-moving truck. "No. She moved to Sarasota with her sister."

"Oh. And where is your—" Merlene faltered midsentence at the thunderous look Cody threw her.

And where is your dad? She could hardly bear not to ask. But something in the tense set of Cody's jaw, the dangerous glint in hard blue eyes, made her hold her tongue. *Thou shalt not go there.*

Merlene stiffened. No way was this detective getting away with prying nonstop into her background but then clamming up about his.

She paused. Well, that wasn't totally fair. He just wouldn't talk about his father. He'd seemed rather proud of his eccentric mother. Great. Now she was even making excuses for him.

Talking about her family made Merlene sad…shoot, it always made her cry. But today she'd discovered something odd. The more she talked about them, the easier the words came. Speaking of the past eased the heavy ache she'd carried around far too long. Maybe she ought to be grateful to Cody.

"My mom's dead," Merlene said. "Killed in a car wreck along with my dad."

"How old were you?"

"Fifteen."

He muttered an oath, then shot her a quick glance. "I'm sorry, Merl. I don't know what to—"

"You could offer me your handkerchief, Detective."

"There's tissues in the glove compartment."

"Thanks." She found a tissue and blew her nose. "Sorry," she said. "It's been a long time. I don't know why I'm crying."

"Did you know your nose gets red when you cry?"

She meant to laugh, but the noise that erupted sounded more like a hiccup.

"God bless you," Cody said.

Merlene rolled her eyes. "You're a big help in a crisis."

"Part of my training." Cody shifted his eyes quickly to Merlene, then back to the road. "How about if we stop for lunch? This Vero Beach truck stop has great food."

She nodded. "I'd like to stretch my legs."

A blast of hot air and the smell of gasoline assaulted Merlene's senses when she exited the air-conditioned comfort of Cody's car. She rotated her left shoulder. Man, it did feel good to move.

Looking reassuringly tall and confident in tan slacks and a navy blue knit shirt, Cody waited for her by the trunk of the car. She admired his strong body, noting how the glint of the sun on his brown hair brought out occasional streaks of blond. Other than the afternoon at the ball field, today was the first time she'd seen him in public without the ever-present tie.

As she moved toward him, she again wondered if he was on or off duty. He considered that stuffy neckpiece part of his no-interfering-with-procedure uniform—even in Miami's heat. Yeah, for sure this was a cop who played it strictly by the book.

She lost her breath when his strong arms encircled her and gathered her close.

CHAPTER EIGHT

"I'm sorry about your parents."

Cody kissed her hair, drawing its lemon scent deep into his lungs. She could push him away if she wanted, but he would hold her close for this one moment. She'd been through so much. He longed to comfort her. Hell, he wanted to protect her from more hurt. That was his job, right? To protect and to serve.

And for a moment she relaxed, seductively soft, feminine and warm. "It's okay," she whispered. "Really. Talking about it helps."

She stepped away, looking up to meet his gaze with dove-gray eyes that had again turned wary.

Nervous little bird, Cody thought. Afraid to trust anyone. He wondered what had happened to her after she lost her parents, guessing a series of foster homes. He could easily imagine the hellish conditions she'd endured. He'd seen it often enough during his years on the job. She'd have been better off if those cops she despised had removed her from a rotten home. But of course a child would never understand that.

He gave her shoulders a light squeeze. Likely there was a hell of a lot more to her story, but now was not the time, not when she was fighting tears again. "I'm glad you told me."

"I don't know why I did." She smiled, and its warmth felt as if the sun had come out after a week's rain. "Must be because of that crackerjack training you're so proud of."

Wearing an uncertain expression, she bit her lip. He knew Merlene wanted to lighten the mood with her teasing, move on to less personal subjects. For now he'd let her off the hook.

Tucking her arm into his, he moved them toward the restaurant. "Oh, I'm trained in any number of things," he said. "Picking places to eat is one of my specialties."

How could anyone dig through the many defensive layers of Merlene Saunders? If he wanted to win her trust, he would have to peel each one away bit by bit to uncover what lay underneath. And earning her trust had become important to him. He wanted her to know not all cops were bad news.

"I'LL SAY ONE thing for you, Merlene—you certainly have a healthy appetite." Cody had watched in awe while she put away a cheeseburger and a huge order of fries smothered with ketchup.

She looked up from a half-eaten piece of chocolate cake and frowned. "Are you criticizing my eating habits again?"

He held up his hand. "I know better than that. But you're such a little thing, I'm wondering where you put it all."

She lifted her chin. "I'm not little."

He didn't immediately reply. He had to admit that there were some delightful parts of Merlene that were definitely not small, but it was probably best that he didn't dwell on *those* particular images.

"How much do you weigh?" he asked.

She dropped her fork, and it hit the plate with an audible clatter. "Where I come from, it's not considered polite to ask."

"Why? Is it confidential?"

"It's like asking a woman how old she is."

He shrugged. "I already know how old you are. Twenty-five."

"How do you know that?" Stormy eyes narrowed in a familiar, suspicious manner. "Oh, that's right. I forgot you ran a check on me."

"Relax, Merlene. Your date of birth is on your vehicle registration."

He reached for the check, watching as her tongue licked a trace of chocolate frosting from her upper lip. She scooped the last bit of fudge cake onto her fork and raised her gaze to his, offering him the bite.

"Last chance," she said.

Cody refused, preferring the pleasure of watching her enjoyment.

She set the fork down and collapsed into the booth with a satisfied sigh. Nodding at the check, she said, "How much?"

"I'll get it."

Merlene shook her head. "I'm on an expense account. I'll pay my half."

"I thought you wanted to save money."

"But of course I'll pay my share," Merlene said as she pulled a leather wallet out of her purse. "This isn't a date. The only reason I let you come along is because you convinced me I was in danger."

"You sure that's the only reason?"

Merlene looked up from counting out bills.

"Would it be so hard to let me buy you lunch?" he asked.

"Yes." There was that flicker in her eyes again. "I need receipts to prove to my client I made this trip."

"I'll give you the damned receipt." He wasn't sure why, but her refusal irritated him. She kept pushing him away. Maybe this wasn't a date, but he was a man; she was a woman. "Hell, you can even charge Pat Johnson for the whole amount. That's what most P.I.s would do."

Merlene's back went ramrod stiff. "So now I'm a big bad mama who pads her bills?"

"I didn't say that."

"Not in so many words, no. Cops always look down their noses at me and my profession."

"I don't understand why you even work considering the pile of cash your ex dropped on you after your divorce."

His anger dissolved as Merlene's face closed off to him. *Just great, Cody.*

"You looked up my divorce file?" she asked, her voice tight and defiant.

"Of course," he said. "It's my job to uncover as much information as possible."

"You needed information about my divorce?"

He nodded. "I needed to know who you were. Fast."

"And you think you know who I am now?" she asked in a hoarse voice. Before he could answer, she rose. "I'm going to the ladies' room."

BACK IN THE car, a delicious lunch expanded into a lump of nausea in Merlene's stomach.

Worse, a shattering sense of intrusion knocked her off center. Amazing how Cody could just push a few buttons and find out anything he wanted, as if her life weren't her own. She hated the powerless feeling his authority gave her. What else had he looked at? Was there any part of her life that was safe from the eager eyes of the police?

Thirty minutes outside of Ocala she stared at graceful oaks, branches dripping with lacy moss, and brooded over Cody's accusations. Finally, tired of the charged silence, she turned from the scenery and confronted him as he drove.

"I'm not rich."

"You're wealthy by my standards."

"Rich is never having to worry about money."

He shrugged. "I don't worry about money."

"Good for you," she muttered. Why did he always deliberately miss the point? "Look, I used that divorce settlement to buy a house and a car. What was left wouldn't support me for long."

"What happened to the Lexus?"

"How do you know..." she groaned, and rubbed her throbbing forehead. "Did you read every clause in that damned divorce decree?"

"Fascinating reading."

"But it didn't have a thing to do with your case, Detective Warren."

"Just digging for clues, Merl," he said.

She sucked in her breath at the soft, intimate tone of his voice. She felt dangerously exposed to Cody and again wondered what else he knew about her. How far back had he dug? Not that she had any deep, dark secrets. She'd never even been arrested. But still. A person should have a right to privacy.

After a moment he spoke again. "Listen, I'm sorry. But my lieutenant gave me orders to find out everything I could about you. You had to know we'd check you out." She felt his gaze rake over her. "This whole case is about money and fraud. We needed to understand where you fit in. What if Sean Feldman had been your lawyer?"

Merlene nodded when Cody finished, concentrating on the ribbon of asphalt straight ahead. He was right. She should have known. She could never forget who he was. Not even for a minute. Cody was a cop all day and all night—her worst nightmare. But that legal garbage he'd pried into revealed nothing about the circumstances of her marriage or divorce.

And why did she feel the need to explain herself to him?

"Have you ever been hungry, Cody? I mean, really hungry when there wasn't any food in the house or even a buck for a burger at McDonald's when you were too young and helpless to do anything about it?"

"No," he said, his voice barely audible over the rush of the road beneath the tires.

"That basically describes my childhood. So when my divorce was final and I was on my own, I sold that over-priced Lexus, bought a used car and stashed the difference in the bank."

She shrugged when he didn't respond. "Besides, the Lexus was red, too flashy for surveillance. I needed a lower profile."

"Well, thanks to Vanessa Cooper, you no longer have a low profile," he said.

She felt his gaze sweep over her again but didn't answer. She'd be damned if she'd offer Cody Warren any more explanations. He thought he had her completely figured out, so anything she said would be a waste of time.

Why the hell had she let him come with her?

Her mind drifted to the night she and Donny had been caught Dumpster diving behind the local supermarket. She'd been rummaging for edible food inside in the huge metal container—or at least it seemed huge to a scrawny ten-year-old girl—when blue lights began flashing on the wall behind her. Donny scampered into hiding, but she had to stay where she was. When down in the bin she always held her breath, but had no choice except to breathe the disgusting stench because the cops hung around so long.

Even today the sight of a full Dumpster could make her nauseous. Lord help her if she got close enough to smell the odor.

She didn't speak again until the turnoff for the ranch. Cody exited, pulled into the first gas station and cut the engine.

He shifted in the seat to face her. "How about a truce?"

She shot him a questioning glance. Distant blue eyes regarded her carefully.

"Your financial arrangements are none of my business. From now on I'll keep my mouth zipped on the subject."

She didn't trust him to keep his word, but they were 300 miles from Miami and life would go much smoother if they were at least civil to each other.

"Okay," she said. "Truce."

"Okay." He nodded toward the convenience store inside the gas station. "Do you want anything?"

She opened her door. "I'll get it," she said.

Cody watched her walk away, wishing he'd never mentioned her divorce settlement or the Lexus. Her story tugged at his heart. Considering her background, how could she help but think she never had enough.

After hearing about her childhood, he'd figured out she equated money with security. Security was what she craved, and cops surely didn't offer a woman that. Not when they took the chance of catching a bullet every day.

He wanted to trust Merlene, needed to believe that she was basically honest. So far she'd been straight with him. Or had she? Money could be a powerful motivator.

He considered Lieutenant Montoya's last words to him. "I want you to stay close to Merlene Saunders, Warren. Keep an eye on her. Remember, she had a key to Johnson's house."

"DID YOU SAY turn east on State Road Seventeen?" Cody asked Merlene when they got closer to their destination.

She glanced up from the map. "Right, Seventeen. The ranch is east of town, close to the Ocala National Forest."

Cody decided she sounded civil. Maybe she hadn't forgiven him, but at least she was speaking to him again.

Acres of green rolling hills lined with white picket fences had flowed past the car since they'd left the interstate. The lay of the land was definitely rural and the pace peaceful.

Merlene rarely spoke, but the nervous crease between her eyes had smoothed out.

The fragile bond between them had evaporated with his harsh words. How had he let her goad him into angry accusations—suppositions, really? He now understood how much she distrusted the police and he'd practically rubbed her nose in his investigation.

But maybe better to keep each other at arm's length. The more time he spent with Merlene, the more he ached to learn everything about her.

"Make a left on this county road," she said. "The turnoff is about a mile south."

A white wooden gate stood ajar at the entrance to the Johnson property.

"That doesn't look right," Merlene said.

Cody exited the car and examined a busted lock, deducing one hard blow could easily have done the deed.

Dropping the lock, he glanced down the long, unpaved entrance to the ranch, a path bordered on both sides by fenced pasture. Maybe three-quarters of a mile ahead, the top of a red roof peeked from a stand of giant oaks.

When he slid behind the wheel, he asked, "Did your client mention anyone else being here?"

"No one is supposed to be here," Merlene said. "Pat was clear about that."

Her eyes met his with a question and an unmistakable spark of excitement. She raised her eyebrows.

"Is there another way in?" he asked.

"Maybe." She consulted the map. "There's an unpaved back entrance through pasture land. It'll take us a while to find it."

An uneasy feeling squirmed in his gut again, that tickle of disquiet that seldom failed him. Sure, Johnson could have

forgotten his key and broken the lock himself last week...
another harmless coincidence?

He considered continuing to the ranch on foot, taking
whoever preceded them by surprise. No. That would cut off
a quick escape. He glanced at Merlene and found her watching him with a worrisome anticipation.

"Who do you think it is?" Her eyes widened. "Do you
think it's Neville Feldman? Or maybe the other man in the
car the night Dr. Johnson was murdered? What's his name?
Ray Price?"

"I don't think it's anyone," Cody said, deliberately keeping his voice calm. "I just don't like surprises. We'll go in
slow. Pay attention and keep your head low."

"It could be Neville, you know." She took a deep breath.
"If he was really in cahoots with Dr. Johnson like you think,
he might be up here looking for evidence that would convict
him. Remember, Johnson was here just before his murder."

"Don't jump to conclusions, Merl."

But her words echoed his own thoughts, thoughts that
pumped a quick rush of adrenaline into his bloodstream.
Lieutenant Montoya had insisted Neville would travel north,
and Montoya was seldom wrong.

Cody navigated the dirt road, making as little disturbance
as possible, silently thankful for recent rain and mud that
helped muffle the noise of the tires. He didn't want Neville
or anyone else at the ranch house to know about visitors any
sooner than necessary.

"Get your phone ready," he said. "Be ready to dial 911
and report the exact address."

Merlene withdrew a small leather pouch from her purse.
A high-pitched tone sounded when she turned on her phone.

"So you *do* think something is going on at the ranch." She
punched in the three numbers but waited to send the signal.

"Just being cautious," he said, his gaze fixed to the road.

When a one-story brick house came into view beneath the trees, he focused on a blue Jeep parked next to a closed white garage door and made a mental note of the license plate.

He eased his foot off the gas. The car rolled to a stop in the mud inches from the concrete driveway. A screen door slammed, and a tall white male rounded the rear of the house.

Hair stood up on the back of his neck.

Merlene uttered a muffled curse and said, "It's him!"

Neville Feldman.

Feldman reacted the same instant Merlene hit the send button on her cell phone. "Stay down," Cody ordered. Merlene released her seat belt and slid low. He drew his Glock, opened the door and crouched behind it.

"Hold it right there, Feldman!"

A volley of shots thudded into the mud near the front of the car. One slammed into the hood.

Merlene screamed.

Cody returned fire, but Neville vaulted into his vehicle and roared off on a rut-filled road behind the house. Cody leaped into his car to follow.

"Officer needs assistance," Merlene shouted into the phone. Hunched below the dash, her body lurched from side to side as Cody bumped over the rough terrain after Feldman. She thought about resnapping the seat belt, but the strap wouldn't reach.

The operator transferred her to a police dispatcher, who requested the direction they were traveling.

She peeked over the top of the dash to figure that out.

Cody placed his hand on her head and pushed. "Stay down." He grabbed the phone, gave his ID and summarized the situation. One hand kept their swerving vehicle on the narrow path.

While he talked, Merlene placed her hands on the dash

and raised her head to peek out again. They raced after the Jeep on an unpaved back road closely lined on both sides by wooden fences.

So this was a high-speed police chase.

Not that she would go so far as to call it high-speed. The mud-filled ruts in the road kept either vehicle from gaining too much speed. Still, a green blur of vegetation flew by at a frightening rate. Sturdy-looking fences loomed way too close. Her mouth tasted dry as dust.

If Cody lost control—this had all happened so fast she hadn't had a chance to experience any real fear, but now her breath came in quick pants. She couldn't seem to get enough oxygen. Her palms were slick with sweat.

Their car rocked forward and shuddered to a wrenching stop. Cody cursed as her head struck the windshield with a painful thud.

CHAPTER NINE

"MERL? ARE YOU OKAY?"

Merlene heard Cody's voice over the deafening sound of the engine's roar but couldn't respond.

"Talk to me, Merl."

She opened her eyes and realized her right hand covered a throbbing lump on her head. He turned off the engine, and the resulting silence made her feel a whole lot better.

"Let me see," he said, pulling her hand away.

"Am I bleeding?" Which she doubted, since nothing felt warm or sticky.

He examined her scalp with a gentle touch. "No."

She met his gaze, and the worry on his face told her more than any words ever could. Her pulse pounded in her ears. Except for her baby brother, no one had ever cared what happened to her before. But right now Cody did.

She looked away, unsure how to react to the relieved smile that softened his face, or the flood of warmth that swept through her, leaving behind a sweet ache mixed with confusion. Cody was worried about her, really worried. And not because she was his star witness.

"I'm okay," she managed.

"Are you sure?"

"I really didn't hit it that hard." She took a deep breath. "What happened?"

He pounded the steering wheel with his fist. "We're stuck."

"So Neville is escaping?"

"No way. Not if I can stop it."

Cody grabbed the map and reconnected with the Marion County Sheriff's Office, explaining Feldman's route and where they were stranded.

She pushed open the car door and stepped ankle deep into cool, wet mud. Yuck. No wonder they'd gotten stuck. The right front tire was buried to the fender in thick ooze. Although she'd jump-started plenty of dead batteries, she knew they'd need a wrecker to pry this heavy policy cruiser out of such a giant mud hole.

Cody joined her outside, pocketing his phone. "Shit," he muttered.

"How in the world did Neville get through this?"

"A Jeep with four-wheel drive."

She balanced against the wooden fence, removed her muddy shoe and tried to clean it as best she could. A strong odor of decaying vegetation and muck surrounded her. "How long do you think it'll take for the sheriff to come get us?"

Cody rested his elbows on the top of the car and exhaled roughly. She read his frustration. He'd have chased Neville all the way back to Miami. She shuddered at the thought of racing down I-95.

He looked around, and she followed his gaze. They were trapped in the middle of a pasture with no buildings in sight. Thick electric lines overhead were the only sign of civilization.

"At least an hour," he said. "Maybe two."

She stood and shoved her toes back into the damp shoe. "How far back to the ranch house?"

He eyed her. "Probably a fifteen-minute walk."

"Let's go check it out while we're waiting. We can tell the cops where we are."

With a faint smile, he said, "The cops, Merlene? You mean the good guys, the ones coming to rescue us?"

She almost said that she didn't consider the cops the good guys but changed her mind. "Whoever."

His smile faded. "Are you sure you're up to walking that far? How's your head?"

She touched the lump and winced. "A little sore, but I think I'm okay. I'd rather go back to the house and get some ice than sit here with nothing to do."

He shrugged. "After you, ma'am."

CODY CHECKED IN with his partner when he could break away from the Marion County deputies. As he waited for Jake to answer his call, he moved outside to the front porch so Merlene couldn't overhear. They'd been separated for a while, each huddled with the local authorities. Jake had phoned twice in the past hour—unusual for his partner—but this was Cody's first opportunity to call back.

Jake answered with his usual "Steadman."

"What's going on?" Cody asked.

"I could ask the same of you."

Cody quickly reported on their encounter with Feldman at the Johnson ranch. "Marion County has set up roadblocks."

"Let them know there's another murder charge added to the list."

"What? Who?"

"Ray Price."

Cody leaned against the porch railing as he absorbed the news. "Neville Feldman killed his accomplice before he left town?"

"That's what it looks like."

"Neville doesn't want any loose ends."

"That's not all. We've heard from an extremely nervous Sean Feldman."

"Yeah? Did he get religion all of a sudden?"

Jake laughed. "Something like that. Sean got a call from his brother swearing any video of him killing Johnson has to be bogus."

"Of course he'd claim that. Next he'll say he was in church."

"Yeah, well, Neville told his brother he'd kill the bitch who faked the video, along with anyone else who got in his way."

Cody straightened up. "Neville Feldman has threatened Merlene?"

"Bingo. Sean's cooperating because he wants nothing to do with a murder charge. Plus, with his brother running wild he's now worried about his own safety."

"Ain't brotherly love grand."

"Yeah, Sean says his bro has gone off on him before. But the thing is, Sean still insists Neville didn't shoot Dr. Johnson. And you'd better prepare your witness. Since Neville has already killed twice, Montoya wants her in protective custody."

"What are you saying? Montoya is putting Merlene in a safe house?"

"It's being arranged. When are you coming back?"

Cody glanced toward the house, unsure he should tell Merlene about the threat. "I'm not sure yet."

"Well, call for the details before you get back to town."

"Will do."

"And watch your ass, buddy."

"You can count on that." Cody flipped his phone shut.

So Montoya wanted Merlene under police protection. Was it to guard her or keep tabs on her? He might want to know where she was at all times. Whichever, she'd hate the whole idea, even if it was for her own good.

Cody stared at the rolling pasture before him, a peaceful scene in conflict with his thoughts. What troubled him most was Neville Feldman's claim that Merlene's video was fake. What did Montoya think about that? His lieutenant was already suspicious of the time it took Merl to produce the video. No doubt he believed she'd delayed to tamper with the recording.

Did she even have the expertise to make changes that wouldn't be noticed? He'd seen none of the expensive equipment necessary for technical editing work in her home, and twelve hours wasn't enough time to send the recording out to a pro.

But, hell, lowlifes like Neville Feldman always claimed they were innocent. It meant nothing.

He needed to talk to Merlene.

He found her at a breakfast bar in the kitchen holding a bag of ice to her head. Even with those expressive gray eyes closed, creases of worry around her mouth and eyes revealed her anxiety.

Damn, but this case just got crazier and crazier. Thank God he hadn't let Merlene travel to Ocala by herself. Had Neville known she was driving to the ranch and waited to greet her? How could he know that?

She lowered the ice when he sat beside her. He returned the bag to her scalp, reliving his fear from when she'd hit the windshield. He'd insisted she stay low so she wouldn't get shot, but in that position she couldn't wear her seat belt. And of course the woman had peeked over the dash. He managed an encouraging smile, thankful beyond words that her hard head remained intact.

"How are you feeling?" he asked.

"I'm okay. Did Neville escape?"

"So far. But right now I'm worried about you. Are you sure you don't want a trip to the emergency room?"

"I'm fine, Cody. Really."

He lowered the ice and checked her injury again. "Didn't break the skin," he reported. "Looks like you'll live." With fingers cold from the ice, he tucked a lock of hair behind her ear. "Be patient," he said. "I'll get you out of here as soon as I can."

"I'm counting on that, Detective."

He studied her, wondering about what went on inside her stubborn brain. She hid something, maybe exhaustion or fear. Maybe she just wanted to go home. Or was it something more sinister?

He was letting Feldman's protestations of innocence play with his head. He knew better than that.

She sighed. "Quite an adventure we're having, huh, Detective?"

He stiffened at her choice of words. He didn't want her to consider this fiasco an adventure. But Merlene didn't know about the threat on her life.

He'd decided not to tell her, thinking it would needlessly frighten her. But what if he'd made the wrong decision? She shouldn't treat the danger as some kind of joke.

"What do you want to do tonight, Merl?"

"Find a motel, I guess," she said.

"You don't want to drive back to Miami?"

"No." She glanced up, eyes widening. "We'd be on the road all night."

He nodded. "Just wanted to be sure. But we're not getting a motel. I'm taking you where Neville will never find you."

He wanted her away from Neville Feldman, this ranch—hell, this case. Once deputies realized an outstanding murder warrant existed for the fugitive, the Sheriff's Office became efficient and thorough. Checkpoints had gone up at major intersections. Cody didn't believe Neville was smart enough to elude capture a second time, but he wanted Merlene someplace safe until they had the bastard in custody.

She'd been shot at this afternoon, and he was angry with himself for allowing that to happen. She hadn't panicked, though. In fact, she'd been too damn exhilarated by what they'd gone through. Even the nasty knot on her head didn't faze her.

But something bothered her now, and he knew it had to do with him. He wanted to gather her close, nuzzle behind her sexy ears, kiss past her prickly defenses and find out what the hell was wrong.

But not in a room full of cops.

"Well?" Merlene raised her eyebrows. "I'm waiting."

"For what?" he asked, fascinated by the fleeting dimples that never failed to appear when she fought a grin.

"Where is this place that Neville won't find me?"

"Shh." He placed his fingers across her lips for no other reason than to touch her. "I'll tell you when we're on the way."

"MY BROTHER-IN-LAW'S FISHING CAMP on Lake Dorr."

"Lake Dorr?" Merlene repeated. They were back on the road, and finally their destination had a name, even if she'd never heard of the place. She opened Cody's glove compartment and reached for her map—now crinkled from being folded wrong.

"How far is it?"

"Not far." He rubbed the back of his neck. "It's in the Ocala National Forest. Probably take us thirty minutes."

"I found it," she said, her finger on the spot. "You have a key?"

"I know where one is."

"Why there and not a motel?"

"Because Neville will never find us. I can hide the car in the garage, and the cabin's got a security system."

Dropping the map to her lap, she said, "You can't believe he'll come looking for us now. He's on the run."

"Maybe." He tightened both hands on the wheel. "I'll feel a lot better when he's in custody."

"Worried about the evidence in your murder case?"

"I'm worried about you, Merl."

The edge in his voice told her more than she wanted to know. Dread knotted in her stomach. "What's happened that you haven't told me?"

She stared at his jaw, waiting for the muscle to twitch, pleased with herself when it did.

"Remember the passenger in the car with Neville that you recorded?"

She thought about the photographs on her dining table and dredged the name up from her memory. "Ray Price?"

"Bingo. My partner finally caught up with him around noon today. Unfortunately, Neville found him first."

She swallowed hard. "So…he's dead?"

Cody nodded, and she noticed he again rubbed his neck.

"Now Sean Feldman is even willing to cooperate. With his brother gone berserk, Sean's worried he could be the next body in the morgue."

"Sean confessed?"

"Not exactly, but he wants no part of a first-degree murder charge…and he wants to stay alive."

"I can't believe Sean ratted on his brother." Shaking her head, she wondered if she could have ever ratted out Donny, no matter what awful thing he'd done.

"Sean's worried his brother wants no witnesses. Not even a brother."

"Wow." Merlene closed her eyes, overwhelmed by the events of the past few days. Murders, chases, bullets, brothers threatening to kill each other. She knew one thing: she was definitely glad to be with Cody. What if she'd driven to the ranch alone and discovered Neville Feldman fleeing out the back door? What the hell would she have done? She shivered, not wanting to think about confronting a murderer by herself.

Would he have shot her? Would she be wounded and bleeding miles from help. Or dead?

"Price's murder rattled Sean big-time," Cody continued, "but he still insists Neville didn't shoot Dr. Johnson. I'll question Sean again when we get back."

"How can they say Neville is innocent when I have him on video? That's ridiculous." She rubbed her temples. Somehow the pieces didn't all fit together, but the more she thought about the case, the more muddled the clues became. The obvious answer was that murderers always claimed innocence.

Cody pulled the car into the parking lot of a small country grocery. He surveyed the area for a moment then turned to her. "I need to go inside and grab something for dinner. We don't want to eat out and risk running into our friend."

"Whatever you say, Detective." She smiled at Cody. He thought of everything.

"I don't like the idea of you staying out here alone. I'd feel better if you came in with me so I can keep an eye on you. Okay?"

She nodded, liking it very much that he asked.

"Come on, then. Stay alert and stay close."

THE FISHING CABIN lay so deep in the woods that Merlene doubted there was a chance of running into anything—except perhaps a bear.

As the vegetation thickened and the asphalt road turned into potholes, she imagined a primitive log cabin with an outhouse. Instead, when it came into view through the trees, the camp consisted of a modern structure with a screened porch facing the lake. A covered boathouse floated at the bottom of a sloping hill dotted with laurel oaks.

Even better, inside she found modest but comfortable furnishings and two bedrooms. The place smelled musty from being closed up but was surprisingly clean for a male enclave. She dropped her bag in one bedroom and checked out an updated kitchen. Then she moved to the porch and discovered Cody stringing a hammock.

"Why don't you relax while I start dinner?" He studied the lake, and she followed his gaze. "Take advantage of it while you can. I don't want to stay out here after dark."

They had maybe an hour of sun left, and the long shadows off the porch fascinated her. Soft light highlighted every trembling leaf and ripple of water with a muted glow. She moved closer to the hammock and Cody.

"Smells great out here, doesn't it?" he said.

She closed her eyes and filled her lungs with the clean air, old memories making her wistful. "Like summer and playing outside as a kid."

He held the hammock steady for her while she awkwardly climbed in. After giving her a gentle push, he disappeared inside the house. She closed her eyes and tried to relax into the sway but couldn't.

She'd never felt safer in her entire life. And why not? She was hidden under lock and key somewhere in the deep woods with a strong, handsome man professionally trained in various deadly weapons, some of which he'd brought along for the ride.

She wouldn't starve to death, either, because he planned on cooking her dinner. So why did she feel so—what was the word? Unsettled.

Strangely, her mood wasn't because she was hiding from a murderer.

No. It was Cody and his kindness. All her life she'd taken

care of herself. Shoot, she'd pretty much taken care of her whole family until it had self-destructed. Her husband had been a big baby, and she took care of him for a while, too.

She stopped the hammock with her foot. The idea of someone doing nice things for her was…well, new.

She needed to talk to Cody. She needed to thank him.

He looked up from organizing groceries when she entered the kitchen.

"Tired of the hammock already?"

"Let me help. Why don't I prep those pole beans I made you buy?"

He shoved a bowl toward her. "Be my guest."

She sat at the island in the center of the room and removed the ends from the beans, each snap releasing a pleasant, fresh odor.

He popped open a beer and took a long drink. "Two is my limit tonight," he said, crushing the side of the can.

She nodded, not speaking, but feeling the weight of his scrutiny. Where to begin?

"We're safe here, Merl. Hell, the CIA would have trouble locating you tonight." He paused. "But you should take what's going on more seriously."

"I know," she said. "I do, but—"

"What?"

"This is—" She stopped snapping beans and dared a look at him. How could she explain this to Cody? Would it reveal too much of herself?

"No one has ever looked out for me like this before," she said. "Well, no one besides D.J. anyway. It's kind of, well, nice, but, I don't know… Hard to get used to." She lowered her gaze, returning to her work, the quick movement of her fingers soothing her nerves. "And I'm such an ingrate I haven't even thanked you."

"You're welcome," he said.

Finished, she rose and carried the beans to the sink. After a quick wash, she searched cabinets for a pot and dumped them inside. She added water, found salt and pepper and set the burner to simmer.

She faced him as he emptied the beer, still watching her. "I've thought of a way to thank you properly."

His eyebrows rose. "Yeah? What's that?"

She dried her hands on a paper towel. "Those beans need to cook awhile. Come on." Grabbing his wrist, she led him to the living room. "Sit on the floor and lean against the couch," she instructed.

"Sit on the floor?"

"You've been rubbing your neck all afternoon, so I'm going to massage your neck and shoulders. You're too tall for me to reach if you sit next to me."

"Ah."

"You should probably take off your shirt if I'm going to do this right."

"Yes, ma'am." He jerked the navy blue shirt over his head and tossed it on the couch. Her sense of security shattered.

She'd thought she was safe, wrapped up tight in a protected cocoon. But the real danger had been trapped inside with her, a masculine threat full of sinew and sleek muscle.

At the thought of placing her hands on Cody's powerful shoulders, she swallowed hard and dug in her purse for lotion.

Maybe this wasn't such a great idea. The best way to manage would be for him to sit with his shoulders between her legs, a position that seemed disturbingly intimate. She sat behind him on the sofa with a knee pressing into each of his arms.

"I thought you were about to chicken out," he said.

I should, she thought, rubbing the lotion between her hands, releasing its citrus fragrance into the air. She stared at the sculpted body before her. He was gorgeous, perfect except for the two-inch raised scar at the base of his neck.

When he turned to look at her, muscle rippled smoothly across his back.

"Is something wrong?" he asked.

"No," she tried to say, but the word came out strangled. Merlene cleared her throat. "I'm just warming up my hands so I can get at those kinks in your neck. Turn around."

She placed her hands on his shoulders and methodically kneaded his muscles. One thing she'd learned while married to a neurologist was how to give a good massage.

"You're tight," she said.

"It's been a hell of a week."

Merlene silently agreed. "What happened here?" she asked, running a finger along the ridge of the scar.

"Another bad guy. This one had a knife and a grudge."

"Did you arrest him?"

"Several times. He's been in and out of jail more times than Doc Johnson diagnosed phony backs or the need for more pain meds. Hopefully he's put away now to stay."

The knots in Cody's back gradually loosened under her probing fingers.

He rolled his neck forward. "Don't stop," he said. "This feels great."

The body beneath her hands felt strong, smooth and pulsing with life. The warmth from his flesh worked its way into her fingers, wrists, arms… Soon her entire body flushed with heat, as if she absorbed his energy, as if they were joined in some real, physical way. And touching him this way, giving him pleasure, somehow gave her pleasure, too. She liked making him feel good.

She'd never felt such a connection to anyone else. It had to be because Cody was being so nice to her. He acted as if he wanted to take care of her. That was the thing she didn't get. Duty didn't require that he put her up like this.

"Wow, sweetheart, you really know how to make a man happy."

"Feel better?" she asked, stilling her hands but holding them flat against his shoulder blades.

"Much." He turned to face her again, and her hands slid across his back as he moved. "Thank you."

Never had she seen bluer eyes. Only a cloudless sky on a clear summer afternoon compared with the clarity of the color.

"I was thanking *you,* remember?" she said.

He touched her cheek, and she fought to draw a breath. She could see each individual hair on his arm, the sharp ridge of veins and the clear definition of muscle.

"Your turn," he said.

"What?"

"I'll rub your back now." His voice held a challenge, as if he didn't believe she'd allow him to.

But she wanted him to. She wanted him to touch her the way she'd touched him, wondering if he'd feel the same odd connection.

"Okay," she said. "Get up."

An expression flashed across Cody's face that catapulted a jolt into her belly. Was his look surprise—or hunger? She didn't know or care, only knew she wouldn't be able to stop herself now. She wanted to feel his hands on her body more than she'd ever wanted anything.

With their positions switched, Merlene felt dwarfed by the muscled strength of his thighs. He rested his hands on her shoulders, which hammered home how small she was. How vulnerable.

He brushed her hair to either side of her neck.

"Unbutton your blouse," he said, his breath warm against sensitive skin usually sheltered by her thick mane.

She released one button, then another and shrugged to allow the soft cotton to fall away, imprisoning her shoulders. She closed her eyes when Cody took her bra straps and gently slid them down her arms.

He kneaded her neck slowly, rubbing away aches and soreness she hadn't known existed. Anxiety melted away, leaving her loose and restless, wanting more.

She couldn't help but release small sounds of pleasure. Maybe something sometime had felt better, but she couldn't remember what. His hands worked lower and lower down her back, her blouse shifting with the movement of his fingers.

She didn't resist when he reached his arms around her and freed the remaining buttons of her shirt, exquisitely aware of the weight of her breasts against her bra as he slid the blouse toward him and slipped the sleeves off her arms. Her pulse drummed in her ears when his hands found the bra's catch.

The hook gave way, and she sighed, knowing that she shouldn't want him to touch her this much.

Neither of them spoke. He continued to massage her back, working even slower now, inching closer to the front of her body. She shifted beneath his touch, subtly encouraging his hands closer to her aching nipples. Still he moved slowly, rhythmically, until a finger brushed the swell of her right breast.

She sucked in a breath, the movement of her chest forcing his hands closer to where she wanted them.

"Merl?" His voice was a breathless question whispered close to her ear.

CHAPTER TEN

SHE DIDN'T ANSWER HIM, couldn't answer him.

He broke the silence by refastening her bra and lifting her onto his lap. She inhaled deeply of his scent, detecting a hint of cinnamon in his aftershave. Pushing away disappointment, she buried her fingers in the hair on his chest and laid her palm against the steady beat of his heart.

She studied his face as he buttoned up her blouse again. Why had he pulled back? There was no way she would have stopped him from making love to her, and they both knew it. She'd done everything but beg him. She closed her eyes at the memory.

"How does your head feel?" he asked.

"Fine." She locked her hands around his neck and placed her cheek against his bare chest. "Thanks, Cody."

For what? dangled in the room between them, but they sat quietly together, and she relaxed into the sensation of Cody running his palm over her hair while she gathered her pitiful defenses.

"What happened to you after your parents died?" he asked softly.

She answered without thinking. For some reason it seemed natural that Cody would ask.

"We had no family to claim us, so my brother and I were put in different foster homes. We hated being apart."

"You have a brother?"

Had a brother, she almost corrected him, but noted the

surprise in his voice. She'd never told Cody about Donny. "Yes, but…"

"Older or younger?"

"Younger. I was fifteen, Donny almost thirteen when we were separated. He ran away all the time trying to find me, got into trouble and eventually landed in juvie hall. He got beat up pretty bad once by an arresting officer." She remembered his battered face a week after that beating. "But I'm sure he fought like a wildcat to avoid being caught."

"They were just doing their jobs, Merl."

She stiffened, the old anger creeping back. "I know, but they didn't have to kill him."

Cody's hand stilled. "What happened?"

"He was killed in some kind of high-speed chase with the Centralia, Missouri, police. I never learned all the details." She stared at her fingers on Cody's chest. "But when Donny was fifteen, he stole a car to find me in Branson. By then I'd dropped out of school and run away to make my break into what I considered the big time."

Cody circled her with his arms. Long-ingrained instincts told her to push him away, remember this man was her enemy, but she didn't. She didn't want to. He didn't act like an enemy.

"He refused to stop when they tried to pull him over?"

She nodded, miserably aware her voice would break if she spoke.

"I'm sorry, Merl."

Brushing away a tear, she said, "Of course Donny shouldn't have stolen that car. He had no clue what he was doing. I know he was terrified while being chased, didn't know what would happen if he stopped. He was just a kid. I keep thinking that if—"

"Shh." Cody placed gentle kisses across her forehead, her brows, her closed eyes. He touched a tear on her cheek with his tongue. "That's just it, sweetheart. Your brother was a kid and sometimes kids do stupid things." His soft words rumbled close to her ear, his breath tickling sensitive skin.

She couldn't breathe. The emotional backlash from talking about her brother was choking her at the same time desire for Cody raged through her. Too much sensation at one time couldn't be good.

His mouth found hers, and she met him eagerly. She had wanted to kiss Cody, really kiss him like this with no interruptions since that day in the ballpark, the first time she'd been able to remember Donny without the huge hole in her heart growing deeper.

Now Cody's mouth against hers blocked any painful memories. She couldn't focus on anything but him. He tasted faintly of beer, and the wet, smooth texture of his mouth stripped her of any thought but of how his bare flesh would feel pressed against hers.

He loosened the buttons he'd just refastened. A sense of freedom swept through her as he tossed clothing to the floor. She registered the chill on her naked breasts, but warmth returned when he shifted to his side, gathering her body close.

His hands were on her zipper, then sliding away her khaki shorts, and she heard the sound of another zipper over her ragged breath. She reached out and stroked his erection through his white briefs until he grabbed her wrist, extended it over her head and crushed into her with another kiss.

He pulled back, and she met piercing blue eyes. He studied her with a quiet intensity that made her feel as if he could see right through her.

"Please don't stop this time," she said, not recognizing her own voice. "Tonight can be our night. Just you and me, Cody Wyoming. We're not letting anyone else in, okay?" He answered by sliding her panties over her hips and cupping her warmth with his hand, fingers gently probing.

She arched beneath his touch, closing her eyes as he lightly kissed her belly. She'd never wanted anything as much as she wanted Cody at this moment.

He pulled away, and she opened her eyes to find him sheathing himself. When he entered her, she didn't know where Cody ended and she began, the boundaries between them blurred by swift, roaring passion. He created a hunger deep inside her, and each powerful thrust made her wanting rage hotter and stronger. She forgot everything but the need to hold on to the man inside her.

"You're beautiful," he whispered, and the yearning deep in her center stretched a little further. She wanted to tell him he, too, was beautiful, but couldn't formulate words. On a moan of desperate need, she closed her eyes. Cody answered with a husky sound of his own, and a rush of warmth triggered her startling release.

MERLENE WOKE TO Cody mumbling on the bed beside her and knew instantly he was having a bad dream. A nightmare. What kind of nightmares did cops have?

So maybe their lovemaking hadn't been the same for him, she worried, as she studied the symmetry of his powerful chest. After the explosive first act of love between them, he'd carried her to the bedroom where they'd explored each other again. She'd thought his lovemaking so perfect, so special, so… She stretched against the memories, remembering the cascade of sensation he'd aroused in her. She'd never experienced anything like it, although, sure, she'd read about such bliss. But her only previous sexual encounters had been with her husband, and those had usually ended in embarrassing failure. She'd never been able to please Peter no matter how hard she tried.

Not that he'd ever pleased her, or seemed interested in trying.

But Cody... Merlene took a deep, satisfied breath. Cody pleased her just fine. She recalled his hoarse whisper of her name while each separate pulse of him flowed into her. Smiling in the dark, she decided maybe she had pleased him, too.

But now some unpleasant memory had come between them. He mumbled again and tossed an arm over his head, so she gently nudged his hip to rouse him from whatever fiend pursued him.

"Cody. Hey, wake up."

He bolted upright.

Clutching a sheet to her breasts, Merlene sat up beside him and placed her hand on his shoulder. "You were dreaming. It sounded like a nightmare, so I thought I'd better wake you."

"Oh. Sorry." He took a deep breath, then pulled her down into the bed with him, cradling her head against his chest.

She settled into his warmth, trailing her fingers across his abdomen. The flesh beneath her fingers began to vibrate, and a rumbling noise erupted from the direction of his stomach. She laughed but had to admit her own hunger had growled its presence a few times since she'd opened her eyes to his restless body. They'd fallen asleep without eating, and she could smell the beans she'd started earlier still simmering on the stove. She glanced at the clock for the time. Not even midnight yet.

"Hey," he murmured.

"Hey," she answered. Suddenly shy, she snuggled her face against his chest, his warmth spreading into her cheek. His stomach growled again and she giggled. "Hungry, huh, Detective?"

He placed his hand over hers and brought her fingers to his lips.

"Very," he said softly.

She grinned.

"I can feel your smile," he said. "I wish I could see it."

She moved her hand back to his heart, wanting to feel the steady rhythm. "I smile a lot when I'm around you."

"I smile a lot around you, too."

They remained quiet for a moment. She suspected Cody was thinking, as she did, that they also argued a lot. But right now she didn't want to think about the differences between them. Curling into Cody's protective embrace was too special, felt too nice. Why couldn't she stay right here, warm and safe, forever? Was that an impossible dream? Other people had happy endings. Why couldn't she?

"What time is it?" he asked.

"Around eleven."

"Do you think the beans are done yet?"

"I'll be surprised if they're not burned." She pushed herself to her arms, then leaned over him and grinned. "Want some?"

He placed his hand behind her head and pulled her back down to him. "Yeah, I want some."

They were kissing then, naked flesh to naked flesh, intent on each other until more rumbling from Cody's belly broke them apart, laughing.

"We haven't eaten since lunch," she said. "And a lot has happened." She gulped back a nervous laugh at her understatement.

He hugged her roughly, exhaling his warm breath against her hair. "Yeah, a lot has happened."

Merlene rose to her knees and swatted Cody's hip. "I need food. Come on. Let's go eat."

HE RAN—RAN HARD, his breath labored as he tried to escape whatever chased him. He had to go faster, farther, work harder and then he'd be able to...

Cody awoke with a start, totally aware of Merlene in the

bed next to him, her breath feathering across his chest. She lay on her side, sleeping with dark, thick hair curling around her shoulders in sexy waves. He lifted a silky strand and let it sift through his fingers.

He closed his eyes against the need to have her again. Had he made a mistake? He'd brought her to this secluded cabin to protect her, not seduce her.

Damn. After that massage he'd wanted to take her wordlessly on the floor of the cabin. He'd wanted her until he was shaking with the need, pulled back only because making love to her like that, no matter how much she desired it, would only push her further way. He'd done enough of that already.

And he'd wanted her to admit she wanted him, too.

She'd been beautiful—exquisite—lying before him, flushed with desire. He'd been aroused to the point of madness by her obvious pleasure with their lovemaking. Now full breasts with rosy nipples beckoned him again.

He hated that his old dream had come again, one that had tormented him since his father's betrayal. He always awoke with a panicked jolt, interrupting a dash away from unknown dangers. He never knew what he was running from.

Exhaling roughly, he swung his legs out of bed and planted his feet on the worn wooden floor. After a moment, he rose and moved out of the bedroom to check the house.

His thoughts remained on his dad as he gazed outside, and the dense woods called to mind happier times. He remembered childhood camping trips with his parents and Annie when Dad had taught them how to fish. Although his sister hadn't liked baiting the hooks, she'd liked catching fish and eating the cooked results with no problem. Maybe that's one reason she'd fallen in love with her husband, a man who loved to fish.

Moving to the living room, he thought about his brother-in-law and their fishing trips before Mark got hooked on his pain meds. Good times. Mark had loved this cabin. He'd been a great guy, a wonderful husband to his sister, fabulous father to Charlie. The man was much missed.

Cody stared out the kitchen window. He had promised Annie he'd put away unscrupulous doctors who turned good men into addicts.

Nobody out there. The demons were inside with him.

Annie never used this cabin anymore. She'd asked him whether she ought to sell. Maybe now was the right time. Maybe it was past time to make other changes, too, time for him to move on, escape the past.

When he'd completed his circuit, Cody paused at the bedroom door to watch Merlene sleep. She lay on her side, her chest rising and falling evenly, a splash of dark hair visible against a white pillow. He longed to feel her beside him again—warm, soft, her breasts pressing into him with each breath.

How would she act in the morning? Would their lovemaking ruin any chances of deepening trust, ripening a relationship that had barely started? She was one complicated lady, and he kept taking missteps. This one might have been fatal.

God help him, how he wanted her. But he wanted more than just raw, shimmering passion, as intoxicating as that had been. She was the first woman who'd ever made him want more, made him think about something permanent. What was it about her? Her petite body made her appear deceptively vulnerable. Did he feel a need to protect her, like some ancient troglodyte? No. Her feistiness appealed to him even more. Her stubborn nature, her independence, her desire to better herself with an education.

"Is something wrong?" she asked, startling him from his thoughts. She propped herself up on her elbow, her face barely visible in the dark.

"No," he said. "Go back to sleep."

"Did you hear something?"

"No. Why? Did you?"

"Just you, breathing hard, then prowling around the house. Another bad dream?" Soft and sleepy, her voice drifted to him from the bed.

He exhaled roughly and leaned against the door frame. "Same damn one."

She sat up against the headboard. "Do you want to talk about it?"

He clinched against a sudden need to feel Merlene in his arms, her smooth cheek nestled on his chest, and moved toward the bed. "I'm not much interested in talk right now."

"I'm not sorry about tonight," she said after a pause. "Are you?"

"No way, pretty Miss Merl. No way."

"But I hate to think I've given you bad dreams."

"You didn't. It's an old nightmare." He lay down beside her. "One I can't get seem to get rid of."

She gathered him close. "I know one sure way," she whispered.

CHAPTER ELEVEN

MERLENE FOUND THE long drive back to Miami a hundred times more pleasant than the tense trip north. She relaxed around Cody, enjoyed his company. They chatted like two old friends while learning all about each other's likes and dislikes. He loved sports. Turned out they were both fans of the Miami Dolphins. She quit looking for hidden meaning in every word he uttered.

She understood nothing was certain between them. He was still a cop and she a P.I. So far all they'd shared was one night of fabulous sex. She glanced at him and smiled. He must have felt her gaze because he reached for her hand and gave it a squeeze.

Yes, it had been fantastic lovemaking for them both.

No telling what might happen. This case could come between them, but the prospect of a future together no longer seemed impossible. What would it be like to date a cop?

Her contented musings lasted until Cody exited the interstate in North Miami, miles from her Coconut Grove address.

"Where are we going?" she asked.

"Now, don't freak out, but I'm taking you to a safe house."

"Safe house?" She sucked in a deep breath and focused on the busy road ahead. "But I want to go home."

"Not until we have Neville Feldman in custody."

She'd been so deliriously happy after what she and Cody had shared, she hadn't considered what would happen when they arrived back in Miami. Yeah, Feldman was still out there and remained a threat.

But a safe house? Why hadn't he told her?

"What's going on, Cody?"

"I arranged with my lieutenant to drive you straight there. He wants you protected—and so do I—until Feldman is behind bars."

"You arranged it with your lieutenant? Why didn't you arrange it with me?"

"This is for your own good, Merlene."

"But I don't want to be your prisoner, and you can't believe Neville will come after me now."

He glanced sideways at her, then quickly back to the road. "He's made threats. You need to stay in protective custody until we get this wrapped up."

"Threats?" A bolt of alarm sent a frisson up her spine, kicking up her heart rate. "How?"

"Yesterday he told his brother he was going to take care of the bitch that filmed him. He meant in the same way he took care of his accomplice."

"His accomplice?" She swallowed hard. "You mean Ray Price."

"The very dead Ray Price." Cody gave her a pointed look as he made a right-hand turn into a middle-class residential neighborhood.

All her old suspicions about Cody came slamming back, erasing the euphoria that had buoyed her since last night. How dare he not tell her about Neville's threat? Maybe he thought he was protecting her, but the whole idea of protection was more than unsettling. It was downright... She paused in her tumbling thoughts.

Unsettling, yes. But not nearly as terrifying as being stalked by a murderer.

"You deliberately kept this from me," she said, fighting

to keep her voice under control. "What else haven't you told me?"

"He claims someone set him up."

"Set him up?" She thought about that allegation. "Of course he does. Don't bad guys always say they're innocent?"

Cody nodded. "But he's blaming *you,* Merl. I hope you don't own any dubbing equipment that could alter a digital recording."

"Of course not. Why would I?"

He nodded. "Good."

She wrapped her arms around herself and wondered how her carefully arranged life had become such a disaster. Her surveillance subject was dead, and his murderer wanted to bump her off next. On top of that, she was involved with a cop, the only person who had ever tried to take care of her. Her face warmed as she remembered how well he'd taken care of her the previous evening.

Still, he had no right to keep the truth from her.

"You should have told me," she said. "I'm not a child."

"Hey," he said, "if I was wrong, I'm sorry. I didn't want to worry you."

"Can't I at least pick up some clean clothes? I only packed for one night on the road."

"Give me a key. I'll go later."

Whoa. Was he kidding? For sure she didn't want Cody Warren rummaging through the private drawers in her bedroom. Her most personal secrets would be his to discover while he remained as closed off about himself as ever.

He reached over to squeeze her shoulder. "You'll be totally safe."

"So you say, Detective."

Frowning, she considered how he continued to run roughshod over her life but refused to reveal anything about himself. Maybe when they were alone together in the safe house—wherever the hell that was—she could get him to open up. She wanted to know why he was so unbending yet so sweet, so sexy—so damned everything.

There had to be something wrong with him. Bad dreams. Never married. The way he encouraged the kids in the ball-park, he ought to have five little rug rats of his own to coach. But he didn't. With sudden insight, she knew Cody would make a fantastic father. She placed her hand over her abdomen. And yet he was always careful.

To think she'd been fantasizing about a possible life with Cody. When would she ever learn? He didn't trust her. Or at least not completely. She'd heard the doubt in his voice when he'd casually asked her about the dubbing equipment.

Oh, no question he was skilled at his job. He'd almost hidden it, but the suspicion was still there.

MERLENE SHIFTED HER weight from foot to foot as Cody knocked twice at a boxy one-story house in a suburban neighborhood consisting of block after block of similar homes. A uniformed officer with wiry gray hair opened the door. His aloof gaze touched hers, then he nodded at Cody and motioned them inside.

"We're all set, Cody. Glad to see you and Mrs. Saunders made it safely."

"Thanks, Johnny," Cody said. "This is Merlene Saunders. Merlene, this is Officer Johnny Newcomb. You'll be seeing a lot of each other."

"Ma'am," Newcomb said.

She attempted a smile. "Hi."

What had she been thinking? Of course she and Cody wouldn't be alone. Unease lodged in her gut as she realized how isolated she'd be from the rest of the world. This was looking more and more like a house arrest.

"Any news on Feldman?" Cody asked as he surveyed the interior of the house.

"Nothing yet," Newcomb replied.

Cody nodded and grabbed Merlene's small suitcase. He flipped open his cell phone and punched in a number as he moved into a bedroom.

While Cody reported in, Merlene explored her safe house. Cody deposited her bag in the largest of the two bedrooms, which contained a double bed covered by a navy blue comforter, an ancient wooden nightstand with a reading lamp and an equally old chest of drawers. Another smaller bedroom was furnished similarly. The living room featured a dark gray cloth sofa, a brown leather recliner and a television set. A dining room with a table and mismatched chairs completed the tiny house.

How nice. Her new home, complete with furnishings straight out of her nightmare childhood.

Not exactly the plush surroundings she'd imagined. Certainly nothing like the flashy modern mansions she'd seen on *Burn Notice* or *CSI Miami*.

She ended her tour in a screened-in patio behind the house, finding one wooden chair borrowed from the dining room and an ashtray on the concrete slab beside it. Newcomb must be a smoker.

The view was into a secluded backyard enclosed by a six-foot wooden fence. Thick grass, lush from summer rains, needed mowing. An orange-and-black butterfly flitted among the weeds.

Towering, moisture-laden clouds dominated the western sky. She stared toward the darkening storm, wondering how soon it would reach their location. She took a deep breath and could smell the coming rain.

Cody stepped through the sliding glass door and joined her on the porch, glancing to the west, as well. The breeze stirred, blowing his hair away from his forehead. She ached to trace the stubble that was beginning to show on his jaw. Low, rumbling thunder boomed in the distance, and she felt an answering vibration deep inside her.

And that frightened her. Her feelings for Cody had come on too fast, too strong. She wanted to touch him, to run her fingers through his windblown hair, to feel his lips capture hers—and now she wouldn't even be able to talk to him.

How long before they could be alone together? A rush of warmth accompanied her reckless imaginings, and she averted her gaze from his face.

He was too much the perfect cop to ever touch her here. The realization that she desperately wanted him to pissed her off.

"Where's the Jacuzzi?" she asked.

"Jacuzzi?" Eyebrows raised, he turned away from the brewing storm.

"This is a safe house, right? Where's the pool, the hot tub?" She folded her arms across her chest. "On TV there's always a view of the ocean."

Grinning, Cody reached for her but stopped. A guarded expression replaced his smile. With a glance at the house, he lowered his arm.

"Damn," he whispered. "This is going to be harder than I thought."

Elation flowed through Merlene, making her feel light as the backyard butterfly. So he still wanted her.

"Are you certain your star witness needs this much protection, Detective Warren?"

"Yes, ma'am." Cody stepped away from her. "I have to go. Give me your key, and I'll bring you some clean clothes later."

She hesitated, her stomach executing a quick cartwheel at the thought of Cody in her bedroom, free to pry anywhere he wanted. There had to be another way. Once again she felt powerless because of his position.

"Wouldn't it be easier if I went with you?" she asked. "Or at least quicker?"

"If Neville Feldman is looking for you, he'll be watching your home."

"But he's in North Florida."

Cody shrugged. "He could have accomplices."

"Ray Price is dead, remember?"

"There could be others working with him. We don't know the full extent of this insurance fraud scheme. That's the point of a safe house."

Realizing there was no hope for it unless she wanted to wear the same filthy clothing for heaven knows how long, she dug in her purse for her key chain.

"Bring the textbook on my dining room table, okay? The one I was reading the other day."

He appeared to be judging the weight of her keys, then his fingers closed around them and he looked up. "Sure. Anything else?"

She sighed and cast an unhappy glance around the porch. "I guess I won't be needing a bathing suit, so just shorts and blouses. The blouses are in the closet, shorts in a drawer in the chest. Oh, and clean underwear."

She expected at least a leer from Cody, but he just nodded and said, "You'll listen to Johnny, won't you, Merl? He knows what he's doing."

"Of course."

"You won't try to leave?"

"I don't have a car."

Still, he hesitated, acting like he didn't want to go anywhere. "You'll be safe here. Don't worry."

She stared at him. "Are you serious? You've put me under

house arrest, telling me it's for my own safety, and I'm not to worry?"

"You're not under arrest."

She raised her chin. "So I could leave if I wanted to?"

Cody sucked a breath deep into his lungs and released it slowly. She held her own breath waiting for his reply.

"Yes, you could leave," he said. "But I'm asking you to remain here."

She nodded. "You're also asking me not to worry."

"That's right. Because if you stay here, you don't need to worry." He took a step away, then turned back with a half smile.

"Besides, I promise you, Merl, I'm worried enough for both of us."

"I'M FINE, D.J. REALLY. Not concerned at all." *At least not about my safety,* Merlene silently added. *My sanity, maybe.*

Soon after Cody's departure, she'd phoned her boss to make her own report. Cody asked her not to use her cell, insisting Feldman might have the ability to trace the call. She seriously doubted he was that talented a crook but complied.

The only landline in her hideaway hung on a wall in the kitchen. She could hear but not see the television Officer Newcomb watched in the living room.

"But I feel like a prisoner," she told D.J.

"Cody said you were doing great—a real trouper."

Merlene quit twisting the phone cord around a finger. "When did you talk to Cody?"

"Yesterday and today. He's been keeping me posted a lot better than you have."

"Sorry. I've been a little…distracted." How could she possibly explain her present situation to D.J. when she didn't understand herself what was going on?

"So I gathered." A coughing fit interrupted anything else he intended to say.

"Are you using your inhalers?" she asked.

A long pause hung heavy over the connection.

"D.J.?"

"I had another…episode last night."

"What the hell happened?"

"Couldn't catch my breath. Scared me a little."

She closed her eyes. Things must be bad for D.J. to admit that.

"Have you been to the doctor?"

"Now, don't start nagging, Merl. I've got an appointment this afternoon."

"Can you cover everything in the field without me? What about that workers' comp fraud case for Sunshine Insurance?" She heard a burst of laughter from the TV. "I don't think the cops will let me out of here to run the surveillance."

"I can handle it," D.J. said. "Oh, Pat Johnson called this morning, and I filled her in. When I told her about her visitor at the ranch, she went a little nuts. She's decided to stay away from Ocala for now."

"I'm sorry about all this, D.J. I'll give her a call later."

"She's at the house in the Gables now tying up loose ends."

"Are the kids with her?" Merlene asked, thinking about her last conversation with Pat.

"She said she left them with friends in the mountains. Is she always so edgy?"

"Pat's been through a lot. She's probably worried sick about her children."

"True." After another coughing fit, his breath ragged, D.J. said, "Tell you the truth, Merl, I'll be glad when you get out of there."

"They can't force me to remain. Do you want me to—"

"No. You hang tight. Do what the police tell you."

She hung up and left her hand on the receiver, worried about D.J.'s lungs, until the phone rang against her palm.

She stepped away. "Should I answer that?" she called to Officer Newcomb.

"No, ma'am. That's for me. I'll get it."

Newcomb hurried into the kitchen and grabbed the receiver. "Yeah," he said, waving her away with a smile.

Police business, she decided, and moved to take the cop's place in front of the TV, where a loud, incredibly obnoxious talk show blared. The host blathered something about women who date their sons' friends. How was it possible the police could find so many ways to make her life miserable?

As she flopped on the couch, her gaze fell on a pack of cards half hidden beneath a sports magazine on the coffee table. Well, well. This looked promising.

"Shut the door, Cody."

Cody entered Lieutenant Montoya's office and closed the door behind him. Looking grimmer than usual, Montoya sat behind his desk, unwrapping a thick cigar. Cody shot a glance at Jake, and his partner shrugged.

"What's going on?" Cody asked.

"Forensics don't match the Saunders woman's story," Montoya began. "I know you trust her, but the medical examiner doesn't believe that the gunshot wounds were from the Glock in the video."

"The recording doesn't clearly show if Price was carrying another weapon, so that could explain it," Jake said. "But we didn't find a gun in his apartment."

"He would have ditched a murder weapon," Cody said.

"Don't you find it suspicious that Mrs. Saunders didn't report the existence of the surveillance until the next day?" Montoya asked. "Maybe she needed the time to doctor it. The lab is checking on that now."

"There's more," Jake said.

Cody straddled a chair beside his partner, not sure he wanted to hear the rest.

"Neville Feldman's been in touch with his brother Sean again," Jake continued. "Neville is on the run and desperate, but insists the doctor was dead when he and Price arrived. He swears they heard shots before entering and that Pat Johnson had requested him to show for the meeting. He expected to meet with her that night."

"*Pat* Johnson?" Cody repeated.

"Mrs. Saunders's client," Montoya said with slow emphasis.

Cody shook his head. "But she was in North Carolina the night of her husband's murder."

"So she says." Montoya pointed the unlit cigar at Jake. "We're confirming that."

"We've requested phone records and are checking airline reservations," Jake said. "Remember, we couldn't reach Mrs. Johnson to notify her of the death until the following day."

"Mrs. Johnson increased her husband's life insurance policy by two million dollars a few months ago," Montoya said. "Maybe she decided to make bilking insurance companies a family business."

"We'll know more soon," Jake promised.

"So maybe your pain-in-the-ass private eye was hired by her client to frame someone else for the death of her husband." Montoya leaned back in his chair. "Clever, huh? While Saunders records Feldman arriving, Mrs. Johnson is inside pulling the trigger."

"If it's true, the big question is whether Merlene knew about her client's plan or not," Jake said.

"Search her home carefully this afternoon, Warren," Montoya ordered.

"Do we have a warrant?" Cody asked.

"Not yet. But her delay in turning over the video gives us probable cause if we need to obtain one. And don't tell her about our suspicions."

"She might run," Jake said.

"Just like a scared little rabbit," Montoya added. "I like knowing where she is."

CODY PUSHED OPEN Merlene's front door, at war with a guilty conscience.

All too clearly, he remembered her stunned face in the diner when he'd mentioned his investigation into her background. He'd promised himself he'd only gather what she needed and not pry into her private life.

But forensic evidence, along with her delay in turning over the video, had now torpedoed that promise. Damn. Could Merlene be trying to frame Neville Feldman in a conspiracy with Pat Johnson? His original investigation had never turned up a hint of Pat's involvement in her husband's criminal activities.

Would Merlene succumb to the lure of a healthy percentage of Pat's life insurance proceeds? No question she craved the security cold cash could provide. But that didn't mean she would act as an accomplice to murder, did it?

No, he didn't believe she had that in her.

After his meeting with Montoya, Cody had reviewed the surveillance video four times and found no discrepancy, no unexpected jump in a frame or other clue that the recording had been altered. Okay. So was it realistic that she forgot about the surveillance? Well, why not?

She'd been terrified. And hadn't he forgotten to ask about one?

Sure, Montoya had good instincts. That's how he got to be a commanding officer. But his lieutenant hadn't been at the murder scene with Merl. Cody would bet his badge that Merlene had been genuinely frightened by the gun-shots she'd heard.

But she was now an official suspect. And now he had to search her home.

It was his job, of course. Oh, he damn well knew his job. He hadn't cut a corner or bent a rule since his rookie year, when he couldn't shake the feeling that everyone silently watched, waiting for him to turn crooked like his old man.

No, he hadn't bent a rule until he met Merlene. For some reason she had changed everything, even the way he felt about being a cop. He pictured her face, her stunning smile. He'd never experienced this tug, this constant pull toward a woman before, wanting to spend as much time with her as he could. He didn't want to unravel the flimsy threads they'd barely begun to weave together.

If he found incriminating evidence, he'd have to report it to Montoya, obtain a warrant and return with a full team to search. She would know what occurred, that he'd been the one to bring her down. She'd hate him forever.

His career had forced him to do a lot of hard things, but that would be the hardest by far.

He shut the door behind him and quickly scanned the front room. Just as he remembered it. Cluttered, warm, pleasant. Stamps of her unique personality—a framed poster of Blake Shelton, well-used video camera, the bag containing her wigs, a quilt in disarray on the couch—registered quickly with Cody.

He felt her presence and doubted he'd find anything suspicious. Merl was smart. Would she have given him a key if there were anything in her home to be found?

A gilt-framed photograph he hadn't noticed before faced him from a table beside the sofa. Cody picked it up and examined the brooding face of a young male teenager. Merlene's brother. The resemblance between this boy and

Merlene struck Cody like a physical blow. Donny was hard where Merlene was soft, but they could have been twins.

Merlene had trusted him when she'd confided in him about her brother. No way would he repay that gift by searching her home. If they were going to bridge the huge gap between them, they had to start somewhere. He'd start right here, right now.

There was an explanation for the discrepancies in forensics; he just needed to find the reasons. He refused to believe she was lying to him. He was a cop. He'd made it his livelihood to read people, to notice when they weren't telling the truth. She'd displayed none of the usual tells.

Trusting her, trusting himself that he read her right, put his job on the line. He knew that. If he was wrong, if she turned out to be dirty despite all his instincts…yeah, it could mean his badge.

He was willing to take that chance. Merl was worth the risk. And maybe he should change professions if a beautiful woman could dupe him so completely.

He placed the photograph and her heavy textbook by the front door. What else should he take for her? He headed purposefully toward her bedroom but halted when confronted with a queen-size bed covered by a pale blue quilted spread. Turning away, he refused to fall victim to imagining her naked body beneath her cool sheets, hot to the touch, dark hair spilling over soft blue…

Willing away the images, he jerked open a dresser drawer. Black silk stared him in the face. The fresh, warm fragrance of Merlene washed over him. He swallowed. Well, good. He'd found her lingerie.

Selecting several pairs of panties, he tried not to notice their softness, tried not to think of the slinky fabric caressing her supple hips.

Moving faster now, with more resolve, he opened more

drawers and found cotton shorts. In her closet he grabbed blouses, careful not to wrinkle them.

What else? She could be stuck at the safe house for days. He hoped not, but it could happen. What would a woman want?

"GIN," MERLENE ANNOUNCED, displaying her cards to Officer Newcomb on the couch beside her.

"Damn," Officer Johnny Newcomb muttered, throwing his cards on the table in disgust.

She grinned at him, adding points to her winning tally. "Are you sure you don't play poker?"

"Not with you, ma'am. You'd clean me out."

Dealing another hand, she said, "Oh, you never know."

She didn't mind playing cards with Officer Newcomb. In fact, Johnny was kind of nice. D.J. called him a dinosaur, a cop who'd been on the force a long, long time. She and her guard had hit it off over pepperoni pizza when she'd suggested they play rummy. It helped pass the time for them both.

She glanced at the digital clock on the wall. Almost nine. When would Cody show up? She fanned her cards before her face, telling herself she only wanted the promised clean clothes so she could take a shower before bed. It'd been a long afternoon.

"How late are you on duty, Johnny?"

"My shift ends at ten, but there'll—" the officer rearranged the cards in his hand "—there'll be someone else here at that time. Don't you worry."

"I'm not worried," she said, as two knocks sounded on the front door. Merlene looked up, then felt herself smile as Cody entered. Her heart thudded at the smile he offered in return.

"Evening," he said.

"Evening, Cody," Johnny replied.

She blinked at the goodies in the cardboard box Cody placed beside her. Clean clothes, several books...oh, her favorite terry-cloth robe. Two days of mail. She pulled out Donny's photo.

"I watered the plants and checked the windows and doors," Cody told her. "Why don't you go on home, Johnny. I'll wait here for the night shift."

Johnny threw down his cards. "You don't have to ask me twice, Detective. I've got an impatient wife waiting. See you tomorrow, Merlene."

"Good night, Johnny."

After her guard had left, Cody stood by the couch, oddly hesitant, watching her. "Sorry to break up your card game."

"That's okay." Merlene grinned. "Poor guy can't play well. I'm hoping his replacement is better."

"Everything okay here?"

"Still no Jacuzzi."

He shook his head and sat beside her. "You're something else, lady."

"Thanks for all this," she said, indicating the personal items he'd brought.

"You're welcome."

He didn't smile. Curious about his strange mood, she watched him struggle for his next words. Clearly something ate at him.

"Any news on the case?" she asked.

"Feldman robbed a liquor store near Tallahassee."

She sucked in a breath. "That's a long way from South Florida. Why can't I go home?"

"He shot the clerk for not moving fast enough."

"Oh, my God. Is the clerk okay?"

"Should pull through. Merl, you're here for your own

safety. Believe me, I'd rather you were home and Feldman in jail."

"So what's wrong?"

"How well do you know Pat Johnson?"

She noted the deliberately neutral tone of his voice, like he was hiding something. Why was he asking about Pat?

"During my marriage, I would see her occasionally at medical association functions. We weren't exactly friends. I was a lot younger, but some of my best clients have come from women I knew during that period in my life." Hugging the soft robe to her, Merlene considered the irony of how other doctors' wives had once snubbed her because of her backwoods accent and country manners but then hired her when they needed help in divorce court. Life was indeed strange sometimes.

"Did you know she increased the life insurance policy on her husband a few months ago?"

"Of course not." Startled, Merlene met Cody's gaze. "Why?"

"I'm tying up loose ends," he said. "I'm sure you've heard about police paperwork."

"Uh-huh," she murmured, not convinced by his lame excuse. Something else was going on. She thought about Cody combing through her closets and drawers and needed to know how intrusive he'd been.

"Did you find anything interesting when you searched my home?"

His expression didn't change. "I didn't look for anything but what you'd need here."

Plucking at a loose thread on the robe, she said, "That's hard to believe, Detective."

He placed his hand over hers. "Maybe, but I want you to believe me." After a pause, he said, "I want you to trust me. You know you can tell me anything."

She wanted to trust him, but she hadn't believed in anyone in a long, long time and wasn't sure if she could start now. Maybe it was too late, remembering he had looked at her divorce file.

As she smoothed her fingers over the familiar fabric, she felt the intensity of his gaze. Heat from his body, so close to hers, warmed the air between them.

She looked up to meet probing blue eyes. "Do you trust me?"

His gaze penetrated hers as if trying to see straight through to her soul. "I'm trying, Merl. You make it damn hard, but I'm trying."

"Then tell me about your father."

CHAPTER TWELVE

CAUGHT OFF GUARD by the unexpected question, Cody sucked in a quick breath. "My father?"

She nodded, gazing at him expectantly, obviously waiting for an answer.

He stared back at her. Where had this come from? What did she know about his father? Once again Merlene had changed the subject. This time to a topic he always tried to avoid, although of course she couldn't know that.

"What about my father?" he finally asked.

"Johnny, my guard, knew him. Why won't you ever talk about him?"

Cody released a breath. "Well, for one thing, he's dead."

"Oh." Her gray eyes widened. "I'm sorry. I didn't know."

"Forget it," he said, certain she wouldn't. He never mentioned his father because he hated revisiting that miserable story. Why was Merlene probing with these questions now?

Delicate brows drawn together, she asked, "So why would Johnny act as if your dad was such a big mystery?"

"Nobody talks about him."

"Nobody?"

"Not around me, anyway."

"But why? You know, trust works both ways, Cody." Her voice softened. "I've told you all my ugly secrets."

He turned her hand and traced the lines in her palm. Had she really told him all her secrets? Or were there little details she'd omitted? Yeah, trust worked both ways, like a double-edged sword.

Then he remembered her broken voice, her hot tears as she told him about her brother, her obvious love for Donny, despite all his problems. If anyone would understand about his father, it would be Merl.

Why not trust her with the truth? With that thought he suddenly wanted her to know about his dad, about the shame he'd been carrying for so long. He wanted to share his dirty secret with her, knowing it would increase their intimacy, the connection growing between them.

"My dad was precisely the kind of cop you despise—greedy and crooked. When he got nailed on the take, he couldn't face the disgrace so he picked up a forty-five and blew his brains out. My mother found him minutes before my sister came home."

Cody closed his eyes when Merlene placed her arms around his neck. Soft and sweet, she hugged him tightly, surprising him with her strength and the comfort she freely offered. Amazing how the story could still hurt after all this time.

"I am so sorry," she murmured.

Cody wrapped his arms around her, accepting her sympathy and pushing away the notion that Merl might have similar traits to his old man when it came to money, rejecting that thought as unfair.

Wiping a tear from her eye, she sat back. "Well, I can see why you don't like to talk about him. I don't think Johnny knows about the suicide."

"He knows, but Dad's death went on record as an accident. The department managed to keep it quiet, so nobody discusses the matter."

Nodding, she released a deep breath, causing her hair to

flutter away from her forehead. "You're nothing like your father, Cody. Don't ever think that you are."

"I'm glad you feel that way." He smiled at her, amazed she'd hit on the very thing that had bothered him for too long: that he'd end up bent like his dad. He knew plenty of people in the department waited and watched, thinking the coconut doesn't fall far from the tree.

She squeezed his hand. "Thanks for telling me. It means a lot."

He closed his hand over hers, admiring her slender fingers, warmed by her concern. "It's hard to talk about my dad. I guess I want to bury that part of my life, pretend it never happened."

"But you can't," she said with a nod. "Because he was your father."

"Right."

"Believe me, I understand about wanting to pretend the past didn't happen."

"I thought you might."

"Focus on the good times," she said. "That's what I try to do. I know there have to be some. And for sure don't let your father's mistakes become your own."

He didn't respond, thinking it was too bad they couldn't both start over and leave painful memories behind.

"Don't you feel better for telling me about it?"

Glancing up, he found her studying his face. "Should I?"

"Whenever I talk to you about my family, I always feel better afterward," she said. "It's like…I don't know, getting rid of a huge weight. At least for a while."

He knew she wanted him to feel better. Well, hell, maybe he did. He'd known telling her would somehow change things between them. Or maybe his attitude came from being around her. She was obviously pleased he'd shared his secret.

"I always feel good when I'm with you," he said, surprised to hear his voice so husky, and even more surprised at the truth of his words. "I'm not sure what magic you work on me, Merl, but when I'm around you…" He trailed off, unsure of how much of his feelings to reveal, unsure of *how* he felt about her. Confused, mostly.

"When you're around me, what?"

"I'm in big trouble." Always wanting to believe her, wanting to trust her, but always hearing his lieutenant's warnings in the back of his head. Warnings he'd chosen to ignore but couldn't quite manage to forget.

"Big trouble, huh?" she murmured.

"Yeah."

She grinned that heart-stopping smile. "Me, too."

Her gaze dropped to his mouth, and she nibbled at her lower lip. He ached to feel the nip of her white teeth against his flesh. He knew he'd forget everything with the taste of her quick tongue in his mouth.

Her chest rose and fell with a deep inhalation. "Why couldn't you be my guard tonight? Why does someone else have to come?"

His groin tightened at her soft, wistful words. "Not a good idea, Merl."

Their eyes met. "I think it is," she said in a seductive whisper.

"But remember I'm the detective with more training."

Eyes narrowing, she shifted away from him.

"Hey, that was a joke," he said, catching her hand. "I can't stay with you because my lieutenant won't let me." Cody groaned inwardly. What would Merl think if she knew Montoya considered her a suspect?

Wrinkling her nose, she said, "Your lieutenant is a pain in the ass."

He pulled her against his chest and nuzzled her hair. "You must know that I'd rather stay."

"And how would I know that?"

How would she know it? She couldn't know that his heart squeezed every time he saw her, or how he thought about her when they were apart, that he'd placed his career in jeopardy by trusting her. Merl had gotten under his skin like no other woman ever had.

How could she know when he was with her he felt like he'd come home? He didn't understand that emotion himself.

"Because I'm telling you," he said.

With a sigh, she wrapped her arm around his waist. "Hurry up and catch Neville Feldman. D.J. isn't feeling well. I need to get out of here and help him."

"Yes, ma'am." Dismissing thoughts that Merl could be in league with her client, they shared a smile interrupted by two knocks at the front door. Cody stepped to the window to confirm the arrival of her bodyguard for the night.

After making brief introductions, Cody stepped into the humid midnight air. He turned, looking back to catch a final glimpse of Merl, and found himself staring into huge gray eyes begging him not to leave. The closing door cut off his view of her face.

He heaved a deep breath as he glanced around, checking out the surroundings for the tenth time, searching for something unusual, anything out of the ordinary for ten o'clock on a weeknight.

No traffic. No citizens around but one fortyish Hispanic woman walking her boxer. Cody listened hard and could barely discern the sound of a television program in the house next door. Sounded like early news.

Definitely a quiet neighborhood, similar to hundreds of residential areas in the South Florida area. Montoya's team had chosen the location for the safe house well.

Yeah, then why did he feel so strangely disquieted? He moved toward his car wondering why he didn't want to leave. He'd told Merl she'd be safe here. Why didn't he believe it himself?

He paused. Well, no. Maybe he didn't. Merl wasn't exactly high on Montoya's list of best-loved suspects. His lieutenant hadn't assigned a specially trained unit to protect her. Hell, her guards were old men, officers treading water on the job until cashing in their first retirement check. Honest men, all of them, no question. Good officers.

But how proactive would any of them be if Neville Feldman burst through the front door with a team of his own intent on eliminating Merlene?

If woken out of a sound sleep, he doubted Johnny could draw his weapon in time to even protect himself.

Cody glanced back to the house. He knew how these assignments worked. With only one guard on duty, on the night shift there would definitely be some dozing. Human nature. Plus, no one truly expected an attempt on Merl. Montoya was performing his due diligence just in case.

But what if Feldman really did have accomplices in the area? What if the leak in the department had communicated the location of the safe house?

Cody rotated his left shoulder then leaned over to survey his front seat. Looked like a great place to spend the night. He'd spent many an hour on long, lonely stakeouts in this fine police vehicle. He could do it again.

He opened the driver's side door, deciding to grab some coffee at the closest fast-food joint, maybe even a burger. It was a long time before morning.

He'd be back within minutes and remain until the guards changed shift. Then he could catch an hour or so of sleep, take a hot shower before going in to the office.

He'd promised Merlene she'd be safe. He intended to make damn sure he kept that promise.

THE NEXT AFTERNOON Merlene dipped a spoon into chicken noodle soup and decided she was going as stir-crazy as the tasteless noodles. She'd spent the morning catching up on her reading for class and hoping Cody would call. He hadn't. She couldn't reach D.J. since he was out in the field doing her surveillance work. She hadn't heard a human voice all morning except a few mumbles from Arturo, today's guard. Regretting her lack of female friends, she wished she had someone to talk to.

Her excitement for the day had been watching Arturo open a can, dump the contents into a bowl and slide it into the microwave. Instant lunch. Exactly the way her mother used to make it. At least this wasn't tomato. After so many cans of tomato soup, she couldn't stand the stuff.

Steam rose from the thin broth, making her wish she had some of the delicious homemade soup Cody's sister had sent via Cody to her stakeout. What was her name? Annie. What was her last name? Merlene thought back to the brother-in-law's fishing cabin in the woods. She'd seen the name there. Gallahan? No. Gallagher. That was it. Mark Gallagher.

Merlene glanced at the phone on the wall. She ought to give Annie Gallagher a call and thank her for such a yummy meal. Maybe Annie would give her the recipe. And maybe she could learn something about Cody.

Directory assistance gave her the number in less than a minute. Annie answered with a cheery hello on the third ring.

"Hi," Merlene said, momentarily at a loss. She'd done this so spontaneously, she hadn't planned what to say to the woman. "I'm a friend of Cody's," she blurted. "My name is Merlene Saunders."

"Of course," Annie said. "I saw you at Charlie's game last week. How are you?"

"To tell you the truth, Cody's got me stashed in what he calls a safe house, and I'm going a bit nuts."

Annie laughed. Merlene liked the sound. Cody's sister had a nice, open laugh.

"I heard," Annie said. "Is it a male fantasy to keep their girlfriends locked away from the world?"

Merlene's cheeks warmed at the idea of being Cody's girlfriend. "I don't know," she said. "Maybe."

"Definitely make him pay for it when you get out."

"Any idea on how to do that?"

"We'll think of something," Annie said. "In the meantime, is there anything I can do to help?"

"Well, actually, I was calling to thank you for that fabulous soup you sent with Cody. You're a great cook."

"You're very welcome."

"Do you share recipes?" Merlene asked, feeling a bit awkward, realizing this was a first. Never in her life had she asked anyone for a recipe. It wasn't so much that she didn't cook, but she'd never had the opportunity to actually make friends to ask. Not while hiding from the authorities as a kid, not waiting tables in Branson when underage and certainly not with the snooty wives of Peter's colleagues. She doubted they cooked much, anyway.

"The secret is enough garlic," Annie confided. "Have you got a pen handy?"

As Annie talked, Merlene jotted down ingredients. She found Cody's sister easy to talk to, maybe because she liked to talk about Cody. Merlene couldn't help but notice the affection in Annie's voice and that she was worried about her brother. Merl thought of her own brother and wondered what it would be like to have a sister.

When Arturo entered the kitchen with a questioning look, Merlene told Annie she had to go. "Thanks. You've really cheered me up."

"Call me anytime."

CODY ARRIVED AT the safe house that evening with ice cream, a DVD and the intention to have a serious discussion with Merlene.

Thanks to his mom, he'd grown up immersed in the code of the Old West, and he intended to start Merlene's education. No one should go through life without a thorough understanding of trail drives, wagon trains and gunfights over honor. And afterward, they would talk.

Montoya's doubts were driving him crazy. He wanted to make sure in his own mind that she wasn't involved in any sort of shady business with Pat.

"The Magnificent Seven?" Smiling, Merlene raised sparkling eyes to meet his. She'd pulled her hair back with a clip, giving her face a fragile appearance. She wore a cobalt-blue blouse that had grabbed his attention in her closet.

"What's it about?" she asked.

"You'll love it," Johnny said. "My all-time favorite movie." He grabbed the disk and shoved it into the slot of the DVD player.

Merlene raised her brows as Cody sat next to her on the couch.

Damn. He'd expected Johnny to leave so he could have a few hours alone with Merl. He needed to talk to her, reassure himself about her honesty.

"Uh, Johnny, you can go on home now. I'll wait here with Merlene for—"

"I appreciate that, Cody, but Cora is at some crazy yoga class tonight." Johnny relaxed in the brown leather recliner and raised the remote. "So I got nothing better to do than enjoy this movie with you two."

He adjusted the volume as soaring music sounded and the opening credits began. "But you don't have to stay if you got things to do. Merlene and I get along just fine." He winked at Merlene. "I let her beat me at cards."

She laughed. "Yeah, right, Johnny." Catching Cody's eye again, she shrugged.

Cursing the old-timer's apparent intention to hang around, Cody loosened his tie and sat back. Merlene grinned at him, seeming to know exactly what he was thinking. He shook his head. No way to get rid of her guard.

Maybe it was for the best. Being alone with Merl would prove a difficult temptation, seeing as how he wanted nothing more than to kiss her into eager arousal, peel away her clothing and feel the way she came unglued when he made love to her. He shifted, vividly remembering the night in the cabin.

Her uninhibited enjoyment of their lovemaking had resonated deep inside him, her passion pulling him with her to a place that he'd long wanted to visit, a place where love could easily grow and flourish.

What the hell was wrong with him, thinking about making love to her? Merlene was a suspect, a woman full of puzzles—like how she didn't behave like an experienced woman who'd been married for years. She acted more like someone new to lovemaking. Could it all be an act? What could she hope to gain?

His cooperation, he realized, if she were involved in murder. Suspicion made him unsure how to act around her. He hated that.

And now she was sitting too damn close. Close enough that he smelled the citrus scent of her shampoo, felt the slight movement of her chest with the rise and fall of each breath. He wanted to touch her more than he wanted to breathe. Knowing that she wanted him just as much didn't make his desire any easier to control.

Or was that all an act, too?

He tried to watch the movie but instead watched Merlene twirl a lock of hair around her finger. He imagined the hair against his palm, soft, silky, smooth. She caught him staring and dropped her hand. Smiling, she laced her fingers into his and squeezed.

He returned his attention to the television screen. He couldn't just sit here and gawk at her, but damn if he didn't want to. With regret, he disengaged their hands.

How vulnerable was he to Merlene? He needed to watch himself. He was a seasoned detective. He knew how to handle himself around suspects.

The initial findings from the crime lab indicated the video had not been altered, but even after Cody reported he'd found nothing in Merlene's home, Montoya refused to dismiss the possibility that she might be dirty, that the whole recording might be a setup.

Cody wondered if his decision to trust Merlene would come back and kick him in the ass. Of course, that would only happen if she turned out to be guilty.

He glanced at her again, wishing he could banish the questions that played with his head.

His partner hadn't yet found anyone to vouch for Pat Johnson's whereabouts the night of the murder. Plus, Merlene's client had already filed a claim for the life insurance policy on her husband. Still, so far the investigation hadn't turned up any concrete evidence linking either Pat or Merl to any murders. God knew he wanted to trust her, but—

Johnny flipped up the recliner and paused the DVD with one fluid motion. "Bathroom break," he said, disappearing into the hall.

"I wish I'd never rented that movie," Cody muttered when the door to the bath latched.

Her dimples deepened in two smooth cheeks. "He would have stayed anyway. I think your lieutenant told him to." She kissed him quickly, lightly, on his mouth. "I guess I'm a bad influence."

He stopped her before she could move away, holding her mouth close to his with a hand on the back of her neck. With his other hand, he tucked a lock of hair behind her ear. His eyes searched hers. If he only understood what lay hidden in those mysterious gray shadows.

She stretched her graceful neck and closed her eyes. "Don't," she whispered. "It only makes it worse."

His gaze traveled a sensuous line from her beckoning lips and got lost in the opening of her blouse. Her chest rose and fell agonizingly close to his, the creamy skin flushed pink. As he hardened, he fought the need to crush her to him and never let go.

He tensed when the toilet flushed.

The tip of her tongue flicked moisture quickly across her lips.

Cody stood and moved into the kitchen to scoop chocolate-chip ice cream and hide behind the counter until he got himself under control.

He was about to cross a line here. The distrust was tearing him apart, the doubt constantly creeping into his thoughts, wondering if Merl was being honest with him. He couldn't stay away from her, even though he knew he should.

While she remained in the safe house, he'd keep their relationship on a strictly professional level. She'd notice the difference, of course, and call him on it. He jammed the spoon deep into the soft ice cream. That was Merlene. She wouldn't back down.

It'd help if he'd quit coming in to see her at night. He'd just wait out in his car while he kept watch. She need never know. He'd fill her in on the latest case developments during the afternoon. Even better, maybe he'd phone in any reports to her, force himself to stay away from her completely.

She'd be pissed, but it was for the best. He met her questioning gaze and tried to smile. In his heart he still didn't believe she was dirty, but Montoya was convinced, and he had to respect that. God, but he hoped the man was wrong.

ON THE FOURTH DAY of her "exile," as Merlene called her stay in the safe house, Cody made an unscheduled afternoon visit to fill her in on the latest developments in the case. He told himself he owed her that, but the truth was he wanted to see her.

He pulled two dining room chairs out onto the screened porch to watch a Florida thunderstorm move south. He and Merl remained dry, but the air around them hung heavy with humidity.

She turned to him expectantly, flashing her most winning smile. "Have they arrested Neville yet?"

"Sorry, not yet."

The smile faded. "Do you even know where he is?"

"He's in Duval County. The sheriff's department almost grabbed him outside of Jacksonville, but he slipped away again."

"This guy must be smarter than you think."

"He's been lucky, but his luck is about to run out. The sheriff has lured him into a trap he can't possibly evade, and we'll have some much-needed answers soon."

They'd already received some answers that didn't help Merlene's case. Like phone records that revealed she'd received no calls from out of state—either cell or landline—for a week before the murder.

Did she know that her client hadn't called her from North Carolina? Did she know where Pat Johnson had been located when the calls were made? He wished he could just ask her, but that would reveal too much about the course of the investigation. Montoya wanted her in the dark as much as possible so she wouldn't rabbit.

"I can't believe Neville got away again." Merlene nibbled

at her bottom lip. "And you wonder why I don't brag much on cops. You're the only one I've ever known that's..." She trailed off, and he heard the blare of the TV from the living room over the sheeting rain.

"That's what?"

"O-kay," she said slowly, emphasizing each syllable.

"Okay?" He narrowed his eyes at her. "So you think I'm okay?"

She smiled, letting her gaze wander up and down his body. "That's the best I can do as long as I'm in prison."

He caught his breath at her meaningful stare and the seductive timbre to her voice, and couldn't help but wonder if Merlene was playing him for a fool, stringing him along to gain access to any developments in the case. How convenient to know someone on the inside of an active police investigation.

"Actually that's not true," she said, her tone again teasing.

"What's not true?" he asked, unable to resist her bait.

"My guards are pretty nice guys, even if they can't play cards worth a damn."

"Nice guys? Hey, what's this? A softening of your attitude towards us nasty coppers?"

She tried to hide a smile, but dimples deepened in her cheeks. "Maybe. It'd help if they played poker."

"Better watch out, Merl. Next thing I know you'll be contributing to the Police Athletic League."

He'd intended to remain professional but found himself slipping back into an affectionate flirtation with her. He loved to watch her smile when they teased each other. It was hard to imagine never kidding around with her again.

But when it came down to it, she didn't trust him; he didn't trust her, so they danced around each other. What a great pair.

"PAL?" She rolled her eyes. "Not likely."

No, he thought, not likely. Montoya's warning clanged in Cody's ear. He thought about the recently increased life insurance policy.

"You're different today," she said. "What's wrong?"

He shrugged. "I guess I'm tired."

"Have you been having nightmares?" she asked, her voice gentle.

He shot her a glance, surprised at the question. He should have just phoned her to tell her about Neville Feldman. Why couldn't he stay away?

"No nightmares," he reported.

After a moment she said, "I talked to your sister again this morning. She's great."

"You can trust my sister." There was that word again. He shifted in his seat. *Trust.* His trust in Merlene was tested daily. So far all Montoya had were suspicions that could just be the result of unfortunate coincidence. It was possible Merlene had only made some bad decisions. Anyway, that's what he wanted to believe.

"Talking to her helps break up long, boring days. I can't wait to meet her." A devilish grin crossed Merlene's face. "And she definitely has a lot to say about you, Cody Wyoming."

He suppressed a groan. "No doubt."

"She thinks you work too hard."

"I know."

Her face grew serious. "You love being a cop, don't you?"

"Most of the time. This week…I don't know." He smiled at her, wishing he could banish his doubts.

She met his gaze with a cool, gray stare. "Johnny told me how you've been paying back the businesses your father took protection money from. Annie doesn't know about that, does she?"

Cody froze. Damn. Newcomb and his dad had been tight,

but Cody had no idea Johnny was privy to that information. Gossip spread through his precinct like the storm surge before a hurricane.

"No, she doesn't know."

Merlene nodded. "Annie thinks you have a bunch of money stashed in the bank or mutual funds because you never spend a dime."

"Well, she's wrong. I never have more than a couple hundred bucks in the bank."

"Going without food taught me the importance of savings." She shrugged. "But why keep the payback a secret?"

Stung at the reminder of her miserable childhood, he captured her hand and squeezed. She gazed at him steadily, waiting for an answer.

"I kept it a secret because I didn't want my sister to feel like she had to contribute. Returning the money is something I felt I had to do."

A flicker of something—he wasn't sure what—swept across her face. Maybe approval or respect. Maybe disbelief. A horrific clap of thunder sounded almost directly overhead, and she flinched.

"You're jumpy," he said, reaching a hand toward her shoulder to steady her. But he dropped his arm to his thigh, her warmth still lingering on his fingers. Best to maintain distance between them, keep his head straight.

"Sorry." She sighed. "Look, I can't stay here forever. It's been four days, and D.J. needs my help. With all this rain my lawn is going to grow like crazy. Plus, I've already missed one class. What if you never find Neville?"

"We'll find him. Sometimes a case takes time," he said, glad to change the subject. He didn't want to discuss personal issues with Merlene, not with this cloud of doubt hanging between them. In fact, he needed to find an excuse to go. He'd plead some kind of police business.

Warning signs or not, he refused to believe Merl could kill for cash. She didn't have that kind of violence in her. She might be stubborn, but not mean. And never cruel.

"Didn't you ever have a case that was hard to crack?" he asked.

"You bet," she said. "My husband's."

He shot her a probing glance, forgetting any idea of leaving. He'd been wondering when she'd get around to telling him about her ex.

"But you finally solved it?"

"Yeah," she said softly, looking out at the rain, "I finally did."

When she didn't continue, he asked, "How did you wind up married to a doctor in Miami, Florida, from working as a waitress in Missouri?"

She gripped her hands tightly in her lap. "About a year after my brother's death, Peter showed up at a medical convention in Branson. I'd lied about my age so I could work as a cocktail waitress. For a week he came to my bar every night trying to get me to sleep with him. I refused, told him I was saving myself for my husband." Her gaze darted to Cody, then away. "Which was true."

"So he married you?" Cody tried to hide his shock but knew he failed. Why would Merlene marry some guy she'd known a week? With a sinking feeling, he guessed the answer. She was actually going to admit what he'd suspected all along.

"Well, he was a little drunk one night and…yeah, we got married."

"But you didn't love him." Cody knew his words sounded like an accusation but couldn't help himself.

Merlene shook her head slightly, as if trying to decide. "I don't know. I don't think I knew what love was."

"Then why did you marry him?"

"Because I was miserable." She looked directly at him then, her face flushed a pale pink. "He promised me the sun, the moon and a red Lexus."

Merlene saw revulsion cross Cody's face and turned to the rainstorm again. A torrent of water rushed from an aluminum gutter into the backyard, creating a small gully that flowed toward the wooden fence. She wished the hurt, the painful memories, could be washed away as cleanly and thoroughly.

"I was nineteen, barely able to pay the rent in my tiny apartment. I had no family." She shrugged. "I don't know. I guess I figured if I married Peter I'd have security, I'd be safe. We should have known better, but...well, it just happened. He tried to turn me into a proper lady, but I never quite came up to his standards." She shrugged. "At least I got my GED thanks to him."

She eventually figured out that Peter married her because he had some sort of a white-knight complex and had wanted to save her. But once she found self-confidence, he completely lost interest.

Plus, her ex had never been as ready and—she swallowed—well, able to make love as Cody, even with all the special pills he popped. This, of course, explained Peter's mystifying satisfaction when she proved he'd cheated on her. He probably thought the infidelity glorified his manhood, for heaven's sake. No wonder her marriage had been such a disaster. She hoped Peter found pleasure with his new wife.

Cody still didn't speak, and his silence worried her. The rain had eased to a sprinkle, and she sensed he'd leave soon. But not like this. What could she say to cut the tension?

"I was a good wife to him, Cody. Really, I was. I just couldn't please him."

"I'm sure you were." His voice was flat, free of any emotion. "Just like you're a good private eye and always know where your client is."

"What are you talking about?"

"Did you know Pat Johnson wasn't in North Carolina when she called you the day before the murder?"

The suspicion in his voice hit her like a bucket of ice water.

"Of course she—" Merlene paused. How would Cody know where Pat was? Unless… "You checked my phone records?"

When Cody remained silent, she asked, "What's going on?"

He stood. "I've got to get back, Merlene." Without another word, he slipped into the drizzle and disappeared.

She sat for a long time and stared after him, the emptiness in her chest growing until she thought she'd disappear inside the hole.

She'd told him the truth. She shouldn't have, of course, but he'd started this big thing about trust. She'd trusted him with the truth, and he couldn't handle it.

AROUND MIDNIGHT MERLENE placed her ear against her bedroom door and listened for activity in the front room. Nothing but soft sounds from the television; last night her guard had fallen asleep around eleven with the TV still on.

Time to get the hell out of here. D.J. needed her. She thought back for the hundredth time to their conversation when she'd finally reached him late this afternoon.

He'd answered on about the twentieth ring. His voice had been tired and thin as he'd said, "Hello."

She'd immediately asked, "What's wrong?"

"Now, I don't want you to worry, Merl."

"Please stop treating me like a child, D.J. Did something happen during the surveillance?"

"I wasn't on your surveillance." He gulped for air, then continued. "I was at Dr. Fortner's."

Dread mushroomed in Merlene's stomach as D.J. got through a horrible cough.

"What did the doctor say?" she asked.

"That I need to rest and start some new expensive treatment."

She closed her eyes. She couldn't lose D.J. He was the best man she'd ever known, her lifeline, her only tether to sanity. "Promise me you'll do exactly what the doctor tells you."

"I guess I don't have much choice. Although I don't know where I'm going to get the money for the co-pay."

"We'll figure something out."

"But he doesn't want me to work," D.J. had said after another gasp for air. "I can't go out in the field for at least two weeks."

So she had no choice. She had to get out of this jail and go back to work to cover their open cases. Thanks to Cody, the agency was already in trouble with the state licensing authority. D.J. sure didn't need another complaint right now, not when he should be starting a new treatment.

How much could a co-pay be? She'd offer to help, but in the past D.J. had refused to take any money from her.

She hadn't wanted to come to this damn safe house anyway. They had no right to keep her here.

Or was she leaving because of her conversation with Cody this afternoon? For the past three days he'd stopped coming at night. In fact, he called her more than he visited. Yeah, his abandonment stung, but that wasn't the reason. D.J. needed her.

Johnny Newcomb didn't even try to hide his disappointment at Cody's absence. Last night, he'd expected Cody to show up with a Western video and chocolate-chip ice cream. Grumbling about *Red River* and how he'd been looking forward to John Wayne, Johnny had left when his replacement arrived, glaring at Merlene as if she'd deliberately kept Cody away.

Did Johnny know what was going on, why Cody had checked her phone records? No question that meant she was now a suspect. But why? What had happened to throw doubt her way? Possibly her delay in turning over the surveillance video. She'd wondered if she'd skate on that point.

Right. So just as she had suspected all along, this safe house was actually a prison.

Where else in her life had the cops poked their intrusive noses? Had they interviewed her neighbors? Pulled her credit card bills? Probably. Damn them all.

But nothing made sense. Pat *had* been in North Carolina. Merlene had dialed the number herself. Pausing her tumbling thoughts, she remembered she hadn't reached Pat until late in the afternoon of the day following the murder. She'd tried all the numbers multiple times. Which had ultimately made the connection?

Merlene thought hard until certain she'd finally talked to Pat on her landline in North Carolina. She'd never answered the cell number, but that in itself didn't mean anything. Hell, the battery could have died.

If Pat hadn't been at her summer home the day of the murder, where had she been? And why would she lie? Merlene shook her head. She couldn't solve anything while stuck in police custody, so she needed to get the hell out of here.

She moved to the rear window to check her pathway to freedom one more time. All clear.

What made her think Cody would understand about her marriage? He'd obviously been disgusted by that sad tale. She'd let down her guard, revealed too much. The man was so straight he repaid debts he didn't even owe. How could he ever sympathize with her desperation all those years ago? It was impossible.

He was a disciplined officer of the law, from his polished shoes to that ever-present tie, not a man who could forgive her mistakes. What was worse, because of his father's crimes, he hated any sort of greed.

She rested her forehead against the cool windowpane. She hadn't meant to be greedy when she married Peter. All she'd wanted was to be safe from a world that had never been kind to her, never given her even the tiniest break.

Merlene straightened her back. Now she knew that no one was ever truly safe. And a girl had to make her own breaks.

Besides, she'd been nuts to fall for a cop; he had one of the world's most dangerous professions. She'd find no security at all with a man involved in police work.

She returned to the door and listened hard again. Still no activity. It was now or never.

She grabbed her purse and stuck Donny's photo inside, imagining the drama if she waited until tomorrow morning. Cody or maybe some other detective would apply pressure, try to talk her out of leaving. They wanted her locked up and out of their way, and she might cave.

That wasn't going to happen. She was through letting the police tell her what to do. She'd been following Cody's orders for days. Yeah, she'd call him later to let him know she was safe, but now she had to help D.J., the man who had taught her how to make a living at a low point in her life. D.J. was family, something Cody would never be.

And she wasn't afraid of Neville Feldman, either. The scumbag's last known location was 300 miles away, headed north. Why would he come back to Miami? Ridiculous. The cops had another reason for keeping her here, and she knew what it was. They didn't have any evidence to formally arrest her—and, of course, never would since she was innocent—but in the safe house they could keep tabs on her. Oh, and she'd made it so easy for them.

Not anymore.

Holding her breath, she turned the knob slowly, silently pulled the door toward her, then slipped through the opening into the hall. Her escape route was through the kitchen and out a side door, which shouldn't rouse her sleeping guard. Fortunately safe houses were designed to keep bad guys out, not the victims in.

She crept down the hallway, cringing with each careful footfall. She caught a glimpse of the guard on the couch, head slumped to one side, chest rising and falling evenly.

In the kitchen, she turned the dead bolt with a quiet click, opened the back door and stepped into a dark and humid night full of chirping crickets. Freedom.

She hurried through damp grass that moistened the bottom of her jeans, intending to phone a cab at the first major intersection. She'd spend the night at D.J.'s and talk him into accepting her help to pay for the new treatment. She couldn't lose D.J. He was all she had left.

What looked like an unmarked cop car sat at the far end of the block, but she hugged the edge of the property, remaining out of sight. She told herself she wasn't doing anything wrong, that she wasn't under arrest. Cody had told her she could leave. Yeah, he would be pissed, but what did that matter? He was done with her. He'd made that pretty clear.

And when had playing by the rules ever done her any good anyway?

Cody drummed his fingers on the desk, glaring at his cell phone, willing the damn thing to ring. Across from him, sitting at his own desk, his partner pretended to be working on overdue paperwork. Jake's cell phone also lay close at hand, right beside the computer keyboard.

They were waiting to hear from Duval County, to receive word that Neville Feldman had been apprehended. The call could come to his cell, Jake's, the department's line… Who knew which?

The desk phone rang, and Jake snatched up the receiver. "Steadman." He paused. "Oh, hi."

Catching Cody's gaze, Jake shook his head. Cody relaxed. Not Duval.

"Slow down, Annie," Jake said. "Okay, okay. He's right here."

Acting as if the phone burned his fingers, Jake punched the hold button and set the receiver back on the cradle.

"Better pick up," he said. "It's your sister, and she's got a mad on."

Cody held the receiver to his ear. "Annie, I can't talk right now. We're—"

"What exactly did you say to Merlene? And when did you become so judgmental?"

Wincing at his sister's furious voice, Cody leaned back, the squad room chair squeaking as if also displeased with his behavior. He knew he shouldn't have taken Annie's call. His partner couldn't get rid of the phone fast enough.

"Annie, I don't even know where the hell Merlene is. She left the safe house." No way could he tell Annie the department suspected Merlene was involved in murder. What would his sister say to *that* stunning news?

"I know where she is," Annie said. "She's out doing her job today."

"How do you know that?"

"She called me. And she told me she left you a message."

Cody didn't answer. True, Merl had left him a cryptic voice mail about some surveillance job and telling him not to worry. As if he wouldn't worry.

"She's hurt that you deserted her."

He sighed. "I haven't deserted her. I saw her yesterday afternoon." But he had left rather abruptly.

He looked up when the second line buzzed. "I've got to go. We're waiting to find out if Duval County's got Feldman in custody."

Jake had already grabbed the phone. Within a few moments he grinned and gave Cody the thumbs-up. "They've got him!" Jake yelled.

Cody loosened his tie and relaxed into his seat to allow the welcome news to sink in. Man, he would have loved to snap cuffs around Feldman's dirty wrists, but no biggie. As long as this perp was behind bars, it didn't matter who did the honors. He took a deep breath of satisfaction, looking forward to the interrogation. Half the job was done.

He could quit worrying about Feldman finding Merlene.

His sense of well-being evaporated. With the danger over, what would happen to the delicate thread between them? Would she lose all interest in a cop who gave away half his salary?

And damn her for leaving the safe house. Why did she do it? Did she really think he'd deserted her?

Maybe. He had to admit, just maybe.

He swiveled in his chair to watch Jake deliver the good news to their boss.

Annie was right. He'd acted like an overbearing jackass. Life had knocked Merlene on her pretty little rear over and over and then kicked her when she tried to get up. Damn, she'd been a kid, searching for the only way out of a miserable existence when she got married. She'd grown up since then.

Right, she wasn't a kid anymore. He closed his eyes and rubbed them, feeling grit from lack of sleep. Did the fact that she'd withheld the video and fled the safe house mean something ominous? If Merl could marry for money, did that mean that she would kill for it?

No way. He rejected doubts that had played with his mind for days. No matter how bad circumstances looked, Merlene was no murderess. If she'd called Annie, maybe she'd still speak to him. He had to talk to her, figure out what was going on, find a way to clear her.

Montoya pointed a fat, unlit cigar at Cody. "Find Mrs. Saunders, Warren. She's your responsibility."

MERLENE UNLOCKED HER front door and entered a house that stank of hot, stale air. She checked her home quickly, looking for signs of disturbance, but nothing appeared out of place. Not even a sign that Cody had been here, other than the missing photo of Donny. She took the frame out of her purse and placed it back where it belonged.

So maybe Cody hadn't searched her home.

The phone rang, but she ignored it. She cranked up the air-conditioning and moved into the bathroom for a shower, needing to rinse away a miserable day of tedious surveillance. For once she'd succeeded at something.

She'd followed her subject—a young man who claimed he was unable to work because of excruciating pain in his lower back—from his residence to a dusty construction site. She'd watched him strap on a belt loaded with heavy tools, tote materials up and down a scaffold and move bricks from one side of the lot to the other.

And she'd managed to record all the damaging details for her client.

Didn't anyone tell the truth anymore?

With the phone ringing again, she stripped off her sweaty clothes, knowing her client would be pleased. She'd saved this insurance company a ton of money, so maybe she and D.J. could get more work from the adjuster. This was exactly the type of work Pat had promised to secure for her. Funny how that idea no longer excited her.

The Johnson case had put surveillance work into a whole new light, one she didn't much like. Catching a cheating husband no longer seemed too thrilling, either.

Merlene stepped into the shower and closed her eyes, allowing the cool water to glide over her skin. Thankfully D.J. felt better. Looked better, too, because he'd spent the day resting instead of baking in the hot sun.

Her thoughts flickered to Cody. Damn. She'd spent twenty-four hours trying not to think about him—without a lot of success. His image inevitably pushed its way into her mind, which either pissed her off or caused the ache in her chest to expand until she couldn't breathe.

What in the world made her think that Detective Cody Warren could accept her past? She was all alone in the world and always would be.

She wondered whether he, Johnny, or one of the other guards would get into trouble because she'd escaped. She hoped not, but she'd done what she had to do. Cody would just have to understand that. Would he? No, most likely he'd view her late-night departure as more proof that she was a murderer. But she hadn't fled to Mexico, for goodness' sake. She'd gone back to work.

And after what they'd shared, how could he think her capable of murder?

Merlene saw Peter's ring flash in the mirror as she combed her wet hair. Lowering her arm, she stared at the diamond for a long moment, then slid it off her finger and tossed it in a jewelry box.

She quickly dressed and hurried into the kitchen in search of something to eat. One look inside her refrigerator told her she needed to order a pizza. She hadn't intended to be gone so long, and all the produce had rotted.

She pulled the garbage can closer to the fridge and tossed out lettuce, smelly onions, soggy zucchini. Her hand stilled when she found a plastic bag of pole beans purchased a few days before the trip to Ocala. Memories of the amazing night with Cody in the cabin came rushing back, followed by a wrenching sense of loss.

For that one night it had seemed as if someone cared about what happened to her. What an intoxicating, empowering feeling that had been, one she'd never forget and likely never experience again.

With the mushy bag of beans swinging in her hand and the cool air of the refrigerator billowing around her, she straightened her back and squeezed her eyes to banish the image of Cody's powerful, naked body moving over hers. She knew she'd never forget the way his flesh felt against hers.

"Damn you, Cody Warren," she whispered, and tossed the beans into the garbage along with the other rotten produce.

She didn't want to love him. She fought against her rising feelings. Fought damn hard. But Cody had been so sweet, so protective, so—Cody—that she'd forgotten all the hard-learned lessons from the past. She'd thought maybe it could work out between them.

So now she had to pay the consequences, go through the pain of recovering from more loss.

Her phone jangled again, and Merlene glared at the receiver. Stupid thing wouldn't shut up. She didn't want to talk to anybody. Her answering machine was full. The caller ID had quit working—probably a dead battery because of the amazing volume of calls since the story of her video broke— so she couldn't tell whether or not Cody had phoned. Her pulse jerked into fast-forward every time she thought of him trying to reach her.

She knew, damn him, he'd say his goodbyes in person.

Good old honorable Cody. He'd eventually tell her to her face that she was just a bit too trashy for him.

The phone continued to ring, and she considered yanking every extension out of the wall. Instead, she grabbed the receiver. Anything to stop the noise. "Hello."

"Merlene Saunders?" a surprised female voice blurted.

Merlene didn't answer.

"This is Vanessa Cooper from Channel Eight. I've left several messages."

"Sorry," Merlene said. She definitely did not want to talk to Vanessa Cooper.

"I'd really like to—"

"I don't have anything—"

"Don't hang up," Vanessa shouted. "We can make it worth your while."

Merlene halted the hang-up midair. She returned the receiver to her ear. "What do you mean?"

"I mean I'll pay you. I know your time is valuable. How much do you usually charge per hour?"

Suspecting that the interview had already begun, Merlene asked, "How much are you offering?"

"Oh, say, triple your usual weekly rate for one hour of time. If that's not enough, we can negotiate. I can sell the spot to a nationally syndicated show."

Doing the math quickly, Merlene sat on her couch. The total impressed her. Maybe with this windfall D.J. wouldn't refuse her offer to pay for the new medication his doctor had prescribed. Cody already thought the worst of her, and having more of a cushion against being a pathetic bag lady presented an inviting picture. She could take a few more classes each semester, she could…

"I won't jeopardize the prosecution," she said.

"Oh, no. Of course not," Vanessa said. "During the interview, I'll just ask you about what you saw. Too bad you don't have the recording. That would really be worth some money."

Merlene allowed a pause to stretch out.

"Ms. Saunders?" Vanessa said. "Are you still there?"

"How much money?" Merlene asked.

Vanessa's response sounded eager. "You have a copy?"

"How much?" Merlene repeated.

"Enough so that you never have to worry about money again."

"Let me think about it," Merlene said, and hung up the phone.

CHAPTER THIRTEEN

CODY PULLED INTO Merlene's gravel driveway and killed the ignition, unsure if he was relieved to see lights on inside or not. After a moment, he saw movement behind her curtains. Yeah, she was home. She was alive. She was okay.

Good. He had one hell of a lot to say to her.

But he waited, drumming his fingers on the steering wheel.

Her phone message had revealed no regret about leaving the safe house. In Merl's mind, the fact that D.J. needed her had left her no choice.

Unfortunately, escaping in the middle of the night made her look even more guilty in his lieutenant's eyes, even if he had nothing on her yet. Red with rage and suspicion, Montoya had held Cody responsible. He was frustrated with this whole damn case—like everyone else on the squad—but they had obtained no hard evidence that she had been complicit in the murder. Absolutely none.

Sure, yeah, maybe some of Merlene's behavior looked a little squirrely—especially withholding the video—but he understood her loyalty to D.J. Or thought he did. Cody tamped down a quick spurt of anger. Why couldn't she have waited until morning?

Had trusting her put his badge in jeopardy? Did he trust her? Yes. Yes, damn it, he did.

Merl might have faults—and didn't everyone?—but she was no murderer. As soon as he interviewed Neville Feldman, they'd learn the truth and find proof of her innocence. Her client? Maybe. His instincts told him Pat Johnson was a little bent, but that didn't mean Merlene had participated in or even known about a murder.

Rubbing his eyes with his thumb and index finger, he thought longingly of an hour's sleep. He'd been running on coffee and adrenaline for days. He'd tried to reach out to Merl hours ago…but Montoya wanted written reports, the prosecutor screamed for evidence and his partner needed help tracing Pat Johnson's movements.

One thing was for sure: the woman sure as hell wasn't behaving like a grieving widow.

Cody relaxed against the seat, mentally preparing himself for the battle to come. Merlene had had over twenty-four hours to work up a good mad. No question she'd let him know her exact opinion of the way he'd thrown Montoya's suspicions in her face and disappeared into the rain.

Well, guess what? She had a disappearing act of her own to account for, and he had plenty to say about that.

He exited the car, slamming the door behind him.

THE DOORBELL INTERRUPTED Merlene's final wipe down of her refrigerator. Bleach always did her soul good when she needed a fresh start. If only it were as easy to scrub a certain detective from her thoughts.

A peek through her window revealed Cody standing on her front porch. She stepped back. Had he come to apologize or kiss her off?

She swallowed. Or arrest her.

She flung open the door with one arm and propped the other on the wall to bar his entrance. "Detective Warren," she said, as coolly as she could manage.

"Can I come in, Merlene?"

She stared into his face for a long moment trying to assess his mood. His lips were tight but his eyes gave nothing away. Finally, she stepped away and motioned him inside.

Peeling off plastic gloves with two sharp snaps, she moved ahead of him into the living room. No handcuffs. So far so good. What did he want?

"What the hell were you thinking leaving the safe house like that?" he demanded.

She whirled. *So it's like that, is it?*

"I was thinking D.J. needed me. I told you that."

"You left a *message*." He emphasized the word "message," as if it were dog droppings.

"Best I could do," she muttered. *And you're lucky I did that.*

"The department committed resources to protect you, and you run off in the middle of the night?"

"You had no right to keep me prisoner."

He took a step toward her. "You weren't a prisoner. It was for your protection and you know it."

She glared up at him. "Really?"

He advanced another step. "Yeah, really."

"I don't think so," she said, refusing to back down. "Not with Feldman located somewhere around the Georgia-Florida line."

"What if he had an accomplice? What if he returned to Miami?"

"So you keep saying. Did he?"

"No, but—"

"D.J. is sick, Cody. Thanks to you, the agency is in trouble. I had to help out, cover our open jobs. I wasn't exactly having a good time on a loud, smelly construction site for eight hours."

His gaze drilled into hers. "You should have discussed it with me."

"Maybe I didn't want to have this conversation." She

threw out her arms. "Or maybe I didn't notice you anywhere in the vicinity for me to talk to."

Cody ran a hand through his hair but didn't reply.

She raised her chin. Good. Maybe she'd gotten the last word for a change.

She watched him take a deep breath, struggle to control his temper. What would he say now? He lowered his gaze to her hands.

"What are the gloves for?"

"What?" His calm, husky voice stilled her mushrooming anger. "Oh. I was cleaning." She tossed the gloves onto a table. She'd forgotten she was even holding them. "Cleaning house is good for the soul, especially when throwing out useless items."

"Do you want to throw *me* out, Merl?" The tender way he spoke the nickname warmed a spot she'd thought frozen over.

This thing with Cody was crazy. Up—and then down. She ought to tell him to leave, remember he didn't trust her, that she never wanted to speak to him again except to tell him off in her best temper. Why couldn't she?

He'd put as much hidden meaning into his words as she had in hers and obviously wanted an answer. Did she want to throw him out? She picked at a seam in her faded denim shorts, not knowing what to say.

Cody grabbed her hand and rubbed his thumb along the back of her index finger. She wondered what he was thinking, what he wanted to say, not sure she wanted to know.

"You have beautiful hands."

Startled, she jerked back, but he held on and raised her fingers to his lips. His breath, warm and soft, rocketed gooseflesh down her arms and legs. She let him nuzzle her palm against the stubble on his face.

"I went nuts when I learned you'd left the safe house," he said softly. "I was crazy with worry about you."

A prickle of guilt made her look away. She hadn't wanted him to fret. Or maybe she had. She sighed and murmured, "I'm sorry if I worried you."

His lips curved into a crooked smile. He reached for her hand again and guided her onto the sofa beside him. After a moment he said, "Are you glad to be home?"

"You know I am." Focused on Cody's thumb rubbing her skin in a languorous circle, she answered without thinking.

"I've missed you. I think Johnny misses you, too," Cody said. "That old dinosaur just loves to play cards."

"Quit trying to make me smile."

"But I love making you smile."

She couldn't turn away from the intensity in his gaze. Butterflies...thousands of migrating monarchs...fluttered to life in her stomach. How did Cody do this to her? Pathetic the way he made her forget her pride, forget everything he'd done and said.

She freed her hand and folded her arms across her chest, searching for something to say. "Annie's worried about you. She says you haven't been home in days."

"True. I've been spending nights in my car in front of the safe house."

"What?" Merlene searched his face, for the first time noticing the creases around his eyes seemed deeper. "You spent nights in front of my safe house?" Had that been him in the car at the end of the street?

He nodded.

"But why?"

"I wanted to make sure Neville didn't get to you, Merl." Soft and seductive, his voice floated over her like silken wings. "That was the only way I could be sure."

"You never said anything."

"I thought it would worry you, that you wouldn't trust the safe house if you knew. You were fine without me. I just couldn't help myself."

"I see." She sucked air deep into her lungs, hoping to steady the quaver in her voice. "Detective Warren needed to protect his star witness."

"Merlene. Please."

The hurt in his voice made her regret the sarcastic words. He pulled her toward him, and she didn't resist, surprised by how much she welcomed his touch.

"You can't believe that was the reason," he said.

She turned her head into his chest and closed her eyes as he gathered her close. He felt strong, solid, warm. "I don't know what to believe."

Being close to Cody made everything all right again. Somehow nothing mattered. Not as long as Cody stroked her back and rubbed his cheek against the top of her head.

"Believe in me, Merl."

She shut her eyes tightly against his words. How could she believe in him?

"You don't believe in me, Cody." She whispered the words, barely able to get them past a tight throat. "I know I've made mistakes, but…"

Cody stopped her with his lips, kissing her hard, deeply, possessively, his fingers buried in her hair.

When he pulled back, she was dizzy, unsure where the lines between them lay.

"I'm sorry," he said. "I acted like a jerk, and I was wrong."

He kissed her again, and she responded with a hunger that frightened her. No one had ever apologized to her before, or at least not about anything that really mattered… Not for hurting her feelings.

That he'd slept in his car outside the safe house touched something deep inside her. His concern stirred to life the long-buried terror of a lonely child, intense longings for someone, anyone, to care what happened to her. With a rush of joy she knew that someone finally did. She released the buttons on his shirt, dimly aware that Cody's fingers plucked at the front of her blouse. She slid her hands across his bare chest, relishing the feel of taut muscles beneath her fingers. No matter how hard she'd tried not to, God help her, she had fallen in love with this man.

His hand encircled her breast, caressing, teasing her nipple. She arched into his touch and was lost when his mouth fastened on her other breast. She groaned his name, not recognizing her own voice.

Ripples of pure pleasure moved with warm breath as he kissed across her neck, nibbling at the edge of her mouth.

"Listen to me, Merl." His voice was raw, edged with an emotion she couldn't define.

She opened her eyes when he cupped her cheeks with his hands. His bright blue gaze burned into hers.

"I don't care about your past. I want you just the way you are right now. We'll move on from here."

Just the way I am? Dazed, she wondered if he meant it, but he sounded as serious as she'd ever heard anyone.

His thumbs moved tenderly across her cheeks. "You're beautiful and smart and sexy. So what if you don't like to be broke?" He attempted a smile, but she felt his tension, his uncertainty.

She ran her fingers across his pecs to his flat abdomen, watching his flesh quiver under her slow, light touch. She halted her movement at his waist. "No one likes to be broke, Cody."

"I never used to mind a lack of cash." Cody inhaled deeply, and his belly moved beneath her fingers. "Now I think I do."

Merlene smoothed her hands up his broad forearms, intoxicated by the hardness of his body. "Why?"

"Because you care a great deal about money. How will I be able to make you happy?"

Merlene looked into his worried, questioning face. A glow of happiness spread from her center, dissolving the despair that had eaten at her since yesterday afternoon.

"It's not money I care about. It's knowing I won't starve."

He stared at her, not answering.

"And I don't think I'd need a lot of money if I had you," she whispered.

His mouth quirked. "You don't think?"

She grinned, loving the way his hands tightened in her hair. "I'll prove it to you when you make love to me again."

CODY GAVE UP RATIONAL discussion when she beamed the full force of her dimpled smile into his face. He felt as if he'd been zapped by a stun gun. "Whatever you say, ma'am."

Oh, he'd be glad to let Merlene prove her point. He'd been wanting to make love to her from the moment she opened the door.

He gathered her against him, closing his eyes. He hadn't lost her. They still had a chance.

She worked feverishly at his buckle, then helped him shed his clothing. Never had a woman been more responsive to his touch, more eager to have him inside her.

"Don't be in such a hurry, Merl," he growled, planting light kisses across her chin. "It's better if we take it slow."

"Is it?" She arched her neck dreamily, her words sounding forced and far away. "I don't see how it could get any better."

He raised his head and watched, fascinated by the pleasure transforming her face. Wanting to remind her how much better it could get, he slid his hand to the warm, moist spot between her legs. She arched and moved against him, breathing his name.

Hearing his name with sweet pleading propelled him over the edge. He kissed her hard, her surrender exciting him beyond any control. Maybe they'd take it slow next time. He'd do anything to win her love, anything to… He groaned when she slid her hand searchingly toward his groin, seeking and finding what she wanted.

Now he couldn't wait, either.

He sheathed and entered her, watching her face dissolve into wonder and passion equal to his own. She gripped his shoulders, her nails digging into his skin. As their rhythm increased, she hoarsely encouraged him not to stop…then pulsed wildly around him as he emptied himself into her.

When his heart stopped slamming against his ribs, Cody rolled over to take his weight off her. Could they never make it to a bed?

He smoothed the hair away from her face to judge her mood. She smiled and nestled her cheek onto his chest. Cody relaxed against the cushions and closed his eyes, softly stroking her skin that felt like satin beneath his hand. He never wanted to let her go.

He loved her.

For the first time in his life, he wished he had more than he did, wished he had something to offer her. How could he even think of life with a woman who wanted to own nice things, to stay in one place, settle down? He'd always been able to change addresses in a couple of hours. He never had thoughts of saving for tomorrow because he never wanted to become a slave to cash, a victim of greed like his dad. It had been more important to repay the debt his father owed than save for his own future…a future he now desperately hoped would include an innocent Merlene Saunders, private eye, country singer and would-be teacher.

But now, yeah, a place of their own would be nice. He wanted a home…a comfortable, modest home that Merlene could decorate in her own unique style. Breathing deeply, he envisioned a big yard with small children laughing and playing. Maybe a dog.

What was it about Merlene that made him long for that stable life? Her bravado, her vulnerability, her willingness to help him through the pain over his father.

She could quit the P.I. routine—he didn't want her exposed to any more danger—and go to school full time to earn her teaching certificate. Wouldn't take long. He'd help her study.

How many kids did she want? He'd always hoped for at least two…but three would be better. She'd definitely have to get rid of that compact car. He'd buy her a minivan and…

Yeah, right. With what? He must have lost his freaking mind. But they could work through all this together. That's what couples did.

"How's D.J.?" he asked after a moment.

"Better," she said. "The rest did him good. What happened with Neville Feldman?"

Cody sighed, hating to return to the subject that always created a wedge between them. "Duval County finally nabbed him. He's on his way back to Miami."

"That's good, right?" Her breath tickled his chest.

"Yeah, but the feds want him now, too. Sean is acting as his brother's attorney, wants him returned home and is demanding a quick preliminary hearing."

Merlene pulled back to look into Cody's face. "Why the rush?"

"Sean insists he can prove Neville's innocence. He'll probably be disbarred soon, but as you once pointed out to me—" Cody smiled "—suspending a license takes time."

"When's the hearing?"

"Could be next week."

"Next week?" She rested her head on his chest. "How could Neville's case get on the docket that fast?"

"Defendants are entitled to a speedy arraignment." Cody tried to see her face. "Is that a problem?"

She took a deep breath, her breasts moving against him. "Will I have to testify?"

"I don't know. That'll be up to the prosecutor, Rafael Alvarez."

Looking worried, she bit her lower lip.

Cody turned on his side and faced her. "I won't let anything happen to you, Merl."

She smiled, but he saw the doubt in her eyes. Yeah, well, he had some explaining to do. He took a deep breath.

"We pulled your phone records because we're trying to determine Pat Johnson's whereabouts the night of the murder."

"You can't think she's involved."

"There's a possibility."

"Because she increased his life insurance? That's circumstantial and ridiculous."

"Forensics have raised some troubling questions. The gun that killed Dr. Johnson isn't the Glock in the video. Hopefully everything will be cleared up when Feldman is back in Miami."

"You're sure there's no mistake?" she asked. "Labs sometimes make errors."

"No mistake. Plus, the records show you received no out-of-state calls on either your landline or cell for a week before the murder."

Merlene remained quiet, obviously digesting this new information.

"We're still developing evidence," he said into the silence.

"Your people think I'm involved, don't they?" she asked in a small voice.

Cody hesitated before he answered. They'd reached a tricky area. "My lieutenant thinks you know more than you're saying."

"Because I didn't turn over the video right away?"

"And because of forensics. We have a lot of holes in this case that we can't figure out. I'm trying to plug them."

"I understand," she murmured.

"Do you, Merl? Do you really? Because—"

"I get it that you're still investigating. I do. I'm a detective, too, remember." After a pause she said, "I just wish you'd told me."

"I couldn't. I was under orders from my lieutenant not to."

"Because if I knew I were a suspect, I'd flee."

"That's what Montoya thinks."

"I know what he thinks." She inhaled a deep, shaky breath. "But what he thinks isn't important to me."

Cody held his breath, waiting.

"Why are you telling me now? Do you think I'm involved, Cody? Do you think I helped murder Dr. Johnson?"

"No."

"That's the truth?" she asked.

"So help me God. And I'm working night and day to prove you're innocent. Montoya has no evidence of your involvement, or you'd already be under arrest."

"I thought maybe that's what the safe house was all about."

"I know you did, but it wasn't."

"Cody, I swear I didn't know anything about the murder. I would never have—"

"And I do believe you, Merl. Trust me, I'm going to find the answers."

"Thanks," she whispered.

"Any more questions?"

"Maybe. I'm thinking."

Cody yawned into the silence, and his eyes drifted shut. Wanting to remain alert to continue this discussion with Merl, he forced them open again. But fatigue dragged him down into a black hole. Her sweet softness curled into him felt so right, so good.

Just five minutes of shut-eye. That's all he needed. The woman was insatiable, and damn if she didn't wear him out.

The tightness in Merlene's chest released as she considered what Cody had told her. Cody believed her even if his boss didn't. Cody didn't think she was an accomplice to Johnson's murder. She felt light enough to float away.

Snuggled close to him on her sofa, their legs intertwined, she continued to process everything he'd revealed. So the police didn't only suspect her, they suspected Pat. Pat's blond coiffed image popped into her head. Was she the kind of woman who would kill her husband? Could she have hired Neville Feldman to be her hit man? But then why would she insist Merlene surveil Dr. Johnson constantly? It made no sense. Pat had to know Merlene might tape the murder.

Ah, could that have been the point? Ridiculous.

Merl thought hard. Had there been any behavior that should have tipped her off? True, she hadn't been able to reach her client for a while. Pat demonstrated amazingly clear thinking after the murder. In hindsight, it seemed odd how Pat constantly moved Merl around, always trying to position her just so, almost like a piece on a chessboard.

At least Cody believed her. That's all that mattered.

Merlene realized he'd fallen asleep when his hand halted its slow movement up and down her arm. His breath became deep and regular, his body relaxed.

Raising her head, she examined his face. How could he pass out on her after what they had just shared?

He'd better not start snoring.

He mumbled something…might have been her name…
and pressed her head back to his chest as he resettled them
on the couch, never opening his eyes.

Then she remembered that for the past week he'd camped
out in his car for her protection, and let him sleep. Besides,
she liked cuddling close to him. He appeared vulnerable and
trusting, totally at her mercy, although she knew he'd be on
his feet at the slightest threat to either of them.

A chill crept up her naked backside, but Cody's skin
warmed her legs where their bodies connected.

Taking advantage of the unexpected opportunity, Merlene
allowed her gaze to roam over his muscled torso. She'd been
this intimate with only one other male. Compared to Cody,
her husband had had more in common with a marshmallow.
Or maybe a corpse. Merlene stifled a groan at her thoughts.

Low on his abdomen, near his groin, a three-inch scar
angled toward his heart. Suspecting appendicitis, Merlene
lightly rubbed a finger across the faded ridge, then onto a
blue vein that passed very close to his skin. Cody shifted
beneath her, and Merlene pulled back, not wanting to wake
him.

With unchecked curiosity, she gazed at his groin, surprised to find him still hard, his arousal nestled in a thatch
of dark hair. What would Cody's reaction be if she stroked
a finger on that part of his anatomy? She bit her lower lip
at the delicious thought, which brought to mind the idea of
placing her lips on him instead. That ought to wake him up!

She swallowed and turned her mind away from fantasy.
Admiring Cody's powerful body while pressed against it
was giving her all sorts of wanton notions when the man
needed his sleep. After all, the reason he was so tired was
because of her. She grinned. Of course, his fatigue now resulted from more than protecting a witness.

Had he examined her as thoroughly the night she'd fallen asleep on his couch? Her cheeks warmed, then she remembered her long T-shirt. But it didn't matter, not really. She didn't want to have any secrets from him.

But she did.

The realization came like a sickening blow to her ribs when she thought about her conversation with Vanessa Cooper. She needed to tell Cody. She hadn't agreed to sell the recording from the night of the murder, but she hadn't said no.

Cody wouldn't understand. He already considered her money hungry. How had he put it? "So what if you don't like being poor?" as if that were some fatal flaw in her character, one he had to work hard to overlook. She didn't want to make it any harder for him.

Well, okay. It was definitely true she disliked being poor, but she didn't need to rub Cody's face in her need for stability.

She'd demanded an outrageous sum of money for the video. No way would Channel Eight come up with that much cash, but she needed to call Vanessa and put an end to the whole idea.

When he'd lapsed into deep, regular breathing, Merlene quietly rose. After one last admiring look, she placed a quilt over his body in case he grew chilled in the night.

She sighed, wishing she could wake him and lure him to her bed. But hopefully tomorrow he'd be full of renewed energy…and still on her couch.

First, she needed to contact Vanessa.

She soundlessly closed her bedroom door and moved to the phone to call the reporter. No answer, so she left a message.

Then she reopened her door in case Cody awoke in the night.

CODY SNIFFED THE air appreciatively while struggling to consciousness. At least that's how it felt: as if he'd been in a coma. Man, he couldn't remember when he'd had such a good night's sleep, and he could swear he smelled coffee.

He forced one eye open, and the second followed quickly.

A vision in a white silk negligee, Merlene was curled up in an overstuffed armchair six feet away, sipping a mug of what had to be the coffee. Her long hair cascaded to her shoulders, providing a sensual contrast to the delicate nightgown. She turned a page of the *Miami Herald,* then glanced his direction.

The smile that washed over her face made him hard. How could anyone look that gorgeous straight out of bed?

"Good morning," she said, placing the newspaper on the table between her chair and the couch. As she leaned forward, Cody caught a heart-stopping glimpse of full breasts barely concealed beneath flimsy lace.

"Come here," he growled.

Cody groaned with pleasure as she crossed to him, suspecting that she'd deliberately worn this seductive nightgown as punishment for his falling asleep the night before.

Man, he must have really been zonked to pass out with Merlene in his arms.

She perched on the couch and brushed a kiss on his lips. He snaked his arms around her, lifting her to lie beside him. She shrieked but then relaxed next to him.

Wired. That was the only way to describe his mood. And ecstatic. He should be groggy from the deep sleep but was wide-awake, aware of every spot on his body where they touched.

"Did you sleep okay out here?" she asked. Her breath rippled across his chest like a soft, warm wave.

"Best sleep I've had in years."

"Did you really stay awake all night, every night in your car?"

"I dozed lightly," he admitted. "But the slightest noise woke me up." He chuckled. "Nothing like last night."

"Nobody has ever looked out for me like you do. Never." She paused, but he knew she had more to say. She placed her palm directly over his heart. "I've decided I like it."

"Good, because I don't think I'm going to be able to stop looking out for you."

When she didn't respond, he rolled her on top of him. He wanted all or nothing with Merlene. He had to know if she could give up her dreams of big cars and big houses, had to hear her say she loved him, that she'd spend her life with him, for richer, for poorer.

"Cody, I need to tell you something," she said.

Impatient, he interrupted. "Do you have time to do some shopping with me today?"

"Shopping?"

"There's something I want to buy you."

She lifted her head, gray eyes sparkling. "I like that idea." Her long hair tickled where it brushed against his skin.

Disquiet rubbed at the back of his mind as he witnessed her pleasure at the prospect of a gift. But everyone likes a present, he told himself. Was it too early to buy a ring? Maybe just a small piece of jewelry—he shook his head when the phone rang.

"Ignore it."

"No problem, Detective. You go right on talking."

Cody smiled but knew he couldn't continue until the phone stopped ringing. The answering machine clicked on.

After Merlene's recording, a female voice said, "Hey, girl. This is Vanessa. I got your messages. I don't know if this damn machine is working, but stop worrying. I got the okay for your money. You'll get a check as soon as we get the video and the interview. My station manager wants to set it up yesterday. Call me."

CHAPTER FOURTEEN

CODY FROZE, EVERY muscle in his body stiff with disbelief. Rolling to a sitting position, he placed his head in his hands and took a deep breath in an attempt to calm the turmoil raging inside him. He had to wait another moment before he could speak. "You've talked to Vanessa Cooper?"

"Yes, but—"

"You promised her an interview?"

"No. I haven't promised anything. But I was thinking about it."

"My God. You made a copy of the recording before you gave it to me?"

"Yes," she whispered.

He turned to look at her. Her pale skin was now tinged a guilty pink.

"That's what caused the delay. Damn."

She didn't deny his accusation.

"And now you're going to sell it?"

She raised her chin. "Honestly, I haven't decided yet. She offered me a lot of money."

"If money is that important to you, Merlene, then…" He trailed off, now anxious to get far away from her, from impossible dreams. He stood and jerked on his pants. "What do you think it'll do to the prosecution if your video is shown on the six-o'clock news before it's placed into evidence?"

"I won't let that happen."

"Yeah, right," Cody said, yanking up his zipper. "Don't

do it, Merlene. You know it will destroy my case. Don't you want Neville Feldman off the streets?" He narrowed his eyes at her. "Or doesn't it matter since you know he's not a murderer?"

"You think I know someone else is?" She reached for him, but he stepped away, avoiding her touch. "Last night you said you believed me."

"And I've been a fool. I'd convinced myself that you— Never mind."

"Cody, slow down. I haven't done anything."

"Do you know how hard I've worked to convince my lieutenant that you weren't involved in this murder? That your video wasn't an attempt to frame men who were already under investigation?"

"Frame? Who? What are you—"

"So you'll do anything for the right price?" He faced her again. "Maybe you and the grieving widow did plan this ahead of time."

Her jaw dropped. "So, because I didn't immediately shut Cooper down, you now think I planned this murder with Pat, that the video is a cover-up?"

"You tell me, Merlene. Are you conning Channel Eight at the same time you and your client walk away with millions in insurance proceeds?"

An angry flush replaced the confusion on her face, but he didn't wait for the denial. He had to get out, away from Merlene, before he hurled something against the wall.

He grabbed his belongings and escaped to his car without looking back.

Her betrayal worked on him like fire devouring a dry, wooden building. Merlene's treachery hurt worse than his father's greed. He wouldn't have believed that possible, but he'd trusted her, believed in her and she didn't see anything wrong with auctioning off evidence to the highest bidder. Why hadn't he seen that in her?

He pounded his fist on the steering wheel. Yeah, okay. Maybe comparing her actions to his father's thievery was a stretch, a leap he was too quick to make because of his family history. Merl hadn't actually stolen anything, but damn, it sure felt like something had been taken from him. Something important.

God, he was a fool. Montoya was right. Her escape from the safe house should have told him all he needed to know. She'd held back her video for some reason—he just had to figure out what. Was she just after the money, or was she a murderess?

Cash definitely spun her world around. Oh, hell, maybe throw in a jewel or two, a fancy car. He'd seen firsthand evidence she'd settle for that. If someone died, so what? Merlene Saunders would have her nest egg, plenty of money so she'd never want for a thing.

And he'd fallen hard into her trap. He must have been an easy conquest, falling all over himself to protect her. But not anymore. She was on her own now. Let her find a new bodyguard. He had better things to do with his life.

Merlene listened to his car roar away, tires squealing as if he were escaping a sniper on the roof.

She'd watched Cody dress and leave, paralyzed by a shattering sense of loss. He wouldn't even look at her. He despised her. They'd been on the brink of something wonderful and, once again, she'd ruined everything.

So what else was new? It was the same old story, just told in a different and incredibly painful way.

Even as a hungry child she'd always been able to imagine some way out of a bad situation, some action to make things better. A place to beg for food, a spot to get warm.

But not this time. She felt as if she'd been ripped into little pieces and thrown into boiling water. Fighting tears, she collapsed on the couch and placed her throbbing head on a leather cushion still warm from Cody's body.

How could he think she was involved in Dr. Johnson's murder? How could he believe her capable of such a brutal act?

Because he considered her nothing but a greedy witch, a gold digger seeking cold hard cash any way she could get her hands on it. With a jolt she realized she had no one but herself to blame for Cody's judgment of her. God, she'd even requested payment the night he asked her to record the comings and goings from the Johnson home. At the time, her plan had seemed like an inventive way to get him out of her car, but all it did was reinforce his negative opinion of her character. After hearing Vanessa Cooper's message, why would he think anything else? Likely anyone would agree she was a calculating shrew who would stop at nothing— even homicide—to achieve wealth.

And that wasn't her. Not truly. She didn't need a lot of money. All she wanted was to feel safe, to never be terrified, cold and hungry again.

If she were honest, she worried too much about having enough security. That obsession always seemed to get her in trouble because she hadn't understood what it was that she lacked. But now she did. Loving Cody had showed her that cash couldn't provide the safety net that she craved. Only love could. And now she'd lost him because he thought her so grasping she was even capable of murder. Murder!

She squeezed her eyes shut, willing back the moisture that threatened to spill down her cheeks. She had to think… not give in to a useless crying fit.

Merl dredged up what she'd considered earlier and dismissed as ridiculous. Could Pat really have hired a private eye only to provide a perfect alibi? It was brilliant, of course. No one would suspect the wife when Merlene had recorded the arrival of men already under investigation minutes before fatal gunshots. Pat had insisted that the surveillance continue, even suggesting the trip to Ocala, and then canceling. Could she have been plotting murder the entire time? Had Pat been positioning dupes where she wanted them on surveillance? Had her client been inside the house pulling the trigger while, right on cue, her P.I. focused a camcorder on the arrival of Neville Feldman?

The police had no concrete evidence against Pat or they would have already made an arrest. And if they thought the wife was responsible for her husband's death, why had they been so hot to apprehend Neville before he shot the guy upstate?

Merlene sat up. And how long *had* she been a suspect? Had Cody kept her locked up in the safe house to keep an eye on her or to protect her?

Had he made love to a woman he considered a murderess?

There were too many questions without answers, and she needed to dig out those answers.

She stood, squared her shoulders and moved to the bathroom for an aspirin. She'd relied on herself since she was a child, and that's the way her life would always remain. She didn't believe in fairy tales where a knight came galloping to the rescue on a white horse.

Damn Cody Warren and the whole damn police department. Who needed them? She'd do her own detective work. If Pat had used her to frame an innocent man, this was one P.I. who intended to set the record straight.

Merlene grabbed the phone and placed a call to D.J.

Her boss was an experienced detective with contacts all over the state, probably all over the country. She needed his help again.

MERLENE MET D.J. in his home office the next morning. Last night she'd laid out the situation for him and asked him to dig up any information he could.

Searching his face for signs of illness, Merlene settled herself in a chair before his desk. Was it her imagination, or did D.J.'s skin tone appear better today, not nearly as pale? Yes. He definitely looked more rested.

"How are you feeling, boss?" she asked, hoping he wouldn't bristle at her question.

"Better, and that's the truth. Nothing like a good mystery to get the blood flowing."

"Glad to be of help."

"Now don't get all sarcastic on me. I know how important this mess is to you. One of the downsides of being a private investigator is sometimes winding up a suspect."

"Has that ever happened to you?"

"Oh, sure." D.J. waved a hand. "I tell you, this *is* a situation we have here," he muttered. "I might even be willing to bend the rules a little. Cody's right. Something doesn't add up."

"So what did you find out?"

"Plenty. I had to call in a bunch of favors, but I've confirmed that Pat Johnson did not fly on any commercial flights into either Miami International Airport or Fort Lauderdale–Hollywood Airport near the time of the murder."

"Of course not," Merlene said. "She's too smart for that. Could she have made the trip by car?"

"No way. I've done the calculations." D.J. turned to his computer and a spreadsheet appeared on the monitor.

"Speeding the entire distance, not stopping to eat or rest, no way could the woman have driven from South Florida back to the North Carolina mountains in the fifteen-hour window between the time of the murder and when you spoke to her the next afternoon." D.J. swiveled back. "You're sure you didn't reach her on a cell phone?"

"Positive," Merlene said. "I quit trying the cell number because I always got some message about the customer being unavailable. What about a train?"

"The service doesn't exist," D.J. said.

"Bus?"

"Nope. No public transportation could have accomplished the journey in the relevant time frame. If Pat Johnson shot her husband, she flew into town that day."

"Or maybe she paid someone else to pull the trigger," Merlene suggested.

"Murder for hire?" D.J. asked.

Merlene shrugged. "Why not? It's happened before in Miami. Remember the Cohen case?"

"Could be," D.J. admitted. "Can't discount that plan. But if so, she hasn't paid the hit man yet. I've seen the Johnson accounts. No big outlays of cash."

"She could have offshore accounts," Merlene persisted.

D.J. sat back, placed his hands on his belly, obviously deep in thought. "I'm digging for that. But where would she get the money to put in offshore accounts? The woman doesn't have a job. Would her husband just hand over that kind of cash?"

"I don't know."

"Do you think she could save that much from the monthly bills?"

"I doubt it."

D.J. sat up. "She didn't hire anyone. Doesn't ring true."

"From what I know of Pat, I don't think she'd trust anyone else to do the job right," Merlene said, believing D.J.'s instincts. Pat hire a hit man? She'd be seriously trusting a paid assassin to never rat her out. Blackmail would always be something to worry about.

"Another thing." Wearing a huge grin, D.J. slid another stack of papers closer to him. "And this bit of info was hard to obtain, but I managed."

"What?" Merlene asked, her curiosity piqued.

"Cody is also correct that Mrs. Johnson recently tripled her husband's life insurance policy. Agent's name is Jeff Kinney." D.J. looked up. "She's already filed a claim."

Merlene nodded. Of course she had. Pat seemed to believe no one was looking in her direction when lots of people, including the police, had eyes all over her.

"The woman made her claim the day she got a certified death certificate, which was expedited, by the way."

By now nothing Pat did surprised Merlene. Why hadn't she seen through her client? Probably because she'd been hot for those lucrative insurance contracts Pat had dangled in front of her nose. Had that all been part of Pat's game, too?

"Anything else?" Merlene asked.

"That's all so far. I'm still working on the possibility of those offshore accounts, but I don't think they exist."

Merlene sighed. "Probably not." What did it matter anyway?

"What are you going to do now, Merl?" D.J. asked.

"Follow Pat around and see what she's up to."

D.J. sat back in his chair and caught her gaze. "Tell me something, Merl. Do you believe Pat Johnson could have murdered her husband? What I've done here is perhaps prove opportunity," he said, placing a gnarled hand on the files. "But murder takes a hard woman. A real hard woman. Is she that kind of person?"

Merlene considered. "Maybe. She was awfully insistent that I never stop surveilling her husband."

"Desperation is another motive," D.J. said. "But I don't know what the woman has to be desperate about."

Two hours later, driving a rented Ford a safe distance behind Pat Johnson's white Cadillac, Merlene sung the words
to an old country-and-western song about being back in the
saddle again. She planned to keep tabs on Pat for a few days,
learn her habits, determine if anything unusual was going
on in her life. See if she made any visits to her husband's
new grave in the Pinecrest cemetery.

Did her client have any reason to be desperate?

Pat maneuvered the Caddie into a parking space near
Sunset Place, and Merlene logged the time Pat entered the
upscale shopping center. Ninety minutes later, Pat returned
to her car with several large shopping bags.

Lagging far enough behind so she wouldn't be spotted,
Merlene tailed her subject for three hours. Mostly shopping, two hours in the beauty salon. Nothing out of the ordinary occurred.

Merlene's stomach did a blackflip when Pat pulled into
the parking lot of South Dade Insurance Group late in the
afternoon. Did Jeff Kinney, the agent that handled the Johnsons' life insurance, have his office inside this building?

As she snapped several photos of Pat entering the glass
front doors, Merlene wondered if Pat was checking on her
claim. Not in itself suspicious but why not a phone call? Or
maybe she hoped to pick up her money. Fat chance. It was
way too soon. Besides, Cody had likely requested the insurance agent to "cooperate" and not issue a check anyway.

Merlene itched to follow Pat inside but knew even with a
red wig and glasses she'd be recognized. Best to wait a few
minutes, then check names on the directory inside for clues
as to what Pat's purpose could be in this building.

With the melody to "On the Road Again" now humming
in her brain, Merlene noted the time and cautioned herself
to be patient.

CODY STOOD AND shook Jeff Kinney's hand. "Thanks for your cooperation."

"We just need a few days," Jake said, rising from another chair.

Kinney straightened the manila files on his desk and also came to his feet. "Believe me, detectives, if there's a chance Dr. Johnson's wife was involved with his murder, I'm happy to hold up the check. She called at ten this morning, however. I expect her any minute."

Cody glanced at his partner. Pat Johnson was coming here?

"Tell her there's been a screwup at your headquarters," Jake said. "Then tell her you have another appointment to get rid of her."

The agent sighed. "She's a good client."

"We appreciate your cooperation," Cody told the agent again, thinking the man probably regretted the loss of future commissions. Yeah, money really did spin the world on its axis, and sometimes allowed people to die.

"Oh, of course," Kinney said, frowning. "Insurance fraud is something we take quite seriously."

In the corridor moments later, Jake punched the elevator call button. "Kinney's probably glad to have an excuse not to pay out a large claim."

"Just hope he doesn't tell the Johnson woman we're onto her," Cody said.

"Or she'll be on the next flight out of town."

Cody thought about Merl. Had *she* blown town because of his warning? Had he given her the information so she could make an escape? No. He'd told her because he believed she was innocent. And he still believed that now that he'd calmed down. Greedy, yes. Murderer, no.

"We need to find hard evidence," Jake said.

"Assuming it exists." Cody ran a hand through his hair. "Pat Johnson might not be involved at all."

Jake shrugged. "Since when is Montoya ever wrong?"

Before Cody could voice a response, the elevator doors opened. Dressed in a stylish black suit, blond hair lacquered into place, Pat Johnson stepped into the hallway. She smiled in a practiced manner and moved between Cody and Jake, leaving behind an expensive floral-scented trail.

Cody watched her enter Kinney's office.

"She doesn't appear grief stricken," Jake muttered.

"At least she's wearing black."

Cody's thoughts again drifted to Merlene on the ride down. He shook his head. He'd disobeyed a direct order from his lieutenant by telling Merlene both she and her client were under investigation.

Cody stepped from the elevator ahead of Jake—and halted midstride. Merlene stood ten feet away, scrutinizing the lobby directory, notebook and a pen in hand.

He cursed under his breath. Here to snag her portion of the insurance, no doubt. No matter how bad the evidence, he'd wanted to believe she was another victim.

"Merlene," he called out.

She whirled. Her cheeks flamed as if she'd been caught with both hands in the cookie jar. "Cody."

Oh, yeah. Here was just another coincidence that she'd showed up at Agent Kinney's office at the same time as Pat Johnson.

"I don't need to ask what you're doing here," he said, a sick feeling twisting his gut.

"Relax," Jake murmured in his ear. "Are you going to introduce me to this lovely lady?" he said in a louder voice.

"Jake, meet Merlene Saunders." Cody uncurled fisted fingers. How could she look so damn beautiful, so innocent and so guilty at the same time? "Merlene, this is my partner, Jake Steadman."

Merlene transferred the pen to her left hand and extended her arm. "Detective Steadman," she said, her voice husky.

"Jake will do."

"Pat Johnson is upstairs," Merlene said, glancing back to Cody. "I think she's gone to see Jeff Kinney, the agent for—"

"We know who Kinney is." Cody folded his arms. "You'll have to wait for your cut. Pat won't get her check today."

Merlene flinched.

Jake said, "Why don't I wait in the car?"

Merlene lifted her chin but didn't speak.

"So tell me, Detective Warren," Merlene asked when Jake was out of earshot, "if Pat Johnson killed her husband, how did she get from Miami back to Blowing Rock so quickly? I spoke to her myself the next afternoon." She narrowed her eyes. "I dialed the number—a landline."

Cody didn't answer. She had a point. They'd run a check on commercial flights but had come up empty. His request for the manpower to check general aviation airports hadn't yet been approved.

"Or do you think I'm lying about that, too? Well, come to think of it, I could be lying about what time I made the recording. Or maybe I tampered with the date stamp."

"I know you didn't alter the video."

She offered a half smile. "Because the lab says so, right? Not because I do?"

Hearing sadness behind the anger in her words, Cody searched for something to say.

"Thanks for the vote of confidence, Detective," she said when he remained silent. Still holding the notebook and pen, she placed both hands behind her. She lifted her chin higher, exposing the arc of her creamy white throat.

"For the police's information," she said evenly, "I'm conducting surveillance on Pat Johnson. I'll try not to interfere with your investigation."

Reaching into her shorts pocket, she withdrew her car keys. She threw them up about two inches and caught them with a jangling clank. "With any luck, we won't run into each other again."

LEAVING CODY IN the rearview mirror, Merlene angrily brushed aside a tear. Why did she always let him get to her? At least he knew she hadn't altered the video. That was something. That ought to keep her out of jail for a while.

Merlene turned right at the first intersection, drove out of Cody's sight and parked. She could see him beneath a tree limb, but a large car between them blocked his view of her vehicle.

He stared after her for a moment, then walked toward his partner on the sidewalk. The two had a brief conversation, then climbed into Cody's police vehicle. Jake rode in her seat.

She shook her head. No, that had been Jake's seat long before hers. And she'd probably never settle her rear in it again.

She waited for Cody and Jake to drive away, then started her car and repositioned so she had a clear view of Pat's Cadillac. Merlene planned to follow Pat the rest of the day at least, maybe into the evening. What else did she have to do except worry about being arrested?

As she raised her digital camera to focus on the glass doors Pat would exit, Merlene wondered what Cody would be doing. Searching for evidence to convict her or exonerate her? Well, he'd never discover any evidence against her because there wasn't any.

Unless Pat had created some.

Merlene lowered her camera at this unexpected thought. She'd never considered that sinister idea before. But why not? If Cody was right, Pat had, in essence, manufactured evidence against Neville Feldman. Why not frame the unknowing private eye accessory at the same time? A great way to eliminate any possible witnesses.

Maybe Cody *had* found something that made her look dirty and that's why he acted so damn judgmental.

Feeling less and less charitable toward her client, her thoughts again drifted to Cody. So what would he do tonight? Surely he didn't work all the time. Did he ever take the evening off and kick back? She was out of the safe house now. If things were different, they could spend the night together. Merlene squirmed in her seat and pushed away the delicious thought of Cody's strong, naked arms wrapped around her own bare shoulders.

She needed to forget about him. Too bad her treacherous mind always betrayed her when it came to Detective Warren.

She tensed as the insurance building's glass doors swung open, then relaxed when a twentyish man in a Dolphins T-shirt exited. But right behind him was Pat Johnson stomping forward in a manner that spoke volumes about her mood.

Pat jerked open the driver's side door, threw her purse inside as if she were tossing a softball and collapsed behind the wheel. Merlene clicked frame after frame of Pat pounding a closed fist on the Caddie's dashboard.

"Temper, temper," Merlene murmured, lowering her camera.

When Pat started the car and drove away, Merlene stayed with her. *Where to now?* she wondered. Home to nurse her wounds?

Merlene followed Pat to a low-income neighborhood in Little Havana. Rusted, obviously abandoned cars crowded swales. Bicycles and other children's toys, their color faded from baking in the hot Miami sun, littered yards full of more weeds than grass. Many of the houses were for sale or rent, too many with foreclosure notices. Merlene shook her head. Not exactly a slum, but a long way from the affluent surroundings of Pat's home in Coral Gables. Why had she come here?

Merlene waited at the end of the street while her client parked in front of a residence slightly better maintained than its neighbors. Merlene videoed Pat exiting her Cadillac and using a key to enter the small home.

Interesting. Merlene drove by the home and made a note of the exact address. Either Pat owned this house or was on intimate terms with whoever lived here.

Very intimate. She hadn't even knocked.

At the end of the block, Merlene turned around and searched for a safe place to wait for dark. She parked her rental next to a wrecked Camaro with a good view of Pat's Caddie. If Pat left the house before dark, she'd never recognize this Ford. Merlene could hunker down behind the wheel and not be spotted.

But Pat's Cadillac didn't move and the neighborhood remained quiet the entire time Merlene waited. She played a little solitaire. She read. Her thoughts drifted to Cody too damn often.

Every hour she created video test footage to prove how long Pat remained inside. Surprising how no kids came outside to play in the street. No one returned home from work. Nobody worked in their yards. This area had been hit hard by the recession.

When it was dark enough that she couldn't be easily spotted, Merlene slipped a black hoodie and loose black pants over her clothing and made her way toward the residence. Beneath her top, she slung her video camera on one shoulder and her still camera on the other.

Her heart pounded inside her chest as she moved. Approaching the targeted structure without someone seeing her and calling the police was always the tricky part. She used to get a thrill out of this kind of work. She'd felt good catching those cheating husbands, doing her job and making money in the process.

But not this time. And likely never again. After tonight, she was done with this work.

Strolling casually, head down, when she reached the property she stepped onto the grass and hurried into the backyard. No alarm sounded from a neighbor.

Experience told her which window would likely peer into a bedroom.

No curtain. Excellent.

Her back plastered to the cool concrete wall, she stood on tiptoe and dared a peek inside. Sure enough, a naked Pat Johnson and equally naked man enjoyed each other so much they wouldn't have noticed an army conducting maneuvers.

So who was this new player in Pat's little game?

Merlene raised her camera.

FOUR MORNINGS LATER, a process server delivered Merlene a subpoena for Neville Feldman's arraignment. The package also contained a brief note from the prosecutor, Rafael Alvarez, explaining that the Feldmans demanded to see the evidence against them. Mr. Alvarez wanted to meet with her to go over her testimony just in case.

But was that evidence trustworthy? Still reading the newly delivered paperwork, Merlene lowered herself to the couch.

She'd retrieved her copy of the video from under her bed and watched it at least a dozen times.

Yeah, two men rushed from the house, one of them carrying an automatic pistol. What did that prove? She'd relived her own memory of the night so many times she wasn't sure what she'd heard or seen that night anymore.

And she hadn't heard a word from Cody. She hadn't expected to, but service from a stranger irritated her. He could have delivered the summons himself.

If he had, she would have told him how much her surveillance had paid off. What would he say when she told him Pat Johnson had a lover? A much younger lover…

A little detective work had told Merlene all she needed to know about Pat's new boyfriend, Mr. Angel Vasquez. For one thing he was unemployed. Every afternoon the merry widow visited Vasquez's Little Havana home, remained over two hours, leaving with her perfect hairdo smashed flat.

God bless telescopic lenses. She'd managed to snap several revealing photographs of the happy couple.

Imagining Cody's reaction to this info, Merlene folded the subpoena in half. She longed to tell him but couldn't bring herself to make the call. Not yet. What she really wanted to tell him was she'd declined the interview with Vanessa Cooper and that the media vultures would never get their hands on the recording. Turning down more money than she could possibly make in her lifetime ought to count for something.

But she wouldn't call him until she'd figured out everything.

Refusing to think about Cody, she climbed into her rented Ford and hoped for better luck this afternoon in her search of general aviation airports. There had to be a record if Pat had chartered a plane the night of the murder.

So far she'd batted zero.

With irrefutable proof that Pat wasn't the devastated spouse she pretended to be, Merlene wondered what else her client hadn't been truthful about. Yeah, Neville Feldman might be a bona fide thief, but no one deserved to be framed for murder. She certainly never intended to partic-

ipate in something so... She shivered, unable to come up
with a word that fit how much she hoped she hadn't been
manipulated into causing a man's death.

An hour later, she parked in front of a low-slung aluminum building with the name Old Cutler Airport across the
entrance. A faded orange wind sock billowed next to the
runway.

When she entered the building, a dark-haired, fiftyish
man stood up from a desk and approached the counter. He
smiled at her, a toothpick dangling from his teeth.

"Can I help you, ma'am?"

"I hope so," she said, deciding the up-front, head-on
approach was the best way to get information out of this
honest-looking man. She held up her P.I. badge. "I'm looking for some information."

"What about?"

Merlene placed four eight-by-ten photographs of Pat taken
during recent surveillance on the counter. "Have you ever
seen this woman? She possibly flew out on a charter flight
early in the morning of August twenty-third."

She waited while the man leafed through the photos.
She'd asked these questions dozens of times in the past week,
most employees at small airports laughing at the idea of anyone departing in the middle of the night, and no one recognizing the woman in the photos.

"She do something illegal?" the man asked, removing
the toothpick from his mouth.

"I'm not with the police," Merlene said, placing a hundred-
dollar bill before him.

The man glanced at a calendar over the counter. "Yeah,
she was here that night," he said. "Paid us five hundred extra
cash to keep us open so late. She was real secretive like,
but didn't say nothing about keeping it quiet." He tossed

the toothpick in a wastebasket. "I remember the pilot. Nice guy, even if he was a Braves fan."

Scribbling notes as fast as she could write, Merlene said, "Do you have a record of her arrival time?"

The man looked in a file and gave her the day of arrival, the pilot's name, and name of the charter company—Lanier Flyers, north of Atlanta. Damn if the scenario didn't plug in perfectly to the theory of her client killing her husband. The cops already had the motive, and this information proved opportunity. Merlene shook her head as she realized the lengths Pat had taken to hide her tracks. An out-of-the-way airstrip almost in the Keys and a rented pilot from Atlanta would certainly confuse anyone trying to follow her movements.

So the cops were right. No one could reach any other conclusion. Pat had murdered her husband.

Theory had been one thing, but reality was something quite different. Feeling as if she'd been punched in the gut, Merlene closed her eyes, nauseous at how easily she'd been duped.

Her unknowing participation had helped Pat kill her husband.

"Could I have a copy of the record?" Merlene asked.

The man shrugged. "I don't see why not," he said, moving to an old machine.

"Thanks," Merlene said. "The police will be in touch for more information."

"What'd she do?" he asked.

"Same old, same old," Merlene said. "She got greedy."

"DAMN, CODY, LIGHTEN UP. You're acting like a wet cat cornered by a dog."

Cody glared at his partner across their adjoining desks. "I don't want to be here all night."

Jake returned the look. "Who said we have to get all this paperwork done today?"

Cody slammed his pen on the desk and started to say something but halted when he caught a glimpse of Jake's grinning face.

Shaking his half-bald head, Jake said, "I take that back. You're more like a rooster without his hens—mean as hell and taking it out on everybody else. Why don't you do your partner a favor and call one of your old flames?"

"Shut up, Jake."

"Come on. How about sweet Melissa? Remember her? I'll bet she can make you forget Mrs. Saunders."

Cody stood suddenly so that his chair scooted on its rollers halfway across the squad room. "Drop dead, partner."

Jake leaned back in his chair and laughed. "Okay, okay. Maybe Melissa is a bad idea, but I'm sure you can come up with someone to scratch that itch."

Cody needed fresh air, fast. Turning away from Jake, he headed for the door while his partner kept blabbering behind him.

"You want my wife to fix you up with one of her friends from aerobics class? She's been after me to have you to dinner for months. Could be fun, old buddy. Exactly what you need."

Cody wanted to flip Jake the finger, but he kept walking out the door. Better to ignore Jake's needling. The ribbing would end sooner if he did.

"Hey," Jake yelled. "I thought you wanted to finish this paperwork."

Outside, the oppressive summer heat hit Cody like a hot, wet sponge. Sweat trickled down his back, but he kept walking, ignoring the outraged stares of other pedestrians as they sidestepped out of his way.

He should never have confided his feelings for Merlene

to Jake. Big mistake. His partner had everyone in the unit treating his failed romance like a joke, but Cody hadn't felt like laughing for a long time.

How long? Time hung around his neck like a .357 Magnum, dragging him down. Had it been only a week? He couldn't sleep, so he spent most of his time at the station, Merlene's betrayal gnawing at him constantly. He slowed his angry walk, his guts twisting into knots as he relived the morning he discovered she was actually considering selling the video. He'd left her pale and quiet, hands clenched at her sides, gray eyes welling with unshed tears.

Then three days ago, head held high, she'd walked away from him, saying she hoped they wouldn't see each other again. How could he bear that?

She wasn't on the run, and that convinced him, if not his boss, of her innocence. Maybe she bent the rules on occasion, but Merlene was no killer. Every time he managed to think it through calmly, he came to the same conclusion.

Problem was, when Merl was involved, he let his emotions trump common sense. He let his temper flare out of control.

Still…he had to give up any fantasies of a life with her. Even if they worked things out, if she agreed to marry him, she'd grow restless, dissatisfied with the life of a working man. Working man? Hell, he was a cop. She hated cops. His friends were all cops. How would she deal with that?

Cody pulled in a deep breath, humidity and anger almost choking him. Maybe he had to forget the idea of a future with her, but he would never forget her. Forget Merlene's haunting face and smile? No way. Not if he lived to be a hundred.

His thoughts clearing, Cody looked around, not surprised to find that his walk had brought him to the steps of the Richard E. Gerstein Justice Building. It was a huge, square structure, rather startling because of its size. But, hey, Miami attracted an overload of criminals.

He counted up to the fifth floor where this morning he'd met with Rafael to go over strategy for the preliminary hearing.

Since Sean Feldman had pushed for a quick arraignment, Rafael still proceeded with the case as if the video were gospel. Until they could sort out the mess, Cody wanted Neville behind bars. He'd shot a liquor store clerk and had defrauded insurance companies out of thousands of dollars. He belonged in prison.

Cody's mind raced as he walked, searching for ways to prove Merlene's innocence to Montoya. If Neville didn't murder Dr. Johnson, then he also didn't kill Ray Price. Why would he? Neville needed Price alive to corroborate the fact that Johnson had already been shot when they'd arrived that night.

If Neville didn't murder Price, then who did? Who had a motive?

Cody glanced at his watch. Merlene should be meeting with the prosecutor right now to run through her testimony.

Pushing through a revolving door, Cody acknowledged that although he had any number of legitimate reasons to see Rafael, he'd come here for only one purpose.

He wanted to see Merlene.

"THAT SHOULD DO IT, Merlene." Rafael Alvarez flipped several note-filled pages in his yellow legal pad and made quick check marks. "I've got all I need." Placing his gold pen on the desk, he smiled at her. "You'll do great."

Merlene nodded, thinking the raven-haired Mr. Alvarez rather young to be the lead prosecutor in this whole medical fraud/murder case. Maybe that was why she hadn't told him about Pat's lover, but deep down she knew it was because she wanted to give Cody the information first herself.

"Remember Feldman can't do a thing to you now. I don't want you to be nervous."

"I'll be nervous, anyway," she said, rising. Mr. Alvarez had been polite and respectful during the interview, and she intended to do a great job when she testified. She'd look like the ultimate professional and give clear, concise testimony that would blow everyone away. Cody would be proud of her in spite of himself.

Rafael came to his feet and extended a hand. "Be in Judge Nelson's courtroom by nine a.m. I might not need you, but…" He trailed off, looking toward his office door. "Cody? Did you forget something?"

Cody? Merlene whirled around, a rush of exhilaration surging through her.

"Oh. Sorry, man." Cody stood in the doorway unsmiling, watching her intently but speaking his words to the prosecutor. "Didn't know you were busy." The muscle in his jaw twitched.

"We're finished," Rafael said. "Just getting Merlene prepped in case Feldman demands her testimony."

Cody nodded once. "Good."

Frozen in place, Merlene didn't utter a word. Cody remained by the door, shifting from one foot to the other, obviously ill at ease. Any hope that he'd come to see her vanished. From his guarded expression, he didn't want to come within ten miles of her. Well, the hell with Cody Warren.

She lifted her chin. "Good to see you, Detective."

"Mrs. Saunders."

She flinched at the lack of warmth in his voice.

"See you at the hearing, Merlene," Rafael said. "And don't worry."

She heard the prosecutor's voice on her long trip to the

door but couldn't formulate a response. Cody stepped out of her way, his gaze never leaving her face.

She attempted a smile, but her lips refused to curl upward, so she passed him without saying another word, kicking herself for her excitement at seeing him. When would she learn?

"MERLENE, WAIT."

Cody caught up with her as she approached the white Ford sedan she'd rented. She unlocked the door and turned, wondering why he'd come after her, wishing her pulse hadn't kicked into high gear.

"Where's your car?" he asked. He crossed his arms and stood with his legs wide apart.

She leaned against the door for support. "Not that it's any of your business, but Pat would recognize my Toyota."

"Do you really think you can learn anything by surveilling your client?"

"I intend to prove or disprove your new theory about Dr. Johnson's murder. You remember, the one where his wife and I did him in for money?"

"I remember," he said.

Merlene ignored the warning that flashed in Cody's blue eyes. Why should she watch what she said to him?

"Pat has a lover at least ten years younger than her late husband," she blurted. The surprise that flickered across his face filled her with such immense satisfaction she almost smiled. So Mr. Hotshot Detective didn't know everything.

She shrugged. "Maybe that's why Pat shot the good doctor, if she did. She wanted his money but not him."

"You're positive she has a lover?"

"Trust me, I have proof." When he didn't answer, she said, "It's what I do, remember?" He nodded and ran a hand through already tousled hair. "That certainly gives Pat another motive for murder."

Recognizing the frustration in Cody's voice, Merlene wondered if he had anything besides a motive. She certainly had a lot more, and she ought to tell him. Had the precious police not found any evidence? She suddenly had to know.

"What proof do you have of Pat's guilt?" she asked.

His lips tightened. "You're still a suspect, Merlene. I can hardly reveal the status of my case to you."

"Of course not," she said, deciding in that instant she'd sing off-key to the jeers of thousands before she'd tell Cody beans about her investigation. Maybe she'd even turn her findings over to Sean Feldman instead of Cody. Let the "good guys" be embarrassed in front of the judge. See how smug Cody acted then.

She bit her bottom lip knowing she could never betray him no matter how furious she got. She scribbled the name and address of Pat's lover on one of her cards and handed it to him.

"The grieving widow should be with lover boy right about now." Glancing at her watch, Merlene said, "I imagine she'll be with him for about two hours, if you're interested."

"Two hours? That's all?" Their eyes met. A jolt of sensation shot to her feet when his warm fingers slid across hers to accept the card.

Refusing to show emotion she was better off denying, she opened her car door and stepped behind it, relieved to have something solid between them. Damn Cody. He always managed to tip her off balance.

"If there are no more questions, Detective, I have business."

His blue gaze bored into hers. "What kind of business? Are you still watching Pat?"

She slid into the seat and shut the door. "Since I'm a suspect, I can hardly reveal the status of my case to you."

As she drove away from Cody's flushed face, Merlene allowed herself to enjoy the delicious notion she'd discovered information he didn't have. Ha! Even if he was the detective with more experience.

Of course, dragging down that tiny ray of sunshine was the cold, wide distance between them.

She sighed, knowing Cody would confirm the report she'd given him. He'd run a check on the boyfriend and hopefully gain a substantial lead.

And while Pat remained busy with lover boy, she'd search the Johnson residence. She withdrew her cell phone and called D.J., who was, thankfully, steadily improving and insisted on helping.

When he answered she said, "Are you in place? I'm on my way."

"I hope you know what you're doing."

"I do."

"Be careful, Merl, and wear gloves."

"Don't worry. Let me know the minute Pat leaves Vasquez's place. Oh, Detective Warren might show up. I want to know if he does."

Flipping the phone shut, she considered what she was about to do but didn't care if she was breaking the law. She wasn't going to steal anything except the truth. She wouldn't sleep easy until she had concrete evidence Pat had hired her to frame men who, while not exactly upstanding citizens, didn't deserve a murder rap. Who knew what clues existed inside the Johnson home? At the very least she could ascertain whether the theory she and D.J. had worked out was feasible.

With a shudder, she remembered the spreading pool of blood reflected in the mirrors of the foyer. Then her memory flashed to the awkward position of Doc Johnson's crumpled body. D.J. figured the doc had been facing somebody in the rear of the house when she described the way the body fell. She didn't know much about crime scenes and entry wounds, but why would he look back if Neville Feldman and Ray Price came through the front door?

Likely part of the troubling forensics Cody had mentioned.

She intended a good look at the layout of the Johnson home, to poke around in a few hiding places. Who knew what she might find?

If she was really lucky, maybe a receipt from Lanier Flyers. No good without a warrant, but maybe Cody could find a way to obtain one.

And since she still had the key, she'd half convinced herself her visit couldn't be considered trespassing. Yeah, right. *Tell that to the judge, Merlene.*

She backed into the Johnsons' driveway so no one could see her license plate from the street, hoping her car wouldn't arouse any suspicion. She bet neighbors speculated every time they drove by this house, forming theories of their own about the murder. But her car was a rental. With a recent death in the family, neighbors would expect out-of-town visitors.

Pat's kids remained in Blowing Rock, so Merlene knew the house would be empty. She intended to be in and out quickly—no more than thirty minutes, tops—although Pat had been spending longer and longer each afternoon with the boyfriend.

Did the woman have any idea that the police were on to her? Probably not or she'd behave with a little more discretion.

Merlene's legs wobbled as she hurried across the front yard, wanting to duck out of sight behind the foliage. With an eerie feeling, she realized she was mimicking Neville

Feldman's actions the night of the murder. She hoped no one watched her with a video camera.

On the porch, she fumbled with her keys, looking for the one Pat had given her. There. She cursed her trembling fingers as it took several tries to insert the key into the lock. She didn't want to touch anything but the key. For a moment, heart rate galloping, she feared Pat had changed the locks...but the door swung open smoothly.

Merlene sucked in a deep breath, knowing she was truly crossing that proverbial line here.

She looked behind her. No one was there.

Trying not think about what she was doing, how much trouble she could get in, Merlene stepped across the threshold and closed the door behind her with an elbow.

She hurried through the chilly foyer, avoiding a glance into the mirrors so she wouldn't relive memories of the doctor's dead body.

Inside the main house, she stopped and listened hard. Nothing but the soft hum of the refrigerator in the nearby kitchen.

As she stepped forward, a loud click echoed through the house. For a heart-stopping second, Merlene knew her life had ended, but soon realized the air-conditioning compressor had automatically rumbled on. She closed her eyes and heaved a shaky breath.

Damn but she was jumpy. And for good reason. She needed to complete her search and get the hell out of there.

She whirled in a circle, looking for the best location to hide from visitors at the front door. *Well, bless my bones if there aren't several such spots.*

She moved into the dining room and decided this room was the ideal spot for an ambush.

Did Dr. Johnson even know that his wife had come home? Or had Pat remained hidden?

How had she felt while she waited? Had she quietly paced, knowing when she heard Neville's knock it was time to blow out her husband's brains? She and D.J. theorized that afterward she'd run out the back door, having scoped out a clear way through a neighbor's yard to safety.

Pat could have been halfway to Old Cutler Airport before Cody had arrived that night.

Merlene snapped on latex gloves and searched drawers for any information that would prove Pat had been in Miami the night of the murder. Inside an old fashioned roll-down desk, she found bank statements with miniature copies of canceled checks. She released a soft whistle when she saw the amount of money Pat had paid to her lover in the past month. No checks for Lanier Flyers.

As she rounded the corner to search kitchen drawers, the front door creaked. She froze at the sound of a step into the foyer.

Terrified that Pat had returned, Merlene ran into the kitchen. She pressed her back against the refrigerator and held her breath.

Why hadn't D.J. called her? Or maybe this wasn't Pat?

Neville? Of course not. He was in jail. Then who?

CHAPTER FIFTEEN

CODY CLOSED THE Johnsons' front door behind him, then turned the dead bolt with a soft snap that sounded deafening inside the marble foyer. Wall mirrors on either side of him reflected his body into infinity.

What would happen to his career if Coral Gables police showed up and discovered him inside this house with Merlene? How would he explain his actions?

No doubt he'd be talking to Internal Affairs for a long, long time.

He paused and listened, but the house remained quiet. Where was she?

"I ought to arrest you for breaking and entering," he shouted.

His response came as a relieved exhalation to his left. Of course, she wouldn't know who had followed her inside. He nodded. Served her right. Merl deserved a good fright.

Holding up a brass key, she emerged from the kitchen, gray eyes wide. "I didn't break in. You know I have a key."

"What the hell are you doing here, Merlene?"

"Looking for clues," she said, moving into the center of the dining room. She extended both arms forward as if gripping a gun. "If someone stood right here, they couldn't be seen from the front door."

"Someone? You mean Pat?"

Merlene faced him, still pretending to aim a weapon. He searched her face. Did she want to shoot him?

"Isn't that what you think?" she asked.

He stared at her. "That's one theory."

"Do you have another?"

"I want to hear yours."

"When the two con men arrived, she could have sprung from hiding and shot her husband."

"The gunshot wound was to the chest."

She lowered her arms. "Maybe he heard her and turned."

"Come on," he said, taking her elbow. "Let's get out of here before Pat returns home."

Merlene jerked away as if his touch burned. Her rejection hurt more than he liked to admit.

"There's no rush," she said. "D.J. will let me know the minute Pat gets in her car."

"D.J. knows what you're doing?"

She lifted her chin and glared at him. "*He* wants to help prove I'm innocent."

"And so do I," Cody said. "Even so, you're in here illegally." He wondered if D.J. knew exactly what Merlene's plan had been.

"Can't we just take a quick look around?" she asked. "We're already here."

Cody hesitated, the idea of a search tempting. It was something he'd never have considered before meeting Merlene. "Nothing we find will be admissible."

"Yeah, yeah," Merlene said with a wave of her hand. "But when will we ever have a better opportunity to hunt for leads?"

"I can't f-ing believe this," he mumbled. Was he really having this conversation with Merlene at the scene of Dr. Johnson's murder?

She placed her hands on her hips. "I won't tell if you won't."

He smothered a smile, thinking she looked anything but intimidating. Damn, but he'd missed that stubborn attitude.

"All right. You keep a watch on the front door, and I'll search."

"But—" she started to protest, then glanced into the foyer. She reached into a pocket, withdrew a pair of latex gloves and tossed them to him.

"Look for anything with the name 'Lanier Flyers.'"

Already hurrying into a room with file cabinets and dark wood furniture, he paused and shot Merlene a look. "Lanier Flyers?"

She leaned into the door and motioned him away. "Hurry up. We don't have much time."

"Let me know the minute your phone rings."

She made a quick X on her chest. "Cross my heart and hope to die. Lanier Flyers. Don't forget."

He pulled on the gloves and thoroughly searched Dr. Johnson's office, finding nothing with the name *Lanier* on it. Nothing interesting at all. In the master bedroom, while rifling through a bedside stand, he remembered he'd fished once on a Lake Lanier, north of Atlanta. What connection could that have to this case? He wasn't letting Merlene out of his sight until he knew.

They hurried out the front door without speaking. Although he could tell she was bursting with questions, they had to wait. Merlene locked the door behind them and got into her car while he slid behind the wheel of his. When she pulled out of the Johnson driveway, she gave him a little wave, as if to say, "See ya later." Yeah, right.

He followed her down Granada and stayed behind her vehicle when she turned onto Bird Road. She was probably on her way home. He hoped so… He liked being with Merlene in her home. They could talk there whether she liked it or not.

Hell, he liked being with her no matter what. Even when making an illegal search. With a cell phone plastered to her ear, she drove well below the speed limit. Cody figured she'd checked in with D.J. after his warning.

He'd have to quit underestimating Merlene. His gut told him she'd dug up some interesting information. Could he trust her? He knew she had nothing to do with Johnson's murder, but had she sold the video to Channel Eight? Maybe not. The recording hadn't been aired on the news yet. Why would Vanessa Cooper wait?

He wanted to trust Merlene, but every time he did she proved him wrong and broke his heart all over again.

WHEN MERLENE PULLED INTO her driveway, she heard the crunch of Cody's tires behind her on the gravel. She supposed she should have expected him to follow her all the way home. They'd reached some sort of truce. Would he want to come in and talk? She heard his car door open and received her answer.

But did *she* want to talk? What good would that do?

She moved to the porch and unlocked the door. Towering over her, his face impassive, Cody pushed through. "I'm coming in."

"I can see that," she murmured, her gaze following his broad back into her living room.

"Tell me about Lanier Flyers," he said before she'd secured the dead bolt.

"Did you find something with that name?" she asked, her hopes shooting skyward.

"Nothing," he said. "Who are they?"

Disappointed, she crossed the room and retrieved a manila file from her glass-topped desk. Time he knew about the charter flight. She opened the file and handed him the surveillance photos of Pat Johnson.

"I showed these photographs to small charter outfits at airports all over South Florida. Yesterday I found a man who remembered Pat departing Old Cutler Airport around two o'clock the morning of August twenty-third."

"What?" The muscle in his jaw twitched as his blue eyes drilled into her face.

Her stomach churning under his disbelieving stare, she handed him a copy of the information and moved away. "Pat chartered a Learjet from Lanier Flyers in Gainesville, Georgia. The pilot's name is there, too."

Shuffling through the papers, Cody asked, "Did you tell Rafael about this today?"

"No."

He looked up. "Why not?"

"What's the matter, Cody?" she asked softly. "Are you afraid I'm going to demand some sort of payment for the information?"

"Stop it, Merl."

"Or do you think I'm lying about the charter flight, too?"

"I believe you." After a pause he said, "And I know you weren't involved in Johnson's murder."

"Since when?"

"I never truly believed you were involved."

Her eyes narrowed. "That's not the way you acted."

"Fair enough. I admit my lieutenant created some doubts, and when you withheld the video... But I know you, Merl." He gave her a slight smile. "You don't have murder in you."

She caught her breath at his intimate, husky tone and looked away, not wanting to reveal her raw emotions to him. Did he really believe her?

"Is this enough to arrest Pat?"

"I'll have to pass it by Montoya," Cody said. "The prosecutor will make the final decision."

"Aren't you even going to question her?" She shot him a quick glance.

"We don't want her to know she's a suspect. Not yet. She could run." After another long moment he said, "I'm glad you didn't."

"You thought I'd make a run for it?" she demanded. "God, Cody. What happened to believing in me?"

He sighed. "I didn't know what to think."

Merlene paced the room, her thoughts tumbling. "And I don't know whether to be furious or sad that you think so little of me."

He raised his arms and dropped them. "I'm sorry."

She stopped moving and glared at him. "Was that an apology for thinking I'm a murderess?"

"Yes."

"I have no reason to run."

"I know that. I was angry for other reasons—out of line."

"You got that right." She glanced down, away from the uncertainty stamped all over his face. Without trust they could be nothing to each other.

She swallowed hard, unsure where they could go from here. "Keep me informed, okay?"

"Sure. I'll call you as soon as I know anything."

She nodded, still examining her sandals, wishing his opinion of her wasn't so important.

"Look, Cody, I—" She took a deep breath, unsure if she could get what she needed to say past her lips. "I know you believe all I care about is money. I even get why you think that since I once asked you for payment and you heard Cooper's message. But I want you to know that— Well, I'm aware that I might have a problem." She shrugged. "And I'm working on it."

"Look at me." Cool fingers cupped her cheek. She looked into his deep blue eyes and simply forgot to breathe.

With a groan, as though touching her had released some long-denied need, he pulled her roughly into his arms.

"Merl," he whispered, his voice a tortured sigh against her hair. She longed to touch her lips to his, but closed her eyes and breathed in the familiar cinnamon hint of his aftershave. Why did she always feel safe wrapped in the sheltering warmth of Cody's arms? Moving deeper into his embrace, she collided with the solid reality of the shoulder harness that contained his gun.

They both backed away.

He cleared his throat. "I need to report this information."

Was it her imagination, or was there regret behind his words? And what exactly did he regret?

"Of course." She wrapped her arms across her chest, aching for Cody's arms instead. "Plus, I'm sure you want to confirm my report."

"I told you I believe you," he said, his voice sharp, edgy. "I meant it."

"Right," she said. But did he really? Could they get beyond their mutual lack of trust?

Didn't seem likely.

As he continued to stare at her, he narrowed his eyes. He shook his head. "So who killed Ray Price?" he asked. "And why?"

"I thought Neville—"

"No way," Cody said. "Why would he? Ray Price was Neville's proof that he didn't murder Doc Johnson. Neville is sticking by his story that Pat discovered the insurance fraud and demanded he come to her home that night to discuss future plans. Neville didn't trust her, so he took Price to watch his back."

"Maybe Pat killed Price to eliminate Neville's alibi. Then it would be just his word against my video."

"But Pat was in North Carolina when Price was murdered. You talked to her and so did one of our officers. Cell and landline records confirm that. We've even discovered footage of her at an ATM machine."

"Right," Merlene said. Had these events only been a week ago? Seemed like a lifetime. "Pat even sent me a key to the ranch in Ocala."

"Probably to prove her location. Or maybe the trip was a diversion, something to get you out of town while things settled down. We can ask her after her arrest." Cody cupped her chin and smiled down at her.

Was he remembering their night in the cabin? She lightly touched his hand. If only they could start over again.

Merlene stepped away. She was a big girl. She knew better than to buy into fairy tales.

"I'll lay you odds Pat didn't know Neville had gone to the ranch," Cody said.

"I wonder where her boyfriend was at the time of Price's murder." Merlene said.

Cody dropped his hand and tapped the manila file against his leg. "I'm looking forward to asking him that very question this afternoon."

"No way, man." Angel Vasquez, Pat Johnson's young, dark-haired lover, pushed away from the interrogation table and crossed powerful arms on his chest. "No damn way. You tell your partner to back off."

"Jake takes murder personally." Taking grim satisfaction in the good-cop/bad-cap routine, Cody watched Vasquez squirm. Tonight Jake had been the "bad" cop. Using his two hundred and thirty pounds of brawn to intimidate the gigolo, Jake had made colorful threats and then slammed out of the interrogation room with a great show of barely restrained anger.

As the sympathetic cop, Cody now hoped to squeeze the truth out of Vasquez.

The weasel leaned forward again. "I had nothing to do with any murder, man. No way. Go talk to Pat Johnson."

"Tell me about Pat Johnson."

"Hey, she's a real generous lady." Angel offered a slight grin. "Okay, I make a living off generous ladies, but I had nothing, nothing to do with any murder. I never heard of this Roy Price."

"Ray Price."

"Whatever. I never heard of him, and I sure didn't kill him."

"Did Pat?"

"Listen, man, I swear I don't know. Once or twice she talked about knocking off her husband, but that was because she knew he was in trouble with the law. She liked the good life and worried she'd lose her meal ticket if her old man went to prison."

"You'd lose your free ride, too," Cody pointed out.

"Hey, I make her happy." Angel placed his palms flat on the wooden desk and leaned forward. "Pat bragged that she was some of kind of…I don't know, wizard with stocks, that she could turn the insurance payoff into some real money that would keep us in high style. She had this big idea about using a bimbo private eye to frame some jerk-off for the murder, but she never said nothing to me about killing any Ray Price. The husband—" Vasquez shook his head "—could be, but I don't know nothing about nobody else."

"She didn't ask you to get rid of Price for her—or her husband?"

"No way. I'll take a lie detector test, man. Bring it on." He waved an arm. "Besides, she makes me nervous now. If she really whacked her old man, what if she gets tired of me?"

Cody laughed. "Do you have a three-million-dollar life-insurance policy?"

With a shake of his head, Vasquez repeated, "I didn't kill nobody, man."

Cody grilled Vasquez for another forty-five minutes, but the guy never changed his story. Cody believed him.

So did Jake and Lieutenant Montoya, who watched the interrogation behind the one-way glass.

"So who killed Ray Price?" Jake stroked his mustache as the three conferred in Montoya's office. "Maybe his death had nothing to do with Doc Johnson's murder."

Montoya placed his unlit cigar in a clean ashtray. "I don't want my ass in a sling for harassing some innocent society woman, so go over everything we've got one more time. If you don't find anything, bring Pat Johnson in for questioning tomorrow morning."

Jake groaned as he came to his feet. "We'll be here all night. I gotta call my wife."

Dreading the tedious evening ahead, Cody remained slumped in his chair. He'd hoped to see Merl. He needed to clear the air between them once and for all and didn't want to wait any longer. Had she sold the video to Channel Eight?

"Looks like you were right about your private eye," Montoya said, sounding disappointed.

"We've been through Merlene's life with a magnifying glass," Jake said, "and found nothing wrong. Hell, she never even requests an extension to file her income tax return."

Montoya nodded. "And since lover boy just confirmed that Pat Johnson's plan was to use a private eye to frame Feldman, I'm satisfied the Saunders woman is clean."

"Pat Johnson didn't care who she destroyed on her quest to get rid of her husband," Jake said.

"Real nice lady," Montoya said. "And her scheme almost worked. So let's focus on nailing down our case against this murdering wife."

HOURS LATER, still at his desk, Cody stared at the phone, wanting to call Merl. She deserved to know she was officially no longer a suspect. She also deserved another apology. And an explanation.

She'd been right. He'd allowed his father's mistakes to become his own, permitting them to color his entire life. That had to stop. He had to forget the past and move on. But could he if she'd sold her recording?

Would she even give him a chance to explain? Did he deserve a second—damn, or was it a third?—chance? He shook his head.

When she answered the phone, her softly accented voice sent a shaft of regret through him. Why didn't it feel as if it was over between them?

"Hi," he said.

"Good evening, Detective."

He couldn't interpret her mood. How angry was she? Beyond forgiveness?

"Your detective work paid off," he said. "Montoya says you're off the hook."

After a long pause she said, "Thank you for telling me."

"We need to talk, Merl. When can I see you?"

"Have you interviewed Angel Vasquez?"

"He confirmed Pat's involvement," Cody said, allowing her to evade his question for now. "Apparently your client decided her husband wouldn't be worth anything to her in jail."

"Man, did I misjudge that woman." Merl's voice softened with chagrin. "I actually felt sorry for her because of her husband's affair."

"Some people can fool you. Listen, Merl—"

"Are you bringing her in?"

"Not until morning. Lock your doors, okay?"

"Why?"

"Just humor me. Vasquez might tip off his free ride."

When she didn't reply, he said, "Merl? Are you there?"

"I didn't sell the video to Channel Eight. It's true, I never said no. I was still considering the idea. They offered me a lot of money. But in the end, I couldn't. I didn't."

Cody closed his eyes. "Why not?"

"Because some things are more important than money to me." The sound of a dial tone echoed in his ear.

Cody replaced the receiver cursing himself as every sort of damn fool. He should consider himself lucky she was even speaking to him. He'd babbled on and on about trust, then hadn't trusted her. Hadn't trusted her or himself. Did they have any chance at happiness together?

He sure as hell would give it another try.

A FEW HOURS later, Cody glanced up at his partner's surprised grunt. Per Montoya's orders, they'd been digging through records for hours trying to find anything they might have missed.

But Jake shook his head. "Nothing."

Cody grabbed another file as the phone rang. The only person he was interested in talking to was Merlene.

"Warren," he said.

"Cody, this is D. J. Cooke."

"D.J." Cody settled back in his chair as Jake looked up with raised eyebrows at the name. "What can I do for you?"

"Have you talked to Merlene lately?"

Cody could tell the investigator was worried about something. "Couple of hours ago."

"Did she fill you in on her, uh, results?"

"She's been very helpful. Why?"

"Well, she was plenty steamed there for a while. I got concerned she might not tell you what she discovered."

"So you were going to clue us in if she didn't?" Cody held out his cup for his partner to fill when Jake rose to pour fresh coffee.

"Something like that," D.J. replied. "I didn't want her in trouble for withholding information. She's really a fine young lady."

"Thanks." Cody suppressed a laugh at D.J.'s obvious attempt to set things straight for Merlene.

D.J. cleared his throat, and Cody knew the old-timer had something else to say. "Did you know that your dad and I were partners for two years?"

Cody sat up straight in his chair. "Yeah, I remember something about that."

"Bill Warren was a good cop for most of his career, Cody. Don't let anyone ever tell you different."

"Don't worry. Nobody so much as mentions his name around me."

D.J. cleared his throat again. "Well, it's damn awkward, you know."

"I know."

"Yeah, I imagine you do."

Cody looked at the crumpled form in his hand and relaxed his fist as D.J. continued. "I remember how pleased he was when you decided to follow in his footsteps and enter the Academy. I'd made detective by then, but he came to my squad room to tell me. Never seen him so happy."

"Then you're one up on me," Cody said, surprised he didn't mind talking about his dad with the old P.I. "Seemed to me he was always angry."

"*Frustrated* might be a better word. It ate at him bad that he couldn't pass the sergeant's exam. All his career plans kind of went up in smoke."

"That's no excuse for turning."

"Maybe not, but his mom, your grandmother, was in a bad way financially, in danger of losing her home. Your dad couldn't help out, and I think that's what pushed him over."

"I never heard anything about that," Cody said after a moment.

"You were too young when it started. Anyway, your dad would be proud as hell to see you now. No matter what anyone says, Bill Warren loved his family."

"Listen, D.J.—" Cody said as he accepted fresh coffee from Jake.

"I'll shut up. I just thought you might want to hear a few nice words about your old man from someone who remembers the good times."

"Yeah. Thanks," Cody said.

"You bet. Now, why don't you and purty Miss Merl make up?" D.J. said, hanging up before Cody could reply.

Cody shook his head as he digested D.J.'s revelation. So Pop had a good reason for the shakedown, a legitimate need for the money. Yeah, that surely helped him understand, but it didn't justify the crime.

An old memory of his parents and Grandma Warren sitting around the kitchen table popped into his head. He'd been—what? Maybe eight or nine years old. He remembered thinking something was up with Grandma because she'd brought all kinds of papers and letters, and his mom and dad were going through everything. His mom kept shaking her head, but the look on his dad's face was what Cody remembered most before being sent to bed. So sad and helpless. So full of what he realized now was the beginning of his dad's bitter anger.

He sat back and closed his eyes, realizing the tension strangling his guts since his father's suicide had loosened its tight grip. He'd forgiven his father and it was all crazily tied up with his feelings for Merlene, her own family history and her need to help D.J. Learning of her own tortured past had allowed him to find this peace.

Way past time he accepted that he wasn't the only human being on the face of the earth with family issues. If Merlene could forgive her parents, he could forgive his dad.

He loved Merl. Now he needed her to forgive him.

He sipped strong, hot coffee, itching to see her, to set things straight. But that had to wait until he'd solved the last piece of this mystery.

Could their love survive his mistrust? He didn't know, but he'd sure try like hell to—

"Now, that's interesting," Jake said.

"What?" Looking up, Cody found his partner examining an old arrest warrant.

"Ray Price and Nurse Linda Cole were arrested together back in 2008." Jake sat back in his swivel chair with a squeak. "Says here she was a physical therapist during that con. The victim decided not to prosecute."

"Ray Price and Linda Cole." Cody whistled. "That *is* interesting. Did they ever share an address?"

"Not now." Jake sat forward and leafed through the file. "But guess what? With aliases, they've had the same address on and off for years."

"I'll bet Linda's not too happy about what happened to Ray," Cody said.

"Probably not," Jake agreed.

Cody stood, his mind racing. Or would Linda Cole have any reason to kill Ray Price? Most murders were impulsive crimes of passion. "Let's find Ms. Cole and have a conversation."

At six o'clock the next morning, the sun barely lighting the eastern sky, Cody turned the unmarked police vehicle into the parking lot of Linda Cole's apartment complex. His partner rode in the seat beside him. At their lieutenant's instructions, they'd gone home the night before to grab some sleep in preparation for the busy morning ahead of them.

"She's got a white 2012 BMW," Cody told Jake.

They cruised through a quiet lot but didn't spot Cole's vehicle. Few people were out this early. Cody glanced toward the spot where Merlene had secreted her car while watching Cole's apartment. He'd called Merl before leaving the station last night, alerting her to the news about Linda's connection to Ray Price.

Cody parked in an empty space, and he and Jake took the elevator to Cole's unit on the second floor. Jake used his cell phone to call her listed number as they proceeded down a long hallway. Close to Linda's unit, Cody heard the phone jangling inside.

They waited ten rings.

"No answer," Jake said, cutting the connection. The ringing stopped.

"Not home," Cody muttered.

"Better make sure," Jake said, and pounded on the door. "Linda Cole," he yelled. "Police."

No response from inside the unit, but a neighboring apartment's door opened and a dark-haired, thirtyish man poked his head out. Cody held up his badge with his left hand. His right hand went to his hip.

"She's gone," the man said.

"When was the last time you saw her?" Cody asked.

"Been a couple of days." The man glanced at Jake, whose jacket was also drawn aside for easy access to his weapon. "Looks like good riddance."

"Please stay inside, sir," Cody cautioned. The man disappeared, slamming the door.

Jake shrugged, relaxing his stance and scanning the exterior wall of Cole's apartment. Cody did the same.

They'd get nothing here without a warrant. Not even a window to peek through. No way to know what was going on inside.

For all they knew, Linda Cole could be in there, murdered herself.

"Damn," Cody said.

"I'll draw up the warrant," Jake said.

On the way back to the station, they drove by Dr. Johnson's office just in case Nurse Cole had final business there, but came up empty. A cruise by the Johnson home gave them nothing but confirmation that Pat Johnson's Cadillac remained in the driveway, parked exactly where Merl's Toyota had sat yesterday.

They checked all known addresses, but Linda Cole was off the grid. Missing. Now they had a waiting game.

At the station, Jake worked on the warrant for Cole's home. Cody put out an All Points Bulletin on her vehicle and arranged for a unit to watch her apartment complex in case she returned.

At 9:00 a.m. Lieutenant Montoya approached Cody's desk. "Fill me in," he demanded.

After receiving a report on their morning activity, Montoya nodded. "Good start. Now get off your butts and arrest Pat Johnson for the murder of her husband."

Cody glanced at his partner and exchanged a grin. At times like this, he loved his job.

Pat Johnson answered her front door in an elegant floor-length silk bathrobe, a garment that covered her better than if fully dressed in street clothes.

Cody held up his badge. "Pat Johnson?"

"Yes." Her gaze jerked from Cody's face to his badge,

then to the two marked units with blue lights flashing parked in her front yard. Their backup of four uniformed officers was posted at strategic locations around her yard. A woman walking her dog stopped to stare.

Cody said, "You're under arrest for the murder of Dr. Richard Johnson."

Her mouth dropped open, then closed. Her eyes widened, and Cody saw acknowledgment. She knew she'd been caught. Then her eyes narrowed as she plotted a way out.

Cody stared at her. There was no way out.

"There must be some mistake," she said, probably to give herself time to think. She stepped backwards into the mirrored foyer. Cody and Jake followed her inside.

"I've seen you before," she said. "Both of you. I saw you at my insurance agent's office."

"You have the right to remain silent," Cody said. "Anything you say can be used against you in a court of law."

"I want to call my attorney."

"You can call your lawyer from the station, ma'am," Jake said.

Cody continued with the Miranda rights. "If you can't afford an attorney—"

"I can afford an attorney, you fool."

"Yes, ma'am. If you can't afford an attorney, one will be appointed for you."

She drew herself taller, as if offended.

"Do you understand these rights?" Cody asked.

She looked down at her clothing. "You have to take me to your station?"

"Yes, ma'am," Jake said.

"I need to get dressed."

"Do you understand these rights?" Cody repeated.

"Yes, I understand. Now may I put on some clothing?"

"No, ma'am," Cody said. "I'm sorry. But you may get a jacket or a coat to put over your night clothes, if you'd like."

"Thank you for that, at least," Mrs. Johnson said bitterly, moving backward. "I have a coat in that closet right there." She pointed to a door across the living room and hurried in that direction.

Why the rush? Cody wondered, staying close behind her.

When she reached the doorway into the kitchen, Pat broke into a run, obviously intent on rabbiting out the back door.

She was quick, but Cody caught her as she flung open the back door. He grabbed her arm to keep her inside the house, but the change in momentum threw her off balance. Cody steadied her before she could fall.

She closed her eyes, leaned against the kitchen counter and slid to the floor without a sound.

Cody squatted, releasing cuffs from his belt. He cuffed her wrists behind her.

"Oh, no," she wailed. "No!"

Jake joined them and shook his head at the sight of Pat Johnson collapsed on the floor, her legs sprawled at an awkward angle.

Cody rose, glancing at his partner. "Help me get her up," he said.

Jake grabbed under one shoulder, Cody the other, and they pulled Pat to her feet.

"How dare you," she said with a sob. "How dare you."

"We could have done this the nice way," Cody said, nudging her toward the front door. "It was your choice."

"Don't touch me," she screamed, pulling away.

Cody released her. Better if the woman calmed down.

"Now, seriously, ma'am," Jake said. "Do you want your neighbors to see you like this?"

She took a deep breath and squared her shoulders. "All right," she said. "Let's get this over with."

"Yes, ma'am," Cody said.

"My attorney will have me out on bond by noon. I promise you that."

"That could be, ma'am," Jake said.

"I'm telling you this is all just a huge misunderstanding," she said.

"I'm sure it is," Jake agreed.

Cody opened the closet door, retrieved a tan trench coat and draped it over Mrs. Johnson's shoulders.

"You'll pay for this," she hissed.

"Are you ready?" Cody asked.

She nodded, tears now glistening in her eyes.

When they stepped into the front yard, a small group of neighbors had gathered, but the uniformed officers kept them at a distance. Pat ducked her head in an attempt to hide her face.

"Watch your step, ma'am," Jake said.

Cody nodded thanks at their backup as they escorted Pat to his vehicle. *Yeah,* he thought, *some days I just love my job.*

Today, hard work paid off and a murderer was going to jail. A few loose ends remained, but soon this case would be wrapped up. He could talk to Merlene, square things with her and they could get a fresh start.

CHAPTER SIXTEEN

MERLENE GRABBED THE PHONE as soon as it rang, hoping to hear Cody's voice. She'd barely slept, waiting all night for him to call.

He had to call. He couldn't leave her hanging after he'd dropped a bombshell late last night about Linda Cole and Ray Price.

Linda Cole and Ray Price. Lovers, ex-roommates? Unbelievable. She'd never been involved in a case with more twists and turns.

She didn't even bother to check caller ID. If Cody called from his desk phone, the display always said, *Unavailable*.

"Hello," she breathed into the phone.

"Hey, Merlene."

"Oh. Hi, D.J."

"You don't sound too happy to hear from me," D.J. said with a chuckle. "Expecting a call from Cody?"

"And what makes you say that?"

"I may be old and sick, but I'm not dense," D.J. said. "It's obvious to anyone paying attention there's something going on with you two."

Merlene started to object, but bit back her comment. D.J. knew her too well. "It's just that I'm dying here waiting to hear if the police arrested Pat Johnson or talked to Linda Cole."

"Linda Cole? Isn't that the dead doc's nurse?"

"Yep. Turns out she and the dead Ray Price have a connection." Setting herself on the sofa, Merlene filled D.J. in on the latest developments. "So of course I can't wait to hear what she has to say. Cody thinks she's involved in Price's murder."

After a pause, D.J. issued a long whistle. "This is one extremely bizarre situation."

"If *you* think so, then I know this case is out there." Merlene considered her next words carefully, knowing how testy D.J. could get when she tried to mother him. "You sound better," she said in as casual a manner as she could manage. "How are you feeling?"

"Much better. I tell you, Merl, modern medicine is a wonderful thing. A week on that new treatment has helped my breathing more than I dreamed anything could."

"Oh, I'm so glad. So are you sleeping better?"

"You bet. Plus, I think putting my brain to work on this crazy Johnson mess got my blood flowing again. Did you find anything when you searched the Johnson home? You never called me back with details."

"I didn't want to go into it while I was driving, but Cody followed me and caught me inside."

This time the laugh from D.J. was far heartier than a chuckle. "So that's why he never showed up at the love nest. You're lucky he didn't arrest you."

"So are you since you'd have to post my bail." Merlene found herself laughing, too, although it rankled that she hadn't noticed Cody on her tail.

"Besides," she said, "I still say I had a right to enter since my client gave me a key."

Her comment prompted another guffaw from D.J., but Merlene didn't mind. After all, wasn't laughter the best medicine?

"Anyway," she said, "we didn't find a thing interesting."

"I'm not surprised. Mrs. Johnson planned this caper carefully."

"Man, I hate how well she played me."

"Don't take it too hard, Merl. It happens to the best of us. Oh, you should know Vanessa Cooper wants to interview me."

An image of Vanessa Cooper grilling her down-to-earth boss made Merlene shake her head. Now, that was some must-see TV. "How much did she offer?"

"Enough to cover my meds for a good long while."

The more she thought about it, the more Merlene liked the idea. D.J. would know exactly how much to tell the media vulture and not compromise Cody's case. "Are you going for the deal?"

"I don't see why not," D.J. said. "She's pissed that you refused her offer and loves the idea that I'm your boss."

"She thinks she's gone over my head to the top."

"Bingo. She's still trying to worm the surveillance out of me. I'll string her along for a bit, then something new will break and she'll move on. Oh, and I know you've been worried about the investigators from Tallahassee, but that's all been squared away. Seems Detective Warren set them straight and we're off the hook."

Merlene closed her eyes and issued a silent thanks to Cody. "That's great, D.J."

"Let me know when you hear about Nurse Cole," D.J. said.

"Will do."

After they disconnected, Merl relaxed into her sofa cushions and thought about her career as a private investigator. Former career. D.J. was right. It was time she started school full time and earned her teaching degree.

With that thought in mind, she reached for her textbook

on the end table beside the sofa. She was too far behind on her reading for class.

Before she finished a page, the phone rang again. She snatched up the receiver.

"Good morning, Merl."

Cody. Finally. She smiled, noting how the sound of his voice released the tension she'd been holding in her shoulders. "Any news?"

"Pat Johnson has been booked and is awaiting arraignment," Cody informed her. "Man, did she ever protest that we had some nerve to arrest her."

"I'll bet," Merlene murmured, imagining Pat's arrogant treatment of police who dared to thwart her wishes. Had they cuffed her? She hoped so. The witch. My, how the mighty had fallen.

"So what did Linda say when you questioned her?"

"Linda wasn't home. We've got an APB out on her and we're watching the apartment."

"Watching Linda Cole's apartment? Gee, that sounds familiar." Merlene settled back in her chair, remembering her visit from Cody while she conducted surveillance on Nurse Cole.

"Yeah, I suppose it does," he said with a soft laugh.

"Any chance Pat will confess?" Merlene asked.

"Nah. She lawyered up quick after learning what we had. Her attorney will cut a deal when he sees the evidence, but she'll do serious time."

"What about her kids?"

"They're still with the grandparents."

"Thank goodness there's family to take them in."

"Are you thinking about what happened to you after your parents died?" he asked softly.

"I guess," she murmured. Funny, but his intimate knowledge of her no longer seemed so scary. What did it matter? Cody knew all her secrets now. Her problems with the police were useless baggage from the past. She closed her eyes, wondering if she dared to hope for a future that included him.

"Merl—are you there?"

"Sorry," she said, realizing she'd drifted into fantasyland, as much of a dream as Opryland had once been. "What'd you say?"

"Will you be home later?"

Her pulse quickened. Cody sounded uncharacteristically nervous. Why?

"Sure, Detective," she said after a brief pause. "I'll be home all day catching up on my reading for class."

She watched the time for the next two hours, finding it impossible to concentrate on her class work, wondering about Cody. What time would he arrive? What would his attitude be when he got here? What would hers be?

What should it be?

She heard car tires crunch the gravel in her driveway around noon and replaced her textbook on the end table. Certain this couldn't be Cody but hoping it was anyway, she went to the window to peek out. A white BMW sat beside her old Toyota.

Linda Cole's vehicle.

Merlene dropped the curtain and slammed her back against the wall. Her heart pounded inside her chest. Why would Linda come here?

Well, it didn't matter why. She needed to inform Cody immediately. She stared across the room at the phone by the couch. Would he want her to try to detain Linda until the police arrived? Or should she keep her door locked, pretend she wasn't home?

That wouldn't work. Her car gave her away. What else—

A polite knock on the front door startled her from her

wild thoughts. Merlene closed her eyes but didn't give away her position. Damn. What should she do?

No, of course she'd be nuts to invite a possible murderess into her home. Better to keep Linda on the other side of a locked door. But if the woman had murdered her boyfriend, why remain in Miami? Did she even know the cops were looking for her?

And again, more importantly, why the hell come here?

Another knock, a short wait, and then footsteps retreated from the porch. Merlene darted for the phone, praying Cody could dispatch a cruiser quick enough to nab their fugitive. She entered his number, but the line went dead before she punched in the last digit.

She dropped the receiver, her mind racing. Where was her cell phone? In her purse. Where was her purse? On the dining room table.

She was racing in that direction when a loud crack at the back door froze her into place. What the—

The door burst open and hurried footsteps echoed on tile. Merlene looked around for a place to hide and took a step, but Linda Cole emerged from the kitchen wearing a nasty smile. As though in slow motion, she raised her right arm and aimed a handgun at Merlene's chest.

Unable to take her eyes off the gun's barrel, Merlene stepped back. Linda followed deeper into the living room.

"What do you want?" Merlene asked, her voice tight.

"Shut up. I'll do the talking."

Her mind whirled between confusion and terror. What the hell was going on? Were Cody's suspicions on the money? Had Linda killed Ray Price? Why?

The nurse's gaze danced around the room, as if she didn't know what to do next. The gun wobbled, and she raised her left arm to support the right hand. God, did Linda plan on shooting her right here? But why? What had she ever done to Linda Cole except follow her around for a few days?

"It's your fault, you know." Linda's voice sounded as shaky as her right arm. "He's dead because of you."

Merlene raised her eyes from the weapon to Linda's pale face. "Who? Dr. Johnson? But I—"

Hysterical laughter cut her off. The wildness of the sound told Merlene she was in real trouble, that a murderess holding a gun on her was about to go postal in the middle of her living room.

"Well, come to think of it," Linda said, "I guess you killed him, too. But I don't give a rat's ass about Johnson."

"Who, then?"

"Ray," Linda whispered. "My Ray."

So Cody was wrong about Linda, Merlene thought, even more confused. The nurse appeared devastated over her boyfriend's death. *But why blame me? Does she think I killed him?*

"We'd finally made our big score and had enough money to get out of this miserable city. We were…" Linda faltered, took a breath, then continued. "We were going to L.A. to get married, start a new life."

"I'm sorry," Merlene said, stunned to see tears gathering in Linda's eyes. The woman had lost her grip on reality. In Merlene's view that made her even more dangerous. No telling how she'd go off. "But it's not my fault that—"

"Yes, it is."

Merlene recoiled from the venom in the nurse's voice. Could Linda know she'd identified Ray for Cody? Was that why Linda blamed her? But how could—

"If you hadn't filmed them that night at Johnson's, there'd be no reason for Ray to leave town without me."

"He was going to leave?"

"I couldn't let him go without me," she said. "Why did he lie? Why—why, after all we'd been through?"

Merlene tried to follow the nurse's twisted logic, to stay focused. She fought the panic crowding the edges of her thoughts, pushed hard against terror threatening to balloon out of control and drag her into chaos. She squeezed her hands into fists, digging her fingernails deep into the flesh on her palms. Her mind flashed to Johnson's body in his foyer, mirrors magnifying the spreading blood.

If she gave in to her fear, she'd be dead, too.

Okay. She needed to calm Linda, pacify her. But how the hell did anyone reason with a woman holding a gun? Merl searched for a way of talking her into putting down the weapon. What possible reason could she offer the nurse? What possible hope?

"He was having an affair with Pat Johnson, wasn't he?" Linda demanded.

"Ray and Pat?" Merlene echoed. "No." Could this really be happening? She'd been hired to get proof of Linda's affair with Dr. Johnson, but now Linda was accusing the doctor's wife of sleeping with her boyfriend?

Linda nodded as if she hadn't heard Merlene response. "Dick Johnson knew his wife was cheating on him. After his murder, I thought about it and realized it was Ray. She killed her husband and was going to…to run away with my Ray. My Ray." Linda's voice broke on the name. She fought for a breath and continued. "I'd waited too long. I had to stop him. I couldn't let him do that to me."

"Of course not," Merlene soothed, silently urging Linda to keep talking. She needed to buy time. Soon or later she'd figure out something. "You did what you had to do."

But Linda's irrationality terrified her. Possibly she knew Cody was closing in, that she'd be arrested soon. Perhaps she decided she had nothing to lose. So why not make a break for it, pausing on her way out of town to get a little revenge on the meddling private eye who'd caused all the trouble in the first place?

Vengeance. Another great motive for murder.

Merlene figured she could take the nurse in a fair fight, but Linda had a loose screw and a loaded gun. Was there any way to trick her? Any way to knock the gun from her hand? Forming and dismissing one impossible plan after another, Merlene drew breath deep into her lungs, forcing herself to remain calm. Terrified people forget to breathe and, short on oxygen, make bad decisions. She needed to keep her head clear.

"I'm not going to make the same mistake twice," Linda said. "You're going to drive my car to the Everglades so I can dump your body on my way to California." Linda's painted lips curled up in an unpleasant grin.

"No one will ever know what happened to you."

ANXIOUS TO GET back out in the field, Cody waited for the printer to spit out his request for a search warrant on Linda Cole's address. Now he had to find a judge to sign off on the search. Judge Gonzalez was usually his first choice, always a safe bet. Considering the latest developments in this case, though, any judge would sign the necessary documents.

He glanced at his watch. If he hurried and was lucky, he could have the legalities completed by one o'clock.

Jake approached his position by the printer. "What's on Oakwood Drive in Coconut Grove? That address rings a bell."

Cody glanced up at his partner's question. "Merlene lives on Oakwood Drive. Why?" Now standing next to him, Jake focused on a computer printout.

"A City of Miami patrol unit spotted Linda Cole's vehicle in the driveway after a disturbance call."

Cody faced his partner and met his gaze. Why would Linda Cole visit Merlene? Impatient with himself, Cody shoved away suspicion, burying it forever. He loved Merl. He believed in her. He trusted her.

So what was going on?

He flipped open his cell and punched in her number. If Nurse Cole was at Merl's, then Merl was in trouble.

"Have they made a move to apprehend Cole?" he asked Jake.

"The patrol unit has the street contained, but they're waiting for backup to move in for the arrest."

His call went to voice mail. Cody disconnected.

Merlene had said she'd be home all day.

"Notify SWAT," Cody ordered on the way to the door. "We have a hostage situation."

MERLENE SCANNED HER living room for something, anything, to use as a weapon or to distract Linda. Maybe if she bumped into the bitch and threw her off balance there'd be an opening to go for the gun.

Bad idea. Too risky. She could end up dead.

No, she should leave a clue for Cody. But what? If Linda intended to dump her in the Everglades, she should leave a hint for Cody to start searching there. Yeah? Like what? Merlene looked wildly around the room but came up empty.

Anyway, the park was, like, sixteen million acres. Where would he even start?

With an APB already out on Nurse Cole, the best thing to do was stall for time. Cody would eventually come looking for her. She knew that, trusted that belief in her heart. So far he'd always been there when she needed him.

But still…the more time she gave him, the better. Again… how? How to slow down Linda?

"Move," Linda said, motioning with the gun.

"Don't you want to think about this?"

"What's to think about?"

"A lot." Merlene decided to just throw the truth out there. Maybe the facts wouldn't save her life, but at least she'd have the satisfaction of telling this stupidly jealous woman about the mistake she'd made.

"Ray wasn't having an affair with Pat Johnson."

Linda stiffened. "You can't know that."

"But I do. Pat has a different lover. I have photos to prove it."

"Photos?" Linda lowered the gun an inch.

"Photographs of Pat and another man. Not Ray."

"You're lying," Linda said, raising her weapon again.

"I'm not. I swear. Don't you see," Merlene continued in a voice she prayed sounded cool and convincing. "The police suspected *I'd* killed Doc Johnson. I had to watch Pat Johnson to prove my own innocence."

Linda didn't respond.

"The proof is on my desk," Merlene said. "I can show you. Ray was true to you. He didn't cheat on you." *Yeah, like I really know that.*

Linda's face softened. *My God.* Merlene thought, *She looks relieved, almost happy. This idiot is about to smile, but she hasn't put all the pieces together yet. She hasn't realized she killed the man she loves for no reason.*

"Then—then where was he going?" The gun wavered. "I saw his packed bags in the bedroom."

"He probably wanted to blow town until the heat was off. He'd have contacted you when he got settled."

Merlene held her breath as Linda finally connected the dots. "Oh, God. God, no." She squeezed her eyes shut, lowering her weapon. "What have I done? Why didn't I believe him when— Ray!"

With the gun's barrel now aimed at the floor, Merlene

took a half step backward. Then another. If she could make it to the front door…

Linda's eyes flew open. "Stop right there."

Merlene froze as Linda raised the gun again. The nurse now gripped the handle with both hands. Her finger twitched near the trigger.

Merlene took a deep breath, hoping it wouldn't be her last. "Don't you want me to get the photographs?"

"No. It doesn't matter. He's gone, and it's your fault."

"But—"

"Shut up," Linda screamed. "It's too late. I don't want to hear another word from you."

"Okay," Merlene said, raising her hands in surrender. Time to play her last card. She took one step forward and collapsed awkwardly, screaming in pain as she hit the floor.

FEAR SEARED CODY'S gut as he rushed to Merlene's address with the siren blaring and lights flashing. He could focus on only one thing: getting to Merlene. He had to reach her fast or he'd never see her alive again. Was he already too late?

He cut the siren when he neared Merl's neighborhood. Per radio transmission he knew the first officer had been joined by three other cars from her squad. They remained on scene but would take no action until the Special Response Team arrived. He'd requested a hostage negotiator and didn't care he didn't have that authority.

He'd seen a negotiator talk a murderer off the edge before. Could be the only thing to save Merl's life.

One of the patrol officers had slashed Linda's tires, and the Miami-Dade police chopper stood by in case Linda commandeered Merl's vehicle. Linda would likely step outside using Merl as a shield.

Relieved to see the BMW still in Merlene's driveway,

Cody braked to a lurching stop behind the barricade of two police cars blocking the north end of Merlene's street. Two other cars blocked the south.

"I need a report," he barked as he leaped from the car, his badge dangling around his neck.

A dark-haired female patrol officer approached and advised him of the situation in a professional way he immediately appreciated. He nodded, relieved he had good people on scene. But where were the specialists? Anything could happen if Linda forced Merlene through the front door.

He leaned against the roof of his car, his gaze fixed on her front door through binoculars. His fingers tightened on the black plastic. Everything appeared normal, but what was going on inside that house? What the hell did Linda Cole want with Merl?

Where was SRT? If things went sour today, he might not ever be able to tell Merl how much he loved her, how he couldn't live without her.

The arrival of three police vans jolted him from his surveillance. Special teams had arrived.

Officers knocked on doors requesting that neighbors remain inside and out of sight. Two snipers took positions, zeroing in on windows and the front of the house. They were expert shots, but if Linda started shooting, Merlene could be the first casualty. As soon as the hostage negotiator arrived, contact would be initiated with Cole.

But Vanessa Cooper arrived first, accompanied by her cameraman. Disgusted, Cody turned from the sight of them setting up for remote transmission. Channel Eight must have picked up the call on their police scanner. The rest of the stations would show up soon.

As he focused on the front door again, a message from one of the snipers crackled across the radio.

"I've got the subject through the front window. Standing by for kill order."

"No," he silently pleaded. *Don't take that shot. Merlene could be hit in the cross fire.*

CHAPTER SEVENTEEN

SPRAWLED ON THE FLOOR in her living room, Merlene silently cursed herself. Faking a stumble had seemed the perfect tactic to slow down Linda. Too bad her brilliant plan had resulted in a real fall and a painfully throbbing right foot.

"Get up, damn you," Linda gritted out between clenched teeth.

"I can't," Merlene said. "I twisted my ankle."

"Tough. Get your ass off the floor."

"Can't I at least get some ice to—"

"You'll be dead in an hour," Linda said, her tone mocking. "A swollen joint is the least of your problems."

Now what? Out of ideas, Merlene crawled to an end table by the sofa. She placed her hands on top and brushed against the textbook she'd been studying all week.

With fingers gripping the book, she glanced back at Linda. "I'm not sure I can walk to your car."

Linda stepped closer. "You'll manage."

"Can I get a broom or a mop to use as a crutch?"

Gripping the gun with both hands, Linda leveled the barrel in the center of Merlene's chest. "Move."

"Okay, okay," Merlene said, noting the nurse was no longer trembling. Hell of a time for her to get control of herself.

She knew one thing: no way was she getting into Linda's car. Talk about a one-way trip. Whatever the outcome, she'd make her last stand right here, right now.

Could she do this?

With her mind focused on what she had to do, maybe her last act ever, she pulled the book toward her and leveraged herself to her feet. *Now or never.*

Pain blasting through her ankle, she lifted the heavy text and spun with all her strength to slam the hardbound book into Linda's arms.

The gun fired with a deafening boom.

CODY FROZE AT the unmistakable sound of a gunshot. Merlene! What was going on inside that house?

"Shots fired," crackled over his earpiece.

"Shots fired," boomed another a voice beside him.

"God damn it. Have you got the subject in view?" Cody barked into the radio. "Have you got a shot?"

Surely the response came in only seconds, but the wait felt like a lifetime. "Negative. The subject is not in sight. Repeat. I do not have a shot."

Cody pounded the roof of his police cruiser.

"Go, go," yelled the Special Response Team commander to his squad. "Go!"

Crouching low, six heavily armed and armored police commandos jogged across Merlene's front yard.

Cody took a step away from his vehicle. Then another. He couldn't go with them. He felt as if he might sink into the earth. He'd promised himself nothing would happen to Merlene. And now—now he could do nothing to help her.

A frigging war zone. All he could think was Merlene's peaceful neighborhood had turned into a war zone.

Would she survive the coming battle?

Or was she already dead?

THE MOMENTUM OF Merlene's do-or-die swing for life carried her to the floor. Her throbbing ankle wouldn't hold her.

She threw out an arm just before her face slammed into hard wood. The book landed beside her with a thump.

Her ears rang from a gunshot too close to her face, the sensation disorienting, nauseating.

Was she hit? No. The searing pain came from her foot.

Behind her the nurse shouted, the sound distorted, as if one of them were wrapped inside thick gauze. Linda scrambled closer, moving across the floor, looking for something.

The gun. Where was the gun?

With a groan, Merlene raised her head. Her stomach roiled. She hurt all over, but she needed to find the damn gun before Linda did. Her only chance to— There!

Merlene spotted the weapon a few feet beyond her left hand. She reached toward it, stretching to grasp the handle.

Linda's fingers snaked out and clutched the barrel.

Merlene made a fist and pounded the nurse's hand.

Linda cursed but didn't move away. Merlene smashed Linda's flesh again and again. If Linda got control of the gun, she was finished. Merlene pivoted her legs toward Linda's body and kicked.

"You bitch," Linda yelled.

Merlene kicked harder, this time connecting with something soft in the nurse's middle. Linda moaned. Her fingers slithered away from the gun.

Merlene grabbed the weapon just as the front door burst open.

"Drop it!" an army of cops shouted in unison.

Merlene jammed her arms into the air as more cops arrived via the back door. "I'm Merlene Saunders," she yelled, never so glad to see the police in her life. "This is my home."

She pushed to a sitting position while what appeared to be a SWAT team approached a now-incoherent and weeping Linda with outstretched weapons.

Merlene closed her eyes and leaned against a wall.

"Merl!"

At Cody's hoarse shout, she turned and sank into the welcome strength of his arms. "Cody," she breathed, tears of relief flooding her eyes.

He hugged her close, murmuring her name, then held her away. His gaze swept her from head to foot.

"I'm okay," she said, watching a female officer cuff Linda's hands behind her back.

"You're hurt," Cody bit out, focusing on Merlene's right ankle, now red and swollen to twice its size.

"Yeah." She drew the misshapen foot toward her. "A failed attempt to slow down Nurse Linda."

Without another word, Cody lifted her in his arms and carried her to the sofa while the cops ushered Linda out of the house. Merlene turned her head into Cody's chest and closed her eyes, breathing in his scent, a scent that whispered of safety and security.

With a stern "Stay here," he disappeared into the kitchen.

Jake, Cody's partner, appeared accompanied by four uniformed officers. Cody returned with a bag of ice and a glass of water. He ordered her to drink the water while he propped her foot on the coffee table on top of the ice.

Merlene drank in the concern in his blue eyes, warmed by the knowledge that he worried about her. He cared about what happened to her. He always had. She knew that now.

Merlene laughed as she stared at her swollen ankle. She knew she'd been grinning like a fool ever since her rescue and couldn't stop. To think her home was crammed with police and she was delighted to have every last damn one of them. She suppressed a ridiculous urge to invite them all for dinner.

When had she ever felt that way about cops?

Trouble was, she wanted Cody alone so they could talk, but she wasn't near ready for the uniformed men and women to leave. For the first time in her life, they made her feel safe. Oh, but she liked that feeling. Really liked it.

"How you doing, ma'am?" a young black paramedic asked as he set a large plastic case on the floor.

Cody patted her hand and rose. "The paramedics want to check you out, Merl."

"Except for my ankle, I'm fine. My ears are ringing from the gunshot, but that's fading."

The EMT took Cody's place beside her. "Let's just take a look at you, talk to you a few minutes," he said, winding a blood pressure cuff around her arm.

"She didn't physically harm me," Merlene protested as the man pumped up the sleeve and placed a cold metal disk against her skin. "Just scared ten years off my life."

"Pressure's normal considering the circumstances," the paramedic said after a moment, releasing the cuff. "You're already doing the best thing for your ankle. I'll leave you an elastic support for later. Do you hurt anywhere else at all?"

"No," Merlene said. "I'm fine, really. The ankle was my own fault. I was trying to stall for time."

"I hear your ploy worked," he said with an encouraging smile.

"Well, well. So I finally get to meet the famous Merlene Saunders."

Merlene looked up and found a stocky dark-haired man in her living room waving an unlit cigar.

Cody rose. "Merlene, this is Lieutenant Carlos Montoya, my boss."

"You don't look like any private eye I know," Montoya stated.

Merlene gave a snappy salute. "I hear I'm no longer a suspect."

"No, ma'am."

"Thanks for the rescue."

"You can thank Cody," Montoya said, shaking his head. "Ma'am, how did you manage to cause me so much trouble?"

REPORTS COULD DAMN WELL WAIT.

Cody decided to take the rest of the night off after Montoya and the Special Weapons Team commander finished critiquing the afternoon's successful operation. No way was he letting Merl out of his sight until they'd worked things out. She might be happy to see him now, but what would happen when they were alone?

If it took him the rest of his life, he'd convince her to give him another chance.

She waved over Johnny, her old guard from the safe house. While they began an animated conversation, Cody stepped across the room to where Jake worked with the police photographer.

"I'll be late tomorrow," Cody told him. "In fact, I may take the whole day off. Montoya's already gone, so fill him in."

Jake nodded and shot a glance at Merlene. "She's damn brave. Make a good cop's wife."

Cody locked the door behind the last of the responders and turned to find Merlene removing the ice bag from her foot.

"I can't stand this any longer," she said, with a shiver.

"Let me wrap it."

She didn't speak while he wound the elastic bandage around her swollen ankle, careful not to cause her any more discomfort. Her flesh felt cool and smooth against his fingers.

How the hell did one start a conversation like this? He had to trust himself as well as Merl.

"Thanks," she said as he secured the bandage with a clip, her voice husky and cautious.

"You're welcome," he said, cupping her cheek. "Alone at last."

"So," she said. "What happens now?"

"What do you want to happen?"

Wariness flared in her gray eyes, but he found warmth behind the caution. And something he hadn't been able to define before: a shy vulnerability behind her usual bravado.

He placed his hand on her shoulder.

"Your fingers are freezing," she said with a nervous laugh.

"Sorry." He grinned and traced his thumb across her parted, moist lips.

"Now you're trying to distract me," she murmured, closing her eyes.

"I love watching your face when you're distracted."

Her neck lengthened in a graceful arc. "You have a way of making me forget what I want to say."

"What do you want to say?" he encouraged, making his voice an invitation to speak.

Her face flushed as her eyes opened. "I don't remember."

He picked up her hand and linked their fingers. "Maybe you were wondering why I always think the worst of you and never give you a chance to explain."

"I know why you do that," she said, raising her gaze to meet his. "Because of your father, you think the people you care about are going to let you down."

He rubbed his chin. "Sounds like a theory."

"Annie Oakley agrees with it." Merlene smiled, her dimples coming into stunning display. "I talked to her quite a bit last week."

"You and my sister?"

"I told her you paid the money back to the guys your dad ripped off." Touching his leg, she said, "You wanted me to, didn't you?"

This was the hard part of trust, he thought. Trusting someone you love with the bad stuff, the stuff that makes you crazy. Trusting yourself to let it go. But his feelings for Merlene gave him the strength to try.

"I guess I did," he said. "When did you come to know me so well?"

"I don't." Shaking her head, she placed her index finger on his temple. "Usually I have no clue what's going on in here."

"Maybe you don't want to know."

"I want to know."

He tucked a lock of hair behind her ear. "And I want to know everything about you, Merl."

"Then you have to stop running away from me whenever I do something you don't like. It hurts too much."

He drew her to him. "I know. I'm sorry." His voice was muffled as he kissed the top of her head. "I'm never going anywhere again."

"I want to believe that, but…"

"You get into too much trouble when I let you out of my sight."

"You sound like your lieutenant." Closing her eyes, she turned into his chest, feeling his body heat slowly seep into her own flesh. He wrapped both arms around her and she released a sigh. Trusting their love was more frightening than anything she'd ever done, but they would make it work. No matter what the cost, a life with Cody was worth fighting for. She believed that with all her heart.

"Trust works both ways, remember?" he said as he nuzzled her hair.

"Well, Detective, you definitely earned my trust today. I really thought Linda was going to—"

He cut off her words with a quick, fierce hug. "Shh. Don't think about that."

The strain in his voice told her about how worried he'd been.

"Don't feel so bad. I was scared for my life a bunch of times as a kid."

"I don't want you to ever be afraid again," he said.

"Wouldn't that be nice."

"I love you, Merlene."

Merlene squeezed her eyes. Could this really be happening to her? Things in her life never worked out.

He lifted her chin and she met his gaze. "No matter what else happens," he said.

Merlene stared into his fierce blue eyes and whispered, "I love you, too, Cody Wyoming. And your love is all the security I'll ever need."

He gazed into her face long and hard, then kissed her with such feeling that Merlene got lost in the hot intimacy of his mouth. She relaxed into the sofa, feeling as if she had melted into quicksilver—no, liquid happiness. Cody lifted her legs and shifted her beneath him, his tongue teasing her, tasting of the coffee they'd had earlier, and Merlene released forever any lingering doubt.

"Will you marry me, Merl?"

Her heart soared. "Yes."

He smoothed hair away from her face, continuing to hold her gaze. "You'll be around cops all the time."

"I'm not afraid of you nasty coppers anymore."

"Brave talk from an unemployed private eye."

"I won't be unemployed for long." Merlene brushed a lock of hair from his forehead. "I have something to tell you, but you have to promise not to go stomping off."

She touched the familiar muscle working in his jaw. It was time to test their newfound trust. No sense putting it off.

"I said I'm not going anywhere," he said. "Have you decided to pursue your singing career again? If so, you must know I support you all the way."

Focusing on the steady pulse in his throat, she spoke slowly. "I know how you feel about selling the video or an interview, but how would you feel about a book?"

"A book?" he repeated, rubbing the stubble on his chin.

"I've been offered a generous advance from a crime publisher to write about the Johnson case. With my abduction, the deal should only get sweeter. What do you think?"

Not daring to breathe, Merlene watched Cody consider her news.

"Merlene Saunders, private-eye author." He grinned. "Sounds great. Good thing I have a lifetime to get used to your surprises."

A lifetime. Merlene hugged the sound of that word close to her heart. "The book won't come out until after the trial," she said, "so—"

"I can't wait to read it, Merl."

"Of course the book will be dreadful," she said. "But the money will go toward completing my college degree."

"Anything you do will be fabulous." He dipped his head and captured her lips again, his possessive kiss promising a lifetime together. Every inch of her skin rippled into gooseflesh as his index finger traced across her blouse and stopped to tease her nipple. "Do you want me to stop distracting you so you can get started right away?"

Merlene couldn't answer, feeling so close to Cody it seemed as if her heart beat inside his chest. She reached for the buttons on his shirt.

"Not so fast, lady," he said, grabbing her hands and pulling her with him to a standing position. Cradling her in his arms, he said, "This time we're using a bed."

* * * * *

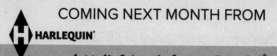

Not Another Wedding

By **Jennifer McKenzie**

"So?" Beck's voice drew Poppy's attention, caused her to turn
before she thought better of it. "Aren't you going to ask how
we know each other?"

Oh, he'd like that, wouldn't he? Though she might not have
seen him for years, she knew his type. He prided himself on
being unforgettable to women. Well, it was time he learned
a lesson.

"No." She couldn't help noting how good he looked. Really
good. However, she'd give up chocolate before admitting it.

She turned on her heel, intending to return to the party and
find someone—anyone else—to talk to, but his hand caught

her bare arm above her wrist. His fingers were warm.

"I guess I've changed. You're as gorgeous as ever, Red." His blatant appraisal of her body should have ticked her off. She was not his to behold, but the attraction sizzling through her was impossible to deny. Poppy shook the thought off. She did not want him looking at her. Not even a little. He'd lost that privilege years ago and a bit of sexy banter and warm hands didn't change anything.

"If you'll excuse me." She pulled her arm free and hurried away before he got a chance to stop her again. As she made her way through the crowd, Poppy did her best to ignore the knocking of her heart. When she sneaked a glance back, Beck was still watching. He even had the audacity to raise his glass toward her as though to toast her running away.

Fabulous.

**Will Poppy be able to avoid Beck?
Or is he determined to renew their acquaintance?
Find out in NOT ANOTHER WEDDING
by Jennifer McKenzie, available October 2013 from
Harlequin® Superromance®.**

REQUEST YOUR FREE BOOKS!
2 FREE NOVELS PLUS 2 FREE GIFTS!

HARLEQUIN®

super romance®

More Story...More Romance

YES! Please send me 2 FREE Harlequin® Superromance® novels and my 2 FREE gifts (gifts are worth about $10). After receiving them, if I don't wish to receive any more books, I can return the shipping statement marked "cancel." If I don't cancel, I will receive 6 brand-new novels every month and be billed just $4.94 per book in the U.S. or $5.24 per book in Canada. That's a savings of at least 14% off the cover price! It's quite a bargain! Shipping and handling is just 50¢ per book in the U.S. and 75¢ per book in Canada.* I understand that accepting the 2 free books and gifts places me under no obligation to buy anything. I can always return a shipment and cancel at any time. Even if I never buy another book, the two free books and gifts are mine to keep forever.

135/336 HDN F46N

Name _____ (PLEASE PRINT) _____

Address _____ Apt. # _____

City _____ State/Prov. _____ Zip/Postal Code _____

Signature (if under 18, a parent or guardian must sign)

HSR13R

She's as voluptuous as
Elizabeth Taylor, yet as
classy as Jackie Kennedy

Audrey Stone and her floral shop are thorns
in Gray Turner's side! All he wants to do is
wrap up his family's business holdings in
Accord, Colorado. But every move he makes,
she's there...in the way. Worse, now he can't
get her out of his mind!

Because of Audrey
by **Mary Sullivan**

AVAILABLE OCTOBER 2013

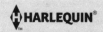

HARLEQUIN®

super romance®

More Story...More Romance
www.Harlequin.com

HSR71883

They say there's always a first time for everything

Mark Sharpe has been torn about JoJo Hatcher since he hired her. Yes, she's a great investigator. Yet she tempts him to cross the line between boss and employee—something he's never done. But when his teenage daughter is threatened, JoJo is the one he trusts to find the truth.

For The First Time
by **Stephanie Doyle**

AVAILABLE OCTOBER 2013

HARLEQUIN®

A *Romance* FOR EVERY MOOD™

Love the Harlequin book you just read?

Your opinion matters.

Review this book on your favorite book site, review site, blog or your own social media properties and share your opinion with other readers!

Be sure to connect with us at:
Harlequin.com/Newsletters
Facebook.com/HarlequinBooks
Twitter.com/HarlequinBooks